PASTEL COLORED DREAMS & HUMAN FLAVORED NIGHTMARES

VINCENT V. CAVA

MIDNIGHTHOUR

Edited by Kirsten Milliron
Design by Kirsten Milliron
Front Cover by CL Smith
Back Cover by Kirsten Milliron
Internal art by Chris "Oz" Fulton

This book is for me.
The next one is for you.

TABLE OF CONTENTS

Contents

FOREWORD

T HERE IS A LINE in Kurt Vonnegut's Slaughterhouse-Five
that I've probably read back a thousand times. I find
myself so drawn to the passage because it grabs me in
a way no other quote ever has. It's near the end of the very
first chapter of the book. To give you a little context, Vonnegut was describing the destruction of Sodom and Go-
morrah, as it is told in the Gideon Bible. Lot was escaping
with his family while fire and brimstone rained down on
the two infamous cities and it was here that I read those
words that stuck with me and will continue to stick with
me for as long as I am alive. They went like this:

*And Lot's wife, of course, was told not to look back where
all those people and their homes had been. But she did look
back, and I love her for that, because it was so human.*

So she was turned into a pillar of salt. So it goes.

It is in my opinion that truer words could not be
penned. Looking back is something that we can't help
but do even though we're continuously warned how fruit-
less of an endeavor it is. I couldn't tell you all the times
I've stayed up at night looking back at my life, reflecting,
remembering, wishing that I could have done things dif-
ferently, all the while hating my mind for punishing me
with memories I ached to forget. I used to think there was

something wrong with me because of that. I even sought professional help and took prescription drugs because I believed these thoughts indicated that there was a problem with the chemical structure of my brain. I didn't want to look back anymore. All I wanted to do was forget.

But forgetting is impossible.

I understand now that looking back on our past is as basic to us as breathing. Reflection makes us better people. It helps us grow and mature. Compiling this book was one big "look back" for me. Each story in this collection is a reflection of different moments in my life over the past couple years. They represent individual instances of heartbreak, frustration, disappointment, even embarrassment. Every tale an echo of my soul at the time when it was written.

You see, writing is my therapy now, and I've decided to replace the drugs with it as well. No longer do I strive to forget the past. Now I thrive on it, I draw from it, and I use it to create something new, something that can (at least I hope) put a smile on someone's face. Maybe I'm crazy, but I'd rather be Lot's wife than Lot. This is the path I've chosen for myself. I understand that it's not an easy one and if it should be the death of me, if it should turn me into nothing but a pillar of salt, then...

So it goes.

AT THE PATIO DOOR

RICK COLLUM STOOD ON HIS PATIO, looking down at the doormat that read: BE NEAT WIPE YOUR FEET in big blocky letters. Right between the 'A' and 'T' of the word NEAT there sat a mushy looking red and white ball and Rick knew at once that Felix had placed it there. Felix was his cat. He had not named the cat himself. In fact, he had argued that Felix was an extremely cliché name for a cat, but his wife, Melanie, had put her foot down on the matter. He hadn't even wanted a cat in the first place. Melanie had put her foot down on that matter as well.

She insisted Felix would be good practice for the young couple before they had a real baby – *a starter kid,* she had told him. *Think of it like a fuzzy toddler with training wheels.*

So Rick had caved and they picked up a kitten from the local shelter, a mostly black and white shorthair, with splotches of blonde fur sprinkled here and there, and Rick grew to love the cat and the cat grew to tolerate Rick.

Rick's backyard was heavily wooded. It sat on ten acres of forestland dominated by evergreens with an occasional cottonwood scattered in like a giant yellow typo amongst a sea of emerald text. The nearest house was six hundred yards down the quiet, scarcely used street that ran past Rick's old Victorian style home. This all gave Felix plenty of space to prowl about, hunting little animals whilst pretending he was a jaguar in the jungle and not just an ordinary kitty.

From time to time, he would leave a mouse head or the half-eaten carcass of a sparrow at the patio door. Rick found Felix's fleshy feline offerings to be sweet in a grotesque and morbid kind of way. It was almost as if the mutilated little critters were his cat's way of saying thank you for cleaning the litter box and filling his bowl with Fancy Feast every day. Whenever Rick would find one of Felix's gifts he'd let out a deep *here we go again* sigh, fetch his work gloves, and dispose of whatever was left of the unfortunate animal in the compost bin.

But there was no frustrated sigh from Rick this time, and trudging off to the tool shed to grab his gloves barely seemed appropriate because once he realized what he was staring at his body froze with dread. The mushy looking red and white ball sitting between the A and T on his doormat was actually a mushy looking red and white ball with a green iris and a black pupil. Felix had delivered a human eye to the patio door.

THERE WERE TWO REASONS why Rick Collum was sure the blood-coated eyeball sitting on his porch had once belonged to a person, the first of which being humans have fairly unique eyes, at least compared to the animals that lived

4

in the woods around his home. If Felix had brought back the eye of a dead deer or bobcat or coyote, Rick would have realized immediately that it was not a human's. It might have been the wrong size or maybe an unnatural color. There were a multitude of tells that could have given this fact away to him, and even though he was no wildlife expert he knew he could spot them.

The second reason why he was sure the eye once belonged to a person was because he thought he recognized it. It looked just like Melanie's, and, Rick surmised, the chances were more than likely that it was hers. It wouldn't have been hard for Felix to find her corpse during one of his backyard, jungle-cat prowls, chew it from her face, and bring it back to the house. After all, Rick had slit her throat and dragged her body into the woods just two days prior.

HE BELIEVED THAT HIS MIND had temporarily cracked the day he tossed her down in the snow, next to the blue-tarped stack of firewood in the backyard, and ground the serrated edge of his handsaw across the front of her throat. For Rick, going crazy hadn't been an instantaneous thing. It had taken weeks, perhaps even months, for him to reach that point. Sleepless nights dominated by angst filled internal dialogues had warped his thoughts; lurid red daydreams had beaten down his psyche. He was as mad as a loon when he murdered his wife, but the moment her blood trickled to the ground, mixing in with the slush like a cherry flavored snow cone, he felt his sanity miraculously return.

He had stood over her dead body that afternoon, fingers shaking, not from the chill of the sharp winter air, but from shock, taken aback with himself, yet remarkably clear minded for the first time in ages. Minutes later, he was lugging Melanie by her ankles through the forest behind their home. He stopped randomly about a quarter mile into the labyrinth of Christmas trees, left her body at the base of a Douglas fir, and started back towards the house.

Now, two days later she had returned – *at least part of her anyway.*

Rick plucked the eyeball up from the porch and walked inside the house. He had never held an eye in his hand before and he supposed he never would again. It was heavier than he expected, but just as squishy. He made a beeline straight for the kitchen sink, dropped it down the drain, then flicked a switch on the wall. The garbage-disposal's blades roared to life. It was a hungry monster that dwelled just beneath the stainless steel basin where Rick sometimes peeled potatoes. It minced and chewed the eyeball to paste with whirling metal teeth, then swallowed it down its crooked, plastic neck.

He wasn't trying to get rid of evidence. Rick was well aware that he would not be getting away with his wife's murder. Eventually, Melanie's mother would wonder why her daughter wasn't answering her calls and ask Rick's brother-in-law, who lived only an hour away, to drive down to the house to check on her. Or maybe it would be that drama queen, Jamie Lynch, Melanie's bestie from the book club, who would become suspicious first and call the police. It didn't really matter. He had nowhere else to go. He didn't own a passport and quite frankly, even if he did, he probably wouldn't have tried to flee. He was too tired to run. No, Rick was going to pay for his crime – he had accepted that – but he didn't want to be reminded of this fact in his last few days as a free man. All he wanted to do was pet Felix and watch sports on the couch.

He flicked off the garbage disposal's switch and the monster beneath the sink went to sleep. Rick marched back across the house until he reached the oak trimmed glass door that opened up to his patio. He tugged at the handle, cracking the door, and icy winter air invited itself into his living room. Rick stepped outside to see if Felix was around, but the kitty was nowhere in sight. He called out his name a couple times and even contemplated looking for him, but decided to retreat to the warmth of his heated home and make dinner instead. Felix would come back when he was good and ready. Sometimes his jungle prowls lasted all night. Besides, it was getting dark and he had a hankering for spaghetti.

THE FOLLOWING MORNING, Rick trudged downstairs in his PJ's and brewed some coffee. Once it was hot and ready, he poured himself a cup, stirred in a teaspoon of sugar, then slogged sleepily through the living room as he sipped it. He stopped once he reached the patio door and peered through the glass to see if Felix was waiting on the porch to be let in. He was not, however, he did see something else sitting on the patio. It looked like uncooked bacon smothered in watery ketchup and he hoped (as ridiculous as the

7

idea sounded in his head) that it was, though deep down he knew this was not the case.

Rick opened the door and strode outside to investigate. The wooden porch burned cold against his warm naked feet. He bent down and picked up the fleshy thing between his finger and thumb. It was part of an ear. A sick feeling crept into his stomach where it mingled with coffee and last night's spaghetti. Without a moment of hesitation, Rick rushed back inside and trotted into the kitchen, taking care not to spill from his mug, then fed the chunk of ear to the monster that lived beneath the sink. Rick would feed the monster the spaghetti from his stomach as well.

ONE HOT SHOWER, two bouts of vomiting, and three swigs of *Pepto Bismal* later, Rick was trekking through the woods towards the spot he had left his wife's body. He had a strange urge to see Melanie after finding her in pieces at his patio door. He was bundled up in a puffy North Face jacket that had fit him better when he was 20 pounds heavier. On his head he wore an ugly knitted cap with an orange puffball at the top and draped around his face was a Christmas themed scarf that had cutesy pictures of elves embroidered into it. Mismatched mittens protected his hands from the biting cold and baggy ski pants sagged awkwardly off his rear as if he was auditioning for a part in the stage production of *Christmas with The Crips: A Holiday Trap Boy Musical*.

Melanie had purchased most of the clothes he was wearing. When she was alive Rick rarely had a say when it came to his wardrobe. It had become commonplace for her to lay his outfit for the day on the bed by the time he came out of the shower every morning. Now that she was dead, he realized he'd forgotten how to dress himself. Or maybe he just didn't care. What did it matter anyway? Soon enough he'd be sporting a prison jumpsuit – probably for the rest of his life. The sun was out that morning, shining bright and ironic in the freezing winter sky. Snow crunched loudly beneath his boots and birds in the trees above his head sang songs about a man who murdered his wife with a handsaw.

Rick spotted Melanie's corpse fifty feet ahead of him. She was still lying at the base of the tree exactly like he left her – dead and nearly headless. The closer he got, the more he regretted setting off to find her. He wondered if it would be better or worse to see her face, sans eyes and ears and whatever else Felix had managed to gnaw off. On one hand, such a sight might give him some macabre sense of closure, on the other-

Rick didn't get the chance to finish his thought. Another one had bulldozed its way into his head, bullying the old one to the back of his mind. This new thought was: *Jesus Christ.*

He was close enough to touch Melanie's body now. Her throat had lolled back unnaturally and the open gash in the front of it made her resemble a human Pez dispenser. Her skin was black and blue, frostbitten from the cold, but her face was still intact, even more so than he had expected it would be. She was not missing an ear nor was she missing an eye. She was however missing the eight and a half month old fetus that had been gestating in her uterus

9

when Rick sawed her throat in half earlier that week.

THE JACKET MELANIE WAS WEARING had been torn to shreds. Her sweater underneath was but a web of tattered cotton ribbons. Melanie's swollen stomach splayed open as if a hand grenade had went off inside it. Felix had not been the one to dissect her. It would have been impossible for a housecat to do such a thing. No, some other animals had gotten to Rick's wife – wolves or coyotes, he assumed.

The baby she was carrying was gone – most likely dragged off and devoured by the scavengers of the forest. An appalling thought then popped inside Rick's head. The body parts that had turned up at his patio door had belonged to his unborn son and not his wife.

He had green eyes, just like Melanie.

The words bore into his mind like an earthworm. Rick doubled over and began to heave. There was no spaghetti dinner this time. He had given it all to the monster beneath the kitchen sink. The only thing that came out was *Pepto Bismal*. It tasted the same coming up as it did going down and it turned the snow at his feet bright pink.

THE BABY WAS THE REASON HE HAD KILLED MELANIE. During the last few years of their marriage Rick had come to hate his wife. He was working up the nerve to leave her before she announced her pregnancy to him. It came as a terrible surprise. Melanie was supposed to be on birth control at the time. She told him the child had been a gift from God, which Rick found odd since he had never known her to be the religious type. He suspected she had secretly stopped taking her pills. Rick pleaded with her to get an abortion. He told her that he was too busy for kids. This was a lie. In truth, he knew a child would make cutting all ties with Melanie impossible, and when he finally did divorce her, he wanted to ensure that she was completely out of his life. But Melanie had made up her mind. She would be having their baby with or without his blessing. This was yet another matter she had put her foot down on.

And so, just like with the cat, Rick had caved and together the two bought a crib, converted his office into a nursery, and did all the other things young couples do when they're expecting their first child. According to their O.B. the baby would be a boy with a late December due date.

Might be a Christmas baby, she had said.

Shortly after that was when the crazy thoughts began flooding Rick's head. Eight and a half months later they finally went away, and all it took was a rusty old handsaw and a few buckets of blood on a cold winter afternoon.

THERE WAS NOTHING LEFT FOR HIM TO SEE. Rick wiped the remaining pink slime from his lips and started his short hike back towards the house. The birds overhead were still whistling their tunes, but now they sung of a baby, ripped from his dead mother's womb and torn to shreds by hungry, wild animals. Rick's brains felt like scrambled eggs. He wondered if the baby was still alive while it was being eaten, then decided he'd rather not know the answer to that and pondered other questions instead.

Was there anything left of his little son out there, hidden under the white sheet of icy slush that blanketed the forest floor? Bones perhaps? *There must have been something,* Rick assumed. Otherwise, he wouldn't have been finding little bits of baby on his porch. A powerful sense of guilt swept over him. Melanie might have been a bitch, but his little boy didn't deserve what had happened to him.

The trees were silent evergreen spectators, rising out of snowy earth. They stopped abruptly twenty yards from Rick's home, circling carefully around it as if they were afraid to root themselves in the soil where Melanie's murder had taken place. Rick's journey had left him fatigued – more mentally taxed than physically exhausted – but still, he felt like he needed to rest, to lay his head down, to close his eyes, and he aimed to do all these things as soon as he got inside the house.

His backyard was an icy desert in the middle of a wintery-green paradise. He lumbered through the last of the trees and across the inverted oasis. The slush beneath his feet seemed tainted. It looked gray and hoary like an ashtray – dead even, if it were possible for ice to appear that way. He halted suddenly when the toe of his boot kicked something hard and rigid sticking out of the snow. It made a metallic *clinking* noise when his foot connected with it. Rick gazed down and noticed the handsaw he had used to kill his wife staring up at him. He bent over and pulled it free from the slush.

He had not held it in his hand since that day. Its teeth were still stained red with Melanie's blood. The saw smiled at him like a satisfied glutton that had just enjoyed a great feast. Its grin was derisive – it mocked him.

Rick spun around and flung the saw as hard as he could. He wasn't aiming for anywhere in particular. All he wanted was to make the damn thing go away, just as he had done with the eye and ear.

The handsaw spun through the air like a boomerang and for the briefest of moments Rick was afraid that – just like a boomerang – it might bend back around and make its way towards him again, grinning its red Cheshire Cat grin. But the saw flew a straight course, sailing out of the yard and vanishing between the trees. Rick watched until it disappeared from sight, then he turned back around and resumed his journey across the yard.

He eyed his porch like the finish line at a marathon. It was eight below freezing outside, but somehow Rick was sweating. He stumbled up the wooden steps and nearly fell flat on his face when his foot slipped on a patch of ice. Without so much as a thought, his hand reached out to grip the rail and he managed to catch himself before spilling onto the deck. He paused at the top of the steps to get his bearings and it was here that he noticed it, sitting neatly atop the doormat like an uncooked cocktail sausage dipped in marinara sauce. The air rushed from his lungs so fast they felt like they were going to collapse in on themselves. He was looking at a human finger, and this time, he was sure that it did not belong to his dead wife or his unborn son.

THE SEVERED DIGIT WAS TOO BIG TO BE A BABY'S and too masculine to have belonged to Melanie. It was thick and stubby and a little bit hairy. It had a cracked yellow nail at one end and at the other was a gnarled mess of stringy pink flesh.

The sight of it evoked a strong disgust in Rick, worse than the other body parts he had found on his patio, worse than the saw with the crimson grin, worse even than his wife lying in the snow with her Pez dispenser neck and a belly like a lunar crater. Perhaps it was the uncertainty that revolted him so much. Where had the finger come from? There were no tracks in the snow around his patio, not even a single paw print. Stranger even, who had it belonged to? It was a question Rick couldn't even begin to fathom an answer for.

Rick staggered towards the finger and snatched it from his doormat. There might have been a million questions streaming through his head, but the one thing he did know was that he needed it off his deck. He cocked his arm like a quarterback and chucked a Hail Mary towards the trees. The finger twirled end over end through the air before spiking itself nail side up in the snow a few feet from the place Melanie had taken her last desperate breaths. It hadn't made it to the forest like the handsaw had. Now it was sitting upright in the middle of his yard like a miniature monument.

Rick stared at it for a few uneasy seconds, contemplating whether or not to walk out across the slush and give it another hurl, but eventually decided to let the finger stand in peace. It was supposed to snow later that afternoon and fresh powder would have it covered up by the evening. He called out for Felix again, but the cat did not appear when he shouted his name, so Rick headed inside his living room and plopped himself down on the couch.

He had only been awake for a couple of hours, but he was wiped. His eyelids were becoming heavy and he could feel himself drifting off, but before the dreams took over, his mind conjured up one more thought – something he had not yet considered.

The body parts were all relatively fresh when he found them on the porch, but the weather outside was below freezing. Exposure for only an hour at that kind of temperature would've been enough to freeze flesh rock solid, yet the eye had been squishy when he held it in his hand and the ear and finger were both warm to the touch. It was an utterly insane conclusion to draw, but this sudden epiphany could only mean that the bits and pieces he had been finding were only just being delivered to his porch minutes before he arrived and that whoever they were coming from was more than likely still alive and breathing when they had been removed.

The revelation was not enough to pull him from sleep's relentless grasp. His body felt like it was sinking into the couch. Just a few minutes, he thought to himself. *I'll turn my brain off for a few minutes and then I'll figure out what the hell is going on.*

Rick would sleep for three and a half hours. During that time he would have a terrible nightmare, but he wouldn't remember any of it by the time he woke up.

THE FIRST THING RICK EXPECTED TO SEE when he opened his eyes was the finger. It was there, still standing upright in his backyard like a tiny pink lawn dart, but something else much more prominent had managed to capture his attention. A black, white, and blonde ball of fur was curled up at the patio door. Rick sprung to his feet at the sight of it. His cat was home. He zipped across the living room in a flash and jerked open the door in the same perfunctory manner Kramer might have entered Jerry's apartment on *Seinfeld,* but the second he got a clear look at his kitty, he knew that something was very wrong.

The black, white, and blonde ball of fur curled up at the patio door was actually a black, white, blonde, and red ball of fur, and it wasn't moving. Felix was dead. Just as dead as his wife, dead as the gray ashy slush that caked Rick's yard. Felix's body was twisted and coiled as if someone had wrung him out like a wet towel. Blood oozed like strawberry syrup from his mouth and eyes.

Rick wanted to cry, but couldn't. Maybe the cold had frozen his tear ducts. More than likely, it was the horror swirling inside him that had put a stop to the tears. He was no longer in denial. It hadn't been Felix, or any other animal for that matter, leaving the body parts on his patio. Rick Collum was being stalked.

He touched a hand to Felix's fur. His body was still warm. The cat couldn't have been killed and placed at his door more than 20 minutes before he woke up. He scanned the yard with wild eyes, searching desperately for some sign of his stalker, but found nothing. Rick's hands were quaking with frustration. He almost screamed out at the trees, but swallowed it down before it could burst free from his mouth. The stalker was no doubt out there watching him, waiting for him to crack. It was clear now that this mystery man had been playing a game with Rick, trying to elicit a certain reaction out of him, but he wasn't about to show that he was rattled. That was what the maniac wanted. He had to stay calm and collected until he could think of a plan.

Rick scooped the poor cat up off the porch and carried him out into the middle of the yard. It was here that he would dig Felix's grave. He grabbed a shovel from the tool shed and went to work. The frozen ground was stubborn and unyielding at first, but Rick chiseled away at the icy upper crust with the edge of his spade until he reached the softer dirt below.

The digging was more for Rick than for Felix. Yardwork helped him meditate. Back when his wife was alive, he had always used it as an excuse to steal away from her incessant nagging. His most peaceful moments had come when he was chopping wood or tending to the vegetable garden during the warm months. He was trying to relax now, but he could feel the eyes of the stalker studying him from the trees.

He didn't know why he was being tormented. Perhaps the psychopath had been watching Rick and his wife for months. He wondered if it could all be some sadistic form of payback – punishment for what he had done to Melanie. His thoughts turned to her, how she had driven him to the brink of sanity, how she had tricked him into getting her pregnant. And then the idea struck him like a bolt of lighting.

Oh God, the baby!

Maybe it hadn't been animals that had torn his son from his dead wife's stomach. Maybe it was the stalker. *Yeah, that was it.* The freak had somehow removed Rick's son before he could die in Melanie's womb, and now he was trying to drive Rick mad.

"He wants me out of the picture so he can raise the baby himself," he uttered under his breath.

He knew now what he had to do. Rick was going to face this mystery man head on. If there was a chance his son was alive, he was going to rescue him from whoever this sicko was. After that, he would own up to his crime and call the police. The baby would most likely be handed over to Melanie's mother while Rick was in prison. She was well-to-do and not *that* old – the boy would have a good life. It wouldn't absolve Rick of his sins, but at least he could do something good with his last few hours as a free man.

RICK SPOONED THE LAST BIT OF DIRT on top of Felix's grave and patted it down with the back of his shovel. The finger stood stoically mere feet from the plot – the sole mourner at the unfortunate kitty's funeral.

Rick tossed the shovel to the ground then whirled around to face the trees. "I know you're out there," he said, "and I know you have my son." His voice was bold, but deep down he was terrified. He pointed to the living room. "I'll be waiting right there. On my couch. If you have any balls, you'll face me. Bring him with you...I'm not moving from that spot until you show yourself."

And with that, Rick marched inside and prepared for war.

RICK COLLUM HAD NEVER BEEN TO WAR BEFORE. If one were to overlook the Melanie incident, he hadn't even been in a fight since the seventh grade, when an older boy named Tommy Harper punched him in the gut for spilling his lunch tray all over the eighth grader's brand-new Denver Broncos jersey after Rick tripped over a backpack in the school cafeteria. Rick had seen movies about war before – he went through a phase in college where he was into old Vietnam movies. He and his roommate had even gotten high one Friday night and watched *Apocalypse Now* three times in a row. But this was not Vietnam or Cambodia and he was not Captain Ben Willard or crazy ass Colonel Kilgore, and he did not love the smell of napalm in the morning. In fact, he didn't even know what napalm smelled like.

His home wasn't a conventional military stronghold. There was a fire burning in the fireplace and his television was tuned into a holiday music station that was currently playing through a Bing Crosby Christmas album. He was sitting on a pistachio green leather sofa and in his lap was a fire-poker that he used to jab kindling when it needed help catching. It was his M1 Carbine. Rick had no real gun (Melanie had never let him own a firearm) and he had no military training outside of what he had seen in old movies, but he readied himself and waited just the same. *Char-*

lie was hiding out somewhere in the woods and he needed to stay alert.

The sun had gone down hours ago and snow was falling heavy. A few inches must have already come down because the finger was finally buried and Rick's dead gray yard had been covered up by a layer of fresh powder. He felt like he had been sitting on the couch, listening to holiday crooners forever. Rick began to wonder if his stalker would ever show, and for a second he even doubted his sanity. Maybe his cracked mind had never really mended itself and everything he'd been experiencing was all one big psychotic episode.

That theory didn't last too long though. It melted away like a dead man's presence in a world that's ever moving, always forgetting. *He was sane, all right.* Rick saw it appear in the darkness. His eyes could just barely make it out, but there was definitely something outside, or someone rather, standing at the edge of his yard, where the tree line began – the figure of a man.

THE MAN STOOD MOTIONLESS, as if completely unbothered by the snowstorm that had rolled in. Rick squinted, trying to make out his features, but the night was dark and the figure was just a black silhouette against a white backdrop. There was no denying what he was seeing though. His stalker had arrived.

Rick leaned forward in his seat, gripping the brass handle of the fireplace poker tight. He tried to swallow, but his mouth was dry. Something was very off about the man.

There was an object in his stalker's hand. It was flat and rigid and he couldn't tell what it was, but the sight sent a shiver down the back of Rick's neck. A rope of some sort hung from the man's waist, dangling down to his mid thighs.

Rick's baby was nowhere to be seen. A disappointed sigh slipped out from between his lips and he felt his heart sink a little in his chest. He had been so sure the stalker would show up with his son. Now his chance at redemption was fluttering away on transparent wings.

The shadowy figure began to move across the yard and as it did, its shape grew larger. By the time the stalker reached Felix's grave, Rick could tell he was dealing with a very big man. The body advancing towards the house dwarfed Rick's much smaller frame. It was tall and broad with thick arms, bulky thighs, and a torso like a mailbox. The stalker's features were beginning to take shape too and now Rick could see that his mysterious pursuer wasn't wearing any clothes. It was both ridiculous and terrifying to see the massive naked man striding through the snow. Rick could tell what he was carrying in his hand now. It was the saw he had flung into the woods earlier that day. The damn thing was still grinning red.

BING CROSBY'S SMOOTH BARITONE VOICE was flowing out of the television's speakers. He was singing of sleigh bells and treetops and snow – the song was White Christmas.

ONCE THE GIANT NAKED MAN reached the base of the patio steps, his features had become as clear as day. The frightening spectacle made Rick jerk to his feet. He knew where the stalker had been getting the body parts that had been turning up at his door – himself. One of his eyes was missing from his face and it looked as if part of his ear had been torn off the side of his head.

Yet the most maddening thing about this man's face was not the disfigurements, but how hauntingly familiar it was. Rick was sure he had never met the nude behemoth before, there was no way he would have forgotten him if he had, but there was no shaking the feeling that he knew his face. *Somehow he knew it.*

The man stomped up the porch's wooden stairs. His footsteps rattled the deck. He was built like an NFL lineman, with huge muscles hidden by a generous layer of fat. He reached the top of the deck, and Rick lowered his poker towards him as if were wielding a spear. The glass patio door was the only thing separating the two. Rick glanced at the rope swinging freely between the depraved man's legs. His eyes trailed it upwards and it wasn't until they reached the top that he realized it wasn't a rope at all. It was gray and fleshy, and it protruded from the stalker's doughy stomach like a growth.

Wait – Rick couldn't believe what he was seeing – *was that an-*

There was no more time to finish his thought. The patio door burst open. In rushed a gust of icy air, but the cold was not the only thing that entered Rick's living room. His stalker was now only a few feet away from him. Rick jabbed at him with the poker, but the hulking man knocked it away with a big, meaty paw and it fell uselessly to the floor. With his other hand, he grabbed Rick by the collar of his shirt, then shoved him down to the sofa.

Rick looked up at his attacker and suddenly it came to him. He knew why the stalker's face was so familiar. It was his face, and Melanie's too – an amalgam of both of theirs. The man had Rick's nose and his dead wife's lips. His one remaining eye was the same color as hers, but damned if he didn't have Rick's chin. He glanced again at the fleshy rope hanging from his attacker's stomach, right where his belly button should be – a rope that had once been connected to Melanie's womb. And so, he understood, the stalker *had* brought his son after all.

The man wrapped a four fingered hand around Rick's face and scowled at him. There was a hateful look in his eye. Rick was sure he would have cursed him if he could talk, but unborn babies don't know how to speak English. A few days ago, Melanie had been carrying his son in her belly. Now that baby was a grown man – a very large grown man – and he was standing over Rick in his living room, palming his face like a basketball.

He raised the saw to Rick's neck. Rick understood then that it was vengeance that had come for him. He would not be getting the redemption he'd been seeking. No, retribution would be had instead, and it would be had at his expense. He was about to be punished for his selfish crime, for ending the life of his baby before it had even begun. And who better to wreak vengeance on him than his son himself? Rick didn't feel the need to question how what was happening was even possible. His mind was sound, that much he knew, but thinking about the ins and outs of what he was witnessing might have caused it to crack again, and he didn't want to die a madman. The teeth of the saw felt cold against his skin. The grinning glutton was ready to feast again – and feast it would.

Bing Crosby's Christmas album was still playing on the TV. The famous crooner's soothing voice blended seamlessly in the air with Rick's screams. He sang of calling pipes and mountainsides, of summer meadows and bleeding throats.

THE OCEAN'S COOL AIR

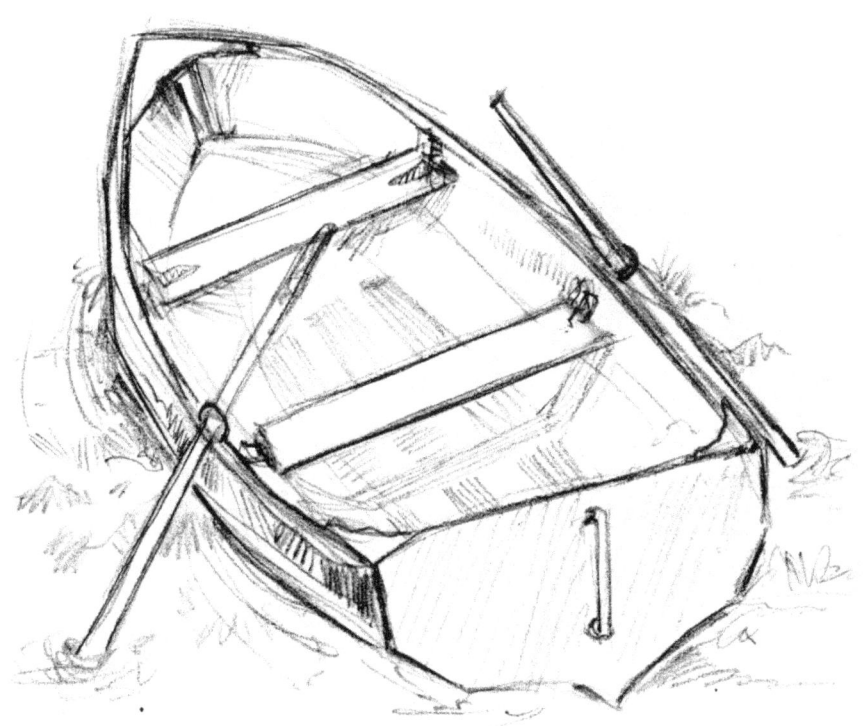

STARED UP AND INTO THE HEAVENS. Stars dotted the evening sky like little white splotches of paint, haphazardly splattered across a black canvas. On a nearly moonless night the tiny twinkling specks of light were the only things illuminating the darkness brought on by dusk. I had grown to look forward to nightfall. The days had become unbearable due to the constant bombardment of UV rays that I had been forced to endure. The evening's cool air tended to my damaged skin, giving reprieve from the daily beatings I took from the sun. The night also provided constellations, which had become a welcomed distraction. The stars told stories – stories that helped me forget – forget about the decrepit old lifeboat in the middle of the ocean that I was stranded in.

I barely noticed the commercial fishing boat as it approached my dinghy – a testament to how far-gone my mind had become from the weeks of isolation out at sea.

"Hey there! Are you ok?"

The young man was looking down at me from the bow of the ship. I gazed up to study him from my rowboat. His piercing blue eyes almost glowed in contrast to the black sky behind him. I could see the whiskers that had begun to sprout from his face — a result of going days without shaving while out on the water. As he scratched his stubbly chin, more of the crew crowded around the front of the boat to take a gander at me. I suppose a half-dead man marooned out at sea was the strangest sight they'd seen in quite a while — an honor I would hold for only the briefest of moments.

"He's alive!" one of the fishermen shouted. "Let's get him up here now!"

As I watched the crew frantically buzz around the ship's deck, trying to figure out how to bring me aboard, a laugh escaped my mouth. Not a loud bellowing one, mind you, just a tiny giggle. It was the irony of the situation that I found comical. Perhaps that last little chuckle was the humor center of my brain finally fading from the weeks of emotional agony I had sustained. Going out not with a bang, but with a whimper — just a tiny giggle.

It started with a loud crash across the starboard side of their boat. The fishermen struggled to retain their footing when the powerful impact caused their vessel to rock onto its side, nearly capsizing it. Shouts and expletives streamed from the mouths of the startled sailors as I watched them desperately try to make sense of what had just occurred.

Another thunderous CLANG rang along the side of their ship and this time it tipped. The once silent ocean air was now filled with the sounds of chaos as the trawler smashed across the surface of the sea, flipping completely upside-down, and sending the men toppling overboard into the cold, murky water. I struggled to lift my head in

28

order to peer over the side of my dinghy at the anarchy taking place around me.

The fishermen barely had a chance to breach and catch their breaths before it began pulling them back down into the abyss. Their panic quickly intensified as, one by one, they started to realize their crewmates were disappearing into the deep, dark sea. You've never truly experienced pandemonium until you've heard a dozen grown men screaming for their lives in the middle of the ocean. The young man who had first greeted me from the ship's bow thrashed and kicked through the water, urgently trying to make his way towards my lifeboat. With salvation mere inches away, he flailed his arms wildly, reaching and grasping with reckless abandon, attempting to grab on to the side. I watched the hope in those piercing blue eyes of his turn to hopelessness as a black, sludge covered tentacle wrapped itself around his ankle and yanked him back down under with one quick jerk.

Then, it was the fishing boat's turn. Still submerged, the sea-beast easily crumpled the already twisted hunk of metal, before sinking it down to the watery graveyard at the bottom of the briny deep. There it would join countless other vessels that had shared a similar fate.

Without warning, the massive creature erupted from the surface of the sea. I wondered briefly if the salty taste of the water that splashed my face when the beast made its appearance stemmed from the ocean itself or the blood of the men who had died in it. I shut my eyes, hoping not to catch a glimpse of its horrible features. The sound of water trickling around the leviathan's body as it waded towards my lifeboat caused me to wince. Though my eyes were clenched tight, I could still feel its awful presence as it closed in on me. The stench of rotten anchovies lingered all around me in the air, and I knew it was near. With a thud, the creature dropped a mangled human limb across my lap – one of the fishermen's arms to be precise.

It spoke only one word. The same word it had said to me many times before and the same word it would repeat many times after.

"Eat."

And with that, it slithered back into the sea, leaving me to myself again. I opened my eyes and stared down at the mutilated piece of flesh lying across my sunburnt thighs. For a moment I was tempted to throw it back overboard, but thought the better of it, fearing retaliation from the creature for not obeying its commands. I was a worm on its hook, and because of this it preferred to keep me alive, but I wasn't about to test my captor's patience. I sunk my teeth into the skin and tore a chunk of muscle from the bone. It had been a week since I had last eaten. I chewed slowly. The taste was almost sweet. The hunger pains in my stomach helped to subdue the horrors in my mind and made the atrocity of cannibalism slightly easier.

I let out a sigh and looked back up to the starry night. I was alone again, and once more only silence reigned over the ocean's cool air.

GAS STATION
BATHROOM

T HE GAS STATION BATHROOM was one of the filthiest, most disgusting places Shelly had ever seen. The nauseating smell that permeated the air wafted into her face, violating her nostrils as soon as she opened the door, invading her mouth and nose before settling on the back of her tongue. Used toilet paper, bloody tampons, and cigarette butts littered the ground like repulsive landmines waiting for some poor unsuspecting sap only slightly more careless than she to trudge through the cesspool in a rush and smear their revolting contents even further across the tiled floor. One of the fluorescent lights above flickered randomly with a sinister inconsistency as if it had a mind of its own. For a moment, Shelly contemplated testing her body's demands for reprieve until she could find another gas station with a cleaner restroom, but remembered the sign she read on the interstate just before taking the rest stop's exit.

NEXT GAS 60 MILES

Besides, nature had been urgently calling for a while and it wasn't dialing number one...

Carefully, Shelly stepped around the nasty obstacles strewn along the ground and made her way towards the bathroom stalls. Another hot wave of noxious odor smacked her across the face when she opened the door to reveal an abhorrent porcelain grotesquery. Vomit began creeping its way up her throat when she took sight of the crap-covered commode, where only dull bits of white and grime were exposed here and there, like the last remaining survivors of some horrific catastrophe, having been caught in this volcanic explosion of feces which now cascaded down in all directions, billowing in and out of the toilet, bubbling like toxic sludge. Quickly shutting the door, she turned away while holding her breath in a futile attempt to prevent anymore of Mt. Evershit's fecal fumes from reaching her already defiled lungs.

The second stall was far less repugnant and aside from the syringe that had sunk to the bottom of the toilet bowl's dirty water, it seemed almost sanitary. Almost. Shelly decided it would have to do, partly because of the pressure building in her bowels and partly because she feared that checking behind door number three might be pushing her luck. Summoning every ounce of courage in her body, she pulled down her undies and squatted over the seat making sure not to touch her skin to the vile porcelain throne.

The young lady had barely even begun to relieve herself when the bathroom erupted in a series of clattering and clanging so loud that it nearly caused her to fall backwards into the water out of shock. Someone had burst through the bathroom door in a flurry and knocked over the metal waste bin that had been standing next to the sink.

Shelly remained silent, hoping that whoever had barged in wouldn't notice her. It was the middle of the night, and as far as she was concerned, anyone causing such a ruckus in a dirty bathroom on the side of the highway was either addicted to smack or a raging lunatic. Either way, she wasn't about to let her presence be known if she could avoid it, so she clenched her cheeks and grimaced, fighting off the backend rebellion.

Loud groans were now emanating from the other side of her stall's door. It was a woman's voice, which only slightly alleviated Shelly's feelings about the predicament she had now found herself in. From under the door she could see the strange woman's legs stumble closer in the direction of the stalls. With a crash and a bang, the woman exploded through door number three, raucously toppling down to the toilet.

The moans turned to cries and suddenly the trepidation Shelly had been feeling melted away only to be replaced by panic as the woman just one stall over from her shrieked at the top of her lungs. She wanted to speak up, ask if everything was alright, but the noises coming from the other side of the flimsy metal barricade between them paralyzed her vocal cords.

The woman began choking, her gags only briefly interrupted by the sounds of screams. A rank potent stench swelled from the third stall and saturated the air in the room, even overcoming the vomit-inducing aroma Mt. Evershit had been cultivating in the first stall. The woman's shadow, cast by the one good fluorescent light in the bathroom, jerked violently on the grimy floor under

Shelly's feet. Shelly tried desperately to drown out the horrific noises taking place behind door number three, but they had gotten so loud that covering her ears barely muffled the woman's sobs.

A symphony of sickening cries burst forth from the strange woman's stall. Shelly began to wonder how much more she could take before the mind numbingly awful sounds and smells would drive her mad. No longer capable of withstanding the war being waged on her senses she tried to work up the nerve to make a break for the door, but before she had a chance to run, the noises abruptly halted – and with a splish and a splash, the room fell silent.

Shelly squatted over the toilet for what felt like minutes, doing her best to remain as quiet as possible. In the third stall, the woman's shadow slowly started shifting again across the dingy bathroom floor. Shelly prepared for the screams to begin anew, but instead of filling the room with more of her ear piercing shrieks the woman fell off the toilet and rolled halfway underneath the divider between the two stalls. She lay there motionless, cheek flush against the urine stained floor and wide eyes looking up to the frightened young lady still squatting over the toilet with her thong around her ankles. Thick black fluid began to discharge from the woman's mouth and nose, dribbling down her face like chocolate syrup on a sundae. With her final few breaths, she forced a couple of tiny grunts out of her oozing mouth in an attempt to speak.

"You- you have to get out of here."

Following these words, the last little bits of life faded from her body. Shelly watched on in terror while the woman's eyes rolled back into her head and the same black ooze started to trickle from her tear ducts.

Something began splashing around in the toilet bowl inside the other woman's stall. A cocktail of confusion, anxiety, shock, and dread swirled around inside the young lady's head as she tried desperately to process what was taking place. From under the divider between the two stalls, Shelly watched a pair of feet covered in the very same black muck that was still seeping its way out of every orifice in the woman's face step down from the toilet and onto the bathroom floor. The rusty hinges fastened to door number three squealed as whatever was inside slowly began to push the door open. Shelly covered her mouth with both hands trying not to even breath audibly, hoping to God that the thing on the other side of the wobbly tin divider between them was not aware of her presence. The slimy feet shuffled clumsily out of the stall and across the scum-covered flooring, as if their owner was using them for the first time. Shelly bit down on her tongue, struggling to fight off the urge to scream as the sludge coated feet stopped and turned towards her stall. A hush reigned over the room for what felt like an eternity. Finally a gravelly cracked voice broke the silence, emerging from the other side of Shelly's door.

"I'm terribly sorry miss, but could you spare some toilet paper? I seem to be fresh out."

THE WOMAN IN THE RED SUNDRESS

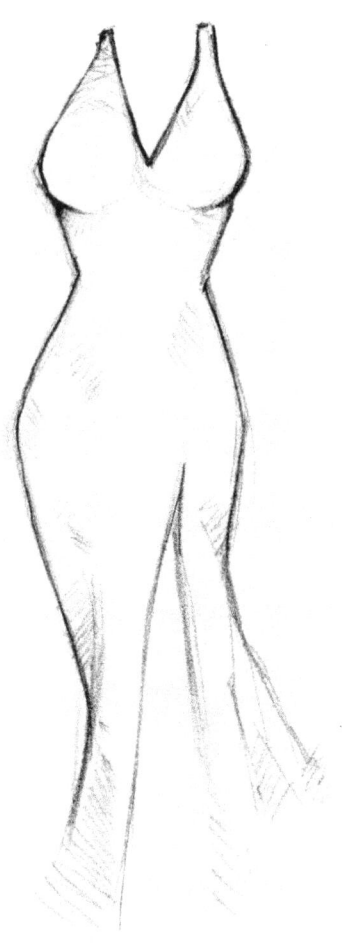

T HE WIND FEELS AMAZING as it whips past my face. There she is. She is but a speck in the distance, but she's there, the woman in the red sundress. She doesn't know me, but I will meet her very soon. This I promise.

I wonder when we meet what she'll sound like, what she'll smell like, what she'll feel like. I wish I could freeze this moment in time just so I could admire her from afar, but alas, the woman in the red sundress grows closer.

You can never truly appreciate the majesty of the city unless you've seen it like I'm seeing it right now. It's breathtaking. The chaos and disorder of this metropolis – rough and rowdy city streets I've traveled so many times. They seem to transform into a picture of serenity from here. *Still, the woman in the red sundress grows closer.*

Her hair is raven colored with auburn streaks. I can see it more clearly now. I close my eyes and stretch my arms like a bird, letting my other senses do the work. The freedom overwhelming my body is intoxicating. It's as if all my sorrows and all my anxiety have escaped me, and though my eyes are shut tight, I know the woman in the red sundress grows closer.

Pastel Colored Dreams & Human Flavored Nightmares

After a few moments I open my eyes again. People are looking at me now. A balding man in a suit with a brief-case points up at me.

"Look out!" he shouts.

I don't care. I feel incredible, like a shooting star that's journey is finally coming to an end after eons of aimlessly wandering the cosmos. I can see her face now. The woman in the red sundress is staring at me. She's so beautiful. Her candy red lipstick matches her ensemble. I can even smell her perfume. Its lavender scented. I had guessed it would have been citrusy, but I am not disappointed. She reaches her hands to the sky as if she's beckoning me. I can almost touch her now. She screams-

Splat

PICTURE THIS

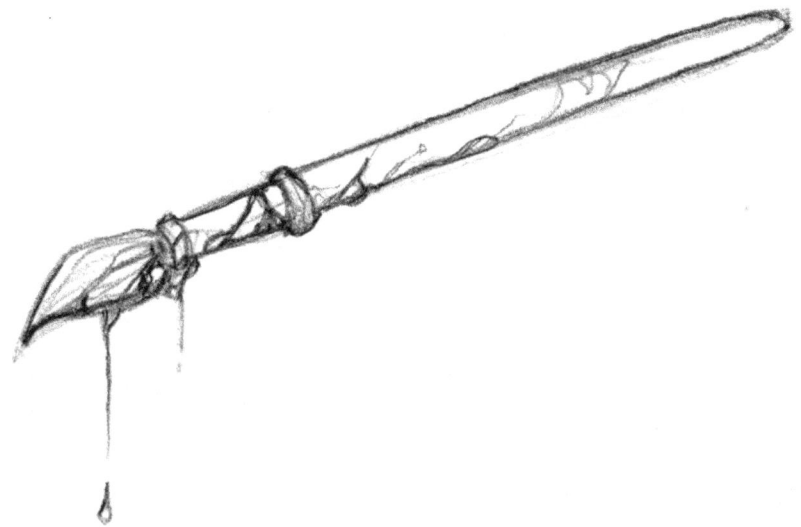

PICTURE THIS.
90,000 people are reported missing every year in the
United States alone. You heard that number correctly.
Don't believe me? Look it up: 90,000 people. A staggering
2,300 people are reported missing daily. Now, let's be clear;
many of these cases are solved relatively quickly, and I'm
not talking about bloated corpses found floating in rivers
or dismembered bodies turning up somewhere off the Jersey Turnpike.

Of the 90,000 people who are reported missing annually, around 85,000 of them are kids. Most missing children tend to fall into one of two categories: runaways who
eventually return home safely, or family abductions. The
latter of which occurs when either the mother or father
runs off with the little ones because of a domestic dispute
or divorce.

As far as adults go, a large portion of missing cases
typically involve people who are suffering from drug or alcohol abuse. These addicts have a tendency to go on bend-
ers, disappearing from their friends and families for days
on end while they pump their bodies full of booze and il-

legal narcotics. A surprisingly high number of reports are concerning senior citizens suffering from dementia or Alzheimer's. You'd be surprised how often they wander away from their caretakers and get lost. Usually it doesn't take very long for the police to locate the disoriented old-timer and bring them back to the nursing home.

Given these facts, we see the number of people (both children and adults) who are abducted by strangers is actually relatively small. Only about 150 of these kinds of abductions are estimated to occur in the United States annually.

Now picture this.

It was 2014. You were an artist – a painter who specialized in impressionism. You loved art all your life. You saw a coffee table book when you were 12-years-old that had a picture of "Blue Dancers" by Edgar Degas and you couldn't look away from it. You were mesmerized by the colors, the pastel strokes, the way the girls in the masterpiece contorted their bodies. To you, they didn't even look like dancers – they were a meadow of morning glories swaying in a gentle breeze. You knew right then and there that you wanted to create something as gorgeous and spellbinding as that picture.

You studied the greats: Renoir, Degas, Cezanne, and of course Monet. When you turned 15, you started taking art classes after school at the local community college, but you never shared your passion with anyone – not even your closest friends and family. You were afraid of what they might say. What if they laughed at you? What if they told you that you that your paintings were sloppy or ugly? What if they told you that you didn't have talent or that you'd never create your own "Blue Dancers" one day?

So you hid your passion from everyone you knew. Whenever you finished a piece you tossed it in the garbage because seeing your art in a dumpster was better than the possibility of hearing your friends make fun of it.

You wanted to study art in college, but society told you that only morons do that. Instead you opted for an engineering degree. Your parents were happy. You graduated from school and got a job where you sat in a cubicle and made $55,000 per year. You spent all day every day musing about what it would be like to wake up each morning and do nothing but paint. You tried to keep up with your art, but you never had the time. Your boss asked you to work weekends every chance he got and when you did have a second to yourself you were too tired to do anything but watch TV or surf the web. You started to hate yourself for being so spineless – for not pursuing the only thing in life that ever made you feel good. You fell into a depression.

Picture this.

An estimated 1 in 10 Americans suffer from depression. That means there are at least 30 million people in the US who feel lost, who feel hopeless, who feel like the world would be a better place without them and you were one of those people.

You wore a mask in front of your friends and family. That part was easy. You had been hiding your passion from them all your life, you could hide your depression too. Nobody at work could see how much you were hurting, but when you got home you lay in bed and you cried. You thought about downing an entire bottle of aspirin, but you were afraid of what people would say if you survived.

You stood on the edge of your bathtub with one end of a belt looped around your neck and the other fastened to the metal rod of your shower curtain while you weighed the pros and cons of suicide. You spent hours surfing the Internet, visiting forums, looking for a way to save yourself. You even went so far as to post questions anonymously, pleading for help.

Then you got the piece of advice that you believed you were searching for – from Reddit of all places, a website famous for stupid cat pictures and bastardizing the word "meme." It came in the form of a comment in a thread you made about feeling suicidal. You didn't see the commenter's username, in fact, you were so excited after reading their advice that you closed your browser's window before checking where it came from. It didn't matter who they were in real life anyways, as far as you were concerned those words were sent straight to you from your guardian angel, watching over from heaven.

Try finding a creative outlet, your web-surfing savior said. *I picked up painting as a means to channel my depression. Whenever I'm feeling down, I grab a brush and get to work. It helps to serve as a fantastic distraction.*

So picture this.

You took that guardian angel's advice and ran with it. You swore off suicide, called your mom and dad and told them you love them. The very next morning you woke up and headed to the library where you spent the entire day reading about your favorite artists – the painters you had idolized your entire life. For hours you looked at photos of their works and it made you feel young again. Then you stumbled upon a book with a picture of "Blue Dancers," and you found yourself awestruck, just like that time when you were 12. It was that moment you decided to quit your job and follow your dreams.

Your mom and dad weren't happy, but they understood when you told them about your depression. They always thought art was just a mild hobby and had never actually seen one of your finished paintings before. It took all of the courage you could muster to show them a piece you prepared for them. After all, it was more than just a picture to you. It was your heart, your dreams – it was a piece of your soul. It went better than you expected. The painting made your dad smile and your mother tear up. Since you had no job, they let you move back in and turn your room into a studio until you could figure things out.

And picture this.

You turned back to the Internet for advice, only this time you weren't looking for someone to talk you off a ledge. You wanted tips on color blending and assistance on applying primer. You started posting pictures of your work to various forums looking for guidance, but you got more than you bargained for. You began receiving compliments – total strangers telling you how much they loved your art.

A few people even commissioned pieces from you. You sold your first painting for $300 to a newly wed couple in Minnesota who said your art would be perfect for their new home. It was surreal. All you ever wanted to do was paint and now people were paying you for it. You opened an online store, started a blog, and even built a website with links to all of your social media accounts. You began to rack up followers on Facebook and Twitter. A couple of your paintings were blogged around the Internet thousands of times. An art enthusiast magazine even did a feature on one of your pieces. It wasn't on the cover or anything, but it was an honor just to get a tiny blurb.

Eventually, you made enough money to move out of your parents' house and get a small apartment of your own. You certainly weren't rich, but you got to wake up and do nothing but paint every day, just like you always dreamed.

One morning you opened your eyes to see a half-finished commissioned piece staring back at you from across the room. Rays of early morning sunshine shimmered in through the window, falling on the partially completed painting. It glimmered in the daylight. You thought about how lost you would have been if not for that guardian angel on the Internet who convinced you to paint your sadness away. You smiled to yourself — the first time in a long time that it wasn't forced because you knew that you were finally happy.

But picture this.

When one begins to receive admirers they also start to attract critics — people who question how or why you got to where you were in your career. Some of them were jealous. They wanted what you had. Many of them were artists in their own right who didn't receive nearly the amount of attention you got. You found their hate silly. After all, it's not like your paintings were touring museums around the country. You were barely scraping by, but they couldn't support themselves with their art so they hated you.

Some of your other detractors weren't artists at all.

They were trolls who couldn't stand to see another person happy so they did their best to knock you down a peg. They used the cloak of anonymity to message you through Twitter just to call you names. They told you that your work was "crap," but when they said that they weren't just insulting your paintings, they were insulting you. Remember, your art was a reflection of your heart, your dreams – it was a piece of your soul and these sorry excuses for human beings, hiding behind idiotic user handles, were shitting all over it.

And then something strange happened. You no longer heard the praise and the compliments. They were still there, but almost muffled in a way – suffocated and drowned out by a vocal minority who only wanted to see you fail.

You fought to prove yourself – to paint something that would make even your most overly zealous hecklers change their minds about you, but the more of your heart you poured into your work, the harsher their words became. The closer you got to creating your very own "Blue Dancers," the more hate and vitriol they spewed at you.

It began to consume you. It was all you could think about.

Picture this.

Hacking isn't nearly as difficult as Hollywood would have you believe it is. You don't need to be a zit-faced computer whiz that spends 18 hours a day in a dark basement eating Cheetos and drinking Mountain Dew to learn how to do it. You don't even need to know how to get around firewalls or disassemble code. All you need is patience. Patience and the understanding that people, even anonymous Internet trolls, get a little too comfortable and give away personal information without even thinking about it.

Now picture this.

The haters kept coming for you. Every time you posted a picture of your work or announced another sale on Facebook, there they were, popping up like a rash of puss filled herpes sores. One commenter in particular really got under your skin. His username was Dark_Painter97 and every remark he made on your art blog was rude and spiteful. "Overrated," he called you – "unoriginal" and "uninspired" as well. You could see the resentment seething out of every comment he left underneath your posts.

You had grown sick of his cyber-bullying. Part of you wanted to see what this keyboard warrior looked like in real life so without thinking you clicked on his username. The link directed you to the profile page of his blog, but he didn't have any pictures uploaded to it. However, a caption in the "about" section caught your eye.

It said: Follow me on twitter @Dark_Painter97.

You checked out his twitter account to see if this anonymous jackass had posted any photos of himself. He hadn't, and his profile picture was just some stupid cartoon character, but you did notice he was very active on his account. He went back and forth, tweeting jokes with one particular user quite frequently – a teenager whose user handle included his real name with a very clear face pic. They appeared to be good friends. You realized then that the "97" in Dark_Painter97 was most likely a reference to the year your tormenter was born. It made sense. It takes a certain amount of immaturity and free time to cyber-bully someone and teenage boys have both of those in spades. You performed a Facebook search of his friend's name and found him pretty easily. His profile page had the privacy functions disabled so it wasn't hard to poke around.

This teenager only had about 125 friends on Facebook, so you began filtering through his list, looking for boys who were born in the year 1997. It only took about an hour of sifting through profile pages until you found something that struck a chord with you. It was a boy who fit the bill. He was a smarmy little weasel who looked like he hadn't been outside a day in his life. Everything about his face irked you, from his bird's beak of a nose, to the pair of bulky, camouflage print Oakley sunglasses he was wearing in his profile pic. You wanted so badly to smash his smug smile into paste.

Then you looked at the info section of his page and you felt the light bulb in your head slowly begin to brighten.

Likes: Gaming, Manga and Painting

Ok, that's a check, but liking to paint doesn't automatically make him the culprit.

Birthday: June, 26 1997

Double check.

And of course...

Follow my art blog @Dark_Painter97

Checkmate, bitch.

You had him. You knew what that insufferable little troll looked like, where he lived, you even knew what high school he went to. In just over an hour and a half you had learned everything you could ever want to know about him, but what were you going to do with your new-found information? According to his Facebook, he lived a state away. That's a long way to go just to tell someone off. You told yourself that driving over state lines for the sole purpose of yelling at some idiot kid was crazy, but you couldn't stop yourself. It was like someone else had taken control of body. Before you knew it, you were on the Interstate, halfway between the teenager's hometown and your apartment.

You stopped off for a burger when you hit his county and looked his parents' information up on your cellphone. Finding their home address was easy. The time was around 4:00PM when you pulled up to his house. According to their Facebook pages, his mom and dad both worked nine to five's so you figured they wouldn't be home yet. You could see the little brat through the window fiddling around on his computer, probably leaving another disparaging comment on the latest picture you uploaded to your blog, either that or looking at porn. Things had worked out too perfectly for you. You had come too far not to give him a piece of your mind so you pulled your car into the driveway and knocked on the front door.

You could tell he was confused when he answered it. He had no idea who you were, which was something you found funny. If you had spent as much time as he did harassing someone on the Internet, you figured you'd at least recognize them if they were standing at your front door.

You opened your mouth to speak. You even pointed an accusatory finger at him, but his entitled little face made you so damn angry. You blacked out.

When you came to your senses, you were standing over him in the foyer. Now that arrogant look on his face was gone. Instead, it appeared as if a cherry bomb had exploded in it. His nose had been mushed into pulp and his left eye was completely swollen shut. You were taken aback with yourself. How had it happened? You weren't even a violent person. In fact, you had never planned on causing the kid any sort of physical harm.

You looked at the grandfather clock against the wall. It was 4:30. Where had the time gone? Who knew how long you had before his parents got home? Charges started to rattle off in your mind: aggravated assault of a minor, burglary. Who knows, maybe even attempted murder? If they caught you then you'd do the next 15 years in prison for sure. Goodbye art career. Then you had another thought. If you just ran off, the snotty little shit might be able to identify you once he came to – so you panicked.

You slung his unconscious body over your shoulder and carried him outside to your car. Lady luck must have been on your side because there was no one else in sight. You dumped him in your trunk and backed out of the driveway as fast as you could before speeding off to make your getaway.

Only about 150 people get abducted by strangers in the United States annually. Now this kid was one of them and he was locked in the back of your trunk.

Picture this.

One in every 15,000 people is murdered in the USA each year. Doesn't that number sound high? It's true though. Don't believe me? Look it up: one in every 15,000 people. Calculate those stats over a 75 year lifespan, and that means there is a one in 200 chance that someone will try to kill you.

It's a terrifying thought, really. In comparison, your chances of getting hit by a car are only one in 600, which means you're three times more likely to get gutted by a knife wielding maniac or shot by a jaded ex-lover than you are to get run over by a minivan that's driver was texting while speeding through an intersection.

Now picture this.

You made it back inside your apartment with the kid. It was late so you were able to smuggle him up to your unit under the cover of darkness. To your knowledge, no one had seen you. You were safe for the moment, but you were sick to your stomach about what had transpired. You remembered the warm fuzzy feeling you got after reading the advice of your guardian angel, and you were pretty sure the mixture of emotions that were now brewing inside you were the exact opposite. You wondered what kind of guidance that anonymous angel of the Internet would give you this time. But what were you going to do? Start a thread on Reddit about it?

Today I Fucked Up By Assaulting And Kidnapping A Minor

The kid was bleeding profusely from the mutilated chunk of flesh hanging off his face that used to be a nose. You placed him in your bathtub to prevent him from gushing all over the floor of your apartment while you thought about how to rectify the situation.

Tears began to well up in your eyes once you realized how screwed you were. You were no criminal, you were an artist, but artists don't beat their critics to within an inch of their lives.

"I'm sorry!" you cried out to the kid, whose body, a

56

broken pile of pulverized meat, lay motionless in your tub. "I never meant for this to happen."

You feared he would die in your bathroom before you could muster up the courage to call him an ambulance. You knew you had made a terrible mistake and needed to own up to it, but you were so afraid of going to prison.

Between your sobs you heard a whimper. You peered up to see the kid begin to stir. The eye that wasn't swollen shut made contact with yours. His sclera was as red as a dog's dick and you could tell he was straining to focus, but he was staring right at you. The teenager's whimpers transformed into something that resembled a low gurgle – almost as if he was drowning on the blood that had pooled in the back of his throat, but you realized he wasn't drowning, he was laughing, causing your concerns to give way to confusion. He forced out a few grunts in an effort to say something, his voice whistling through the broken teeth, jagged shards of bone, that you had shattered with your fists.

"Y-you're that fucking shitty artist, aren't you?" he groaned.

His gurgling laugh began again and you understood it was directed at you. He had won. With nothing but an Internet modem and a laptop he had successfully derailed your career and he knew it too. You were going to spend the rest of your life in prison. With that thought, a fiery rage swelled inside your chest. You didn't deserve what the little shit had done to you. All you wanted to do was make art, to paint your own "Blue Dancers," and this entitled piece of trash had taken it away from you.

There was no blacking out the second time. You were

fully aware of what you were doing when you mounted his body and began to pummel his face. With each blow, you could feel his cheekbones collapse more and more underneath your knuckles. You clawed at his eyes like a rabies stricken animal then forced your hands inside his mouth and pulled at his jaw, popping it from its hinges, and when your arms got sore, you stood up and let your boots take a turn at the kid's cranium.

Picture this.

It takes 200 pounds of pressure to crush a human skull.

By the time you had finished wailing away on the teenager, his head looked like a plate of pink and purple mashed potatoes. One in every 15,000 people in the United States is murdered every year, and now the kid whose brains were currently spilling down your bathtub's drain was the newest casualty of that statistic.

You washed his blood off your hands in the sink and tried to calm down a bit. After looking back at the headless corpse in your tub, you realized you were a little frightened with yourself, but it wasn't because you had just murdered a teenager in cold blood. It was the sensation of ecstasy overtaking your body that worried you. It felt amazing, like you had just lived out a fantasy. Not a sexual one — stomping the kid's skull in didn't get you off, but it was more than a little empowering. The snotty turd deserved everything he got, but now you had a new problem on your hands.

It didn't take a criminal mastermind to know that keeping the kid's body in your tub was a bad idea, but getting rid of it wasn't as simple as chucking it down the trash shoot. You were an artist though, and artists have creative minds. So you did what creative minds do. You got creative.

Picture This.

On average, 75 people are arrested in the United States for having sex with the deceased every year. Don't believe me? Look it up: 75 people. This is especially concerning considering there are four states, Louisiana, Kentucky, Oklahoma, and North Carolina, where necrophilia isn't even against the law.

Of the 75 people arrested for making love to the dead annually, nearly half of them work in mortuaries. Given these facts, one can assume that funeral homes are a magnet for necrophiliacs. It makes sense when you think about it. After all, it seems like the dream job for someone who indulges in that kind of fetish.

Many psychologists believe that only a small fraction of these people actually have sexual attractions to dead bodies. Most engage in necrophilia due to social anxieties. It's the fear of rejection or the body's inability to perform under pressure that causes people to stray down this path. Corpses can't laugh at the size of your penis or roll their eyes if you can't get it up, so people find comfort and safety in the dead. It is for that reason that a staggering 94% of necrophiliacs are men.

Just like any sexual fetish, necrophilia has its own dark little community on the Internet. If one looks hard enough, they'll be able to find forums where users anonymously trade pics and tell stories of their latest sexual conquests. Well, I say anonymously, but as I explained before, when it comes to the Internet, people have a tendency to get a little too comfortable and give away their personal information without even thinking about it.

So picture this.

You opened up your laptop and did a little digging. Google is magic. Within minutes you were perusing a forum full of cadaver-loving freaks. An hour or two of browsing and you stumbled upon a thread that sparked your interest. In an off topic, throw away comment, one of the perverts claimed to regularly visit a pizza joint not more than five miles from your apartment before engaging in his grotesque sex adventures.

After scanning his comment history you saw that he often bragged about how his job supplied him with an end-less stream of what he called his "real love dolls". It turned out he was a mortician who really enjoyed the alone time he spent with the corpses he was supposed to be beautify-ing.

You created an account and messaged him, claiming to be a 19-year-old girl who was into watching guys screw stiffs. When he asked for verification you scrounged up some pictures of your friend's little sister and sent them to him. People are gullible when they want to believe some-thing and this guy really wanted to believe that a cute coed was interested in perverts who fuck dead bodies.

He sent you a face pic. When you performed a reverse image search it directed you right to his Facebook page. The idiot had even messaged you his profile picture. His Facebook page did indeed confirm that he was a mortician and even listed the name of the funeral home he worked in. You smiled to yourself when, after looking the place up, you read that it had a crematorium. However, there was something else you found out about him after digging through his information – something you found very useful. The pervert had a family too – a wife and an 11-year-old son.

You sweet-talked the mortician through the night, encouraging him to tell you about the disgusting things he does to newly arrived cadavers. He said that he wanted to fuck you on top of them. It turns out he was one of the few necrophiliacs that didn't have a fear of performing. This sicko was just genuinely attracted to dead bodies. You told him all the nasty things you knew he wanted to hear. When you asked for a dick pic, he was more than happy to oblige. The picture he sent you was a full-body nude with his erect cock and face clearly visible in the frame.

The two of you made plans to meet up at the mortuary after hours for a little ménage et trois with a 24-year-old model who had recently died from a coke overdose. For some reason, he always seemed excited to tell you how his "real love dolls" had passed. You assumed it was part of the fetish.

You showed up at the funeral home the following evening with a manila folder full of hard evidence. He broke down and started crying when you explained to him that he'd been duped. You presented him with the photos he sent you and explained to him that you had screenshots of the previous night's conversation saved and backed up. The mortician begged you not to show his wife. Apparently she had caught him once on top of a 17-year-old girl who had perished in a car wreck. His wife was pregnant at the time and only stayed with the mortician for the baby's sake, but she had informed him that if she ever found out he was doing it again, she'd call the cops and take his son away from him forever. He tried to make you go away by writing you a check, but you refused the bribe. You hadn't come for money.

You explained that you needed him to help you make a body disappear. The plan was simple. The funeral home had a crematorium and all you needed was access to it. The mortician reluctantly agreed to help you in exchange for keeping his revolting secret under wraps so the two of you headed out to your car and hoisted an oversized duffle bag containing Dark_Painter97's body out of your trunk. You carried it inside, but when you asked the mortician to direct you to the furnace he waved his hand.

"I've got it from here," he told you.

You shot him suspicious look and informed him that if he was planning on going to the police, your evidence would be in his wife's inbox the next day.

"Don't worry," he said. "You're safe. The kid will be ashes by the end of the night."

He asked you how the teenager died, so you told him your story.

"Wow, I get murders from time to time, but that sounds especially brutal," he responded after hearing your grisly tale.

When you were finished, you thanked him for his help and started out the door.

"No, thank you," he said.

His remark left you puzzled. It wasn't until after you started your car and pulled out of the parking lot that you realized what the mortician was showing his appreciation for. You had delivered him a new play toy – a "real love doll" and he was going to have some fun with it before he sent it off to the incinerator.

Picture this.

Roughly 85% of the country's population has access to the Internet. That means approximately 270 million people in the United States alone are connected to the world-wide-web. Of that 270 million, a little over half have profiles on active social networking sites, which makes the number of people using Twitter, Facebook, Snapchat, Tinder, and all the other flavors of the week tally somewhere around 135 million.

You were one of the 135 million. So what did you do after having just gotten away with murder? You hopped on social media to help yourself forget about the past couple days. The problem was, images of Dark_Painter97's caved in skull kept flashing through your mind. Even worse, you couldn't help but picture what that perverted mortician was most likely doing to the partially headless cadaver you had brought him.

Your thoughts turned back to your guardian angel. You hadn't revisited your old suicide thread since that anonymous hero of the Internet had rescued you from your depression. It wasn't necessary. Up until a few hours ago, you had believed yourself to be relatively happy, but the day had been a traumatic one, so you decided to check in on the cyberspace superman to see if he was still crusading around, searching for lost souls to save.

It took a minute for you to remember your password, but once you logged in you began to navigate the site, looking for the familiar forum. It stung more than you thought it would to reread the post. It reminded you how black the world seemed back then. You scrolled down the thread, searching for your guardian angel – the one person on the planet who seemed to understand you.

The comment was still there so you began to read it, hoping that you would again be able to pull something useful from the sage advice that had once saved your life, but you stopped halfway through. You had seen something that made your heart rise in your throat because for the very first time, you had read your guardian angel's user name.

Dark_Painter97

You rubbed your eyes and looked again just to make sure you weren't hallucinating, but the text on your monitor hadn't changed. You came to a realization that made you feel physically ill.

Approximately 135 million Americans are active on social media sites and you murdered the only one that had given you a reason to wake up in the morning.

It was utterly ridiculous. How could a human being be so sympathetic and understanding one day and such an obnoxious little twat the next? It was like a bad dream. You felt as if a war for your sanity was being waged inside your head. Part of you wanted to laugh at the irony of the situation. Another part of you wanted to cry. You ended up spending the entire evening staring at an unfinished piece leaning up against the wall of your apartment, not even able to remember whom you were even painting it for. Did it matter? It was like the whole damn world had lied to you.

It wasn't until morning that reality started to sink in. Perhaps the sun helped to burn off the fog that had been shrouding your brain since your revelation, but for whatever reason you no longer felt helpless. You realized that all this time, you had been using your guardian angel as a crutch – leaning on their words of wisdom whenever you felt like you couldn't stand on your own. Unfortunately, it turned out you had been worshiping a false idol. In reality your champion had been a chump all along – just another jealous wannabe who only cared about seeing you fall. The sick part was, you knew Dark_Painter97 was just the tip of the iceberg. You had other critics. Worse ones – and they deserved everything he got. Maybe even more. That strange feeling of ecstasy had once again returned, only this time it didn't make you feel frightened. It made you feel unstoppable.

Picture this.

Every avalanche starts with a single snowflake. Contemplate that for a second. It's a crazy thought, but it's absolutely true. The fact that a force so deadly and dangerous can come from something so innocent and harmless is remarkable.

When you first started snooping around that annoying Internet troll's twitter account you couldn't have had any idea what it would lead to. There was no way to predict that mere hours later you would be passing off his headless corpse to a mortician with a fetish for the dead. There was also no way to anticipate the other murders it would lead to, but after discovering that you had killed your guardian angel, you felt like there was no point in simply ignoring the rest of your critics.

So you sought them out and made them pay for every hurtful comment they ever messaged you. You started with those who only lived a day's drive away. Like a predator hunting its prey you'd stalk them, laying in wait for the perfect time to strike. Their deaths were usually agonizing ones. You made sure that each and every one of your victims suffered painfully. The mortician was in your back pocket. You still had the ability to blackmail him. He feigned frustration with his predicament, but both of you knew he was happy with the arrangement. After about the third or fourth "love doll" you brought to him, he began making requests.

"I'd really appreciate it if the next one you brought in didn't have teeth," he would say to you. "Can you get me someone who maybe has a genetic birth defect?"

You entertained his bizarre fetish. After all, it didn't matter to you what happened to the bodies you were bringing in, as long as they were a pile of ashes in the morning. The mortician had a network of people like him – hardcore cadaver humpers across the country. Many of them also worked in funeral homes and had access to their own crematoriums. Things probably started to snowball out of control when you found yourself going on vacation just to off another critic.

Painting had become secondary to you. It no longer thrilled you the way murder did. You only kept doing it and posting photos to the Internet as a means to find more people to kill. You no longer strove for perfection in your art. "Blue Dancers" had drifted further away than ever. You started to purposefully make mistakes in order to attract more negative opinions. After a while, you didn't even care if the people you were hunting were offering genuine constructive criticism or not. No one was safe.

But even an avalanche finally reaches the bottom of the mountain.

One day a detective showed up at your apartment and started asking questions. He was trying to connect the disappearance of two of the people you had killed. You could tell by the look in his eye that he didn't consider you a suspect yet, but you knew that he was smart. It would only be a matter of time before he put the pieces of the puzzle together and realized what you had done.

So picture this.

You packed up your belongings, emptied your bank account, and left town that night. You didn't want to rot in prison, so you moved to the other side of the country and changed your name. With a haircut and a pair of colored contact lenses (you always wanted hazel eyes) you started a new life for yourself.

In a few days you would read about yourself in the news – an up and coming painter who suddenly disappeared without a trace. 90,000 people are reported missing every year and now you were one of them. A few days after that, you were the main suspect in the deaths of the two people that detective had questioned you about. The cops were never going to find you, though. You were too smart for them.

But there was a problem. People still needed to die. Laying low for the rest of your life just wasn't an option, but you knew the police would be looking for a painter so you picked up a new type of art, one that was sure to attract its fair share of critics – writing.

Given your actual motives, you figured horror was an appropriate genre to publish in. You created new social media accounts under your fake name, and even used photos of a guy you went to high school with who had died in a motorcycle accident for your profile pics. People seemed to enjoy the stories you posted on the Internet and after a little while you began to get popular. Your tales were read on forums, translated into other languages, some of them even published in books.

Now that your work had become well known, you began to do little things that you knew would encourage criticism. You used run-on sentences and purposefully made small grammatical mistakes in hopes that someone would try to correct you. From time to time, you even wrote stories in a second person narrative, knowing full well just how polarizing it can be for readers.

You stayed connected to the mortician and his network of perverted funeral workers. Your trap had been set and now all you had to do was wait for critics to come along who couldn't resist tearing your work to pieces — and along they came. Like a moth to a flame, people were drawn to the flaws you had engineered into your writing. They pointed them out, under the cover of anonymity, but the masks they wore were as flimsy as papier-mâché.

There is no privacy anymore — no way to truly remain faceless. If someone wants to dig hard enough, they can learn as much about you as your closest and dearest friends.

So let me ask you a question. One that I'm sure a lot of you will laugh off once you realize whom this story is about, but one that you'd be wise to take very, very seriously next time you post to the Internet.

Are you picturing it yet?

THE **AFRICAN** BOWANA **SPIDER**

D R. TWEED, SO NICE TO FINALLY SEE YOU AGAIN. I trust you
have many stories to tell me about your adventures
deep in the heart of Africa?"

Dr. Tweed beamed with sheer delight as he greeted
his colleague at the door. A red bowtie attached to the top
of his khaki blazer gave the fellow an eccentric yet scholar-
ly appearance. The old man squinted through his bifocals
while beckoning Robert to the table where two cups of hot
tea had already been poured.

"Hullo! Robert, my good man," he began, "Yes, yes,
of course. Join me for some tea and I shall regale you with
a tale regarding the most curious creature this old man
has ever had the pleasure of coming across in *all* his years
gallivanting around the globe."

A friendly exchange of smiles and a pleasant handshake later, the two men had taken their seats.

"So Doctor," began Tweed's guest, "tell me about this
mysterious creature of yours."

Dr. Tweed's eyes lit up like a pair of bright blue sap-
phires, "Ah yes! The African Bowana Spider – named after
the indigenous people who reside in a section of the jungle

where the creature originally hails. It's a massive arachnid! I dare say, the thing is about half a meter in diameter, but that's not even the most interesting tidbit about it- "

"Good god, man!" Robert gasped. "I beg your pardon Doctor, but I'm finding it quite hard to swallow that your interest in the tremendous girth of this spider would be eclipsed by an even more fascinating factoid?"

The old man's lips curled into the slightest smirk upon hearing Robert's retort. "Oh, but eclipsed it is, my dear friend. Perhaps you'll understand once you hear this remarkable anecdote.

"On my 21st night exploring the Dark Continent, we found that one of our pack mules had begun to demonstrate bizarre and erratic behavior. The beast had started to crow and moan as though it were suffering from some sort of horrible illness. Our guides had previously warned my party that the primeval forest we made camp in was rife with poisonous asps, adders, and mambas, among other deadly serpents, so naturally I hypothesized it had fallen victim to the bite of one of the jungle's venomous vipers. However, upon further examination I could find no evidence of teeth marks on the animal – no wounds, no pricks, not a single thing that would indicate it had been attacked."

"Sounds like quite the conundrum, Doctor."

"Indeed it was. Even more curious was the fact that, though I found the animal's behavior to be somewhat unnerving, many of our party's guides appeared to be downright terrified! At the sight of the mule's predicament, a few of them even ran off from our campsite and into the darkness of the untamed jungle by themselves, *the fools!* I loaded my rifle in order to put the creature out of its misery, as it was now writhing on the ground and seemed to be suffering quite considerably, but before I had the chance to pull the trigger my eyes witnessed a truly incredible sight."

"No Doctor, you aren't about to say-"

"Oh but I am! Out of the animal's mouth crawled the Bowana Spider!"

Dr. Tweed took a sip of tea. Robert could tell by the old man's reaction that it was still a bit too hot to drink.

"Like I said before, it was colossal! Now, while I haven't quite figured out how the giant thing was able to contort its body enough to crawl its way out of the beast's jowls, I do have a theory about what it was doing there in the first place." Tweed paused a moment for dramatic effect, reveling in the mystery of his account.

"Well? Out with it then! I must say, good doctor, I am absolutely enthralled by this story of yours. You must tell me what happened next!"

"As it turns out, this particular species of arachnid has become quite feared by the natives, hence the reason why some of my party's guides had decided to take their chances out amongst the ferocious wildlife and poisonous flora of the jungle instead of staying at camp once they realized what was behind all the ruckus. The remaining guides insisted that I shoot the spider, but you know me Robert, I'm a man of science! What kind of academician would I be if I ended the life of such a spectacular specimen? An arthropod of such astonishing peculiarity must be studied alive!"

Robert interjected once more, "But Doctor, you still haven't explained what it was doing inside the mule's mouth."

"Have patience my good man, all will be revealed in time. You see, the natives believed the spider to be some sort of soul-sucking demon — one that feasts upon the very life force of a man, bleeding him dry until he becomes nothing but a useless withered husk. Obviously, any educated bloke like myself would dismiss such silly notions as nothing but foolish superstitions, but I do believe these primitive myths were on to something. Nevertheless, there is always a scientific explanation for these things.

"From my brief encounter with the creature, I have gathered that the eight-legged goliath has evolved the most extraordinary of survival tactics. It appears that the spider entered our pack mule through its oral cavity. From there, it may have in some way attached itself to the beast's nervous system, granting it full access to the mule's movements and vocal patterns, essentially rendering the animal a useless puppet. What I'm saying, Robert, is that this creature was wearing our unfortunate ungulate like a hat on Sunday and all of us were none the wiser! I have since postulated that the arachnid made itself at home in the body of its hoofed host, feeding off its cerebral spinal fluid just long enough for it to plant a revolting sack of eggs."

Robert's eyes widened with interest, "What an intriguing yet horrifying creature, Doctor! Ha-ha! Perhaps the guides who fled into the night weren't as foolish as you say? Could you imagine what would happen if a thing like that was on the loose here in England? The country would be in panic!" He and the old man shared a chuckle.

The doctor took another sip of his tea, "Could I imagine, Robert? I dare say, it already is!'"

Dr. Tweed's head cocked back in a violent manner. Terrible gagging noises emanated from his throat as blood began trickling from his eyes, ears, and nose. Eight long spindly legs emerged from his mouth.

FAST ENOUGH

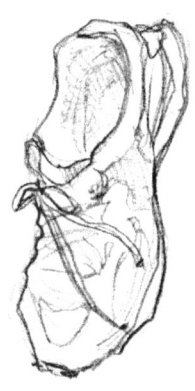

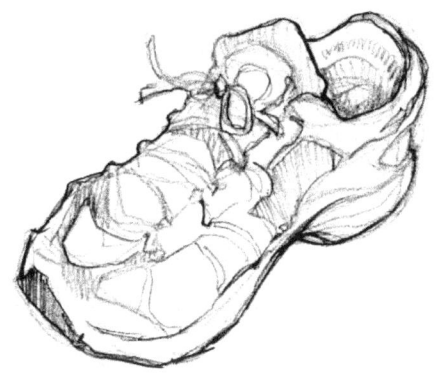

RUN DOWN THE BLOCK — just as fast as my legs can possibly take me - and as I move into a full on sprint, so too does the beast. I think to myself that the sidewalk looks as though it must be ten miles long. It's amazing how the street of an ordinary residential neighborhood can transform into what feels like an endless stretch of road given the right circumstances. My heart is beating a million miles per hour and I don't know if it's from fatigue or panic. The demon, doubt, is screaming inside my head. It wants me to stop, to give up. It tells me there's no use in running, but I know I can't listen.

The dog is massive, 150lbs easy — a rabid blur of black matted fur, charging with the rage of a thousand nuclear blasts. As it snarls, mid gallop, I can see its horrible teeth. Teeth designed for ripping apart and tearing into flesh. Teeth that it has every intention of using. It doesn't have the controlled, focused look of a predator. Instead its eyes are wild and ruthless. It wants to do more than kill, it wants to maim, inflict pain. I'm moving faster now than I've ever moved in my life. Terror is an unbelievable motivator.

Pastel Colored Dreams & Human Flavored Nightmares

There may be even more adrenaline pumping through my veins than blood at this point. My legs burn as lactic acid starts to flood my quadriceps and hamstrings like it's flowing from a broken levy. The muscles in my neck go tense. With every fiber of my being, I will myself to speed up even more, but deep down in the pit of my stomach, I know that I won't be fast enough. The dog is too quick and I'll never catch it. Not before it gets to my three-year-old son in the driveway.

THE CLEAR, BLUE SPRING

THE FOREST WAS SINGING TO US that muggy afternoon — singing the ballad of summer. Its melody swooshed beneath the hooves of doe and fawns bounding through the brush and harmonized with the far away knock of a woodpecker's beak against the bark of a sweetgum. It was the croaky caroling of toads and the murmur of the creek where they dwelled, the chorus of the katydids hiding in the undergrowth, and the call of the birds fluttering over the treetops.

The day was hot, the air thick and humid. It wrapped its heavy arms tight around my chest, swaddling me in its embrace. Its hug was sweltering. I remember how my sweat-drenched t-shirt clung to my back, how the cool, soaked cotton against my skin served as my only refuge from the oppressive August heat.

Lynne was just a few paces ahead of me. I followed her as she ambled down the trail, eyes wandering purposelessly, her hands in the back pockets of her denim shorts like a child lost in thought. Occasionally she'd glimpse over her shoulder and flash me a smile, but despite the hot summer sun beating down on us that day, a storm cloud was hanging over my head and not even the sight of her face could brighten me up.

Lynne's smile capsized once she realized our walk through the woods was doing little to relieve my burden. She turned and hurried towards me and when she got near, threw her arms around my waist, burying her head in my chest. She hugged me tight – tighter even than the heat – and when she relaxed her grip and backed her face away I could see her smile had returned. I looked into her smoky, gray eyes. We were just kids – only seventeen at the time – but in that moment I knew she was the most beautiful thing in the world. We held each other in silence for a while before she finally spoke to me. Her words were gentle; they fell smooth and soft from her tongue like velvet.

Everything would be okay, she said to me.

And that's when she inched herself closer, leaned into my ear, and whispered her secret – a secret I wish I had never heard uttered from those full, sweet lips of hers – the secret of the clear, blue spring.

Everything would be okay because the clear, blue spring would show me so.

Lynne broke free from my arms and snatched my wrist. She started to run, pulling me behind her as she led us from the path. Together we sprinted through the un-tamed brush, trampling bushes and ducking under tree branches. I followed her trustingly. She was more than fa-miliar with that forest. It was like a second home to her. I had walked the trails many times myself, but Lynne spent so much time out among those trees that they *belonged* to her.

I'm not sure how long we were running, but when

we stopped my lungs felt like they were on fire. Lynne's cheeks were flush, the sweat on her forehead glistened in the little bit of afternoon light trickling through the trees, her sun-streaked blonde hair had become so wild and tousled that it reminded me of a tumbleweed, yet somehow through all this, she was even more striking than ever. Her splendor was effortless and I loved her for it.

The two of us laughed for minutes before we finally caught our breaths. I grinned and pulled her close to me. It had been weeks since we had kissed. She stroked my face with the back of her hand then ran her fingers through my hair. We pressed ourselves together until our noses were practically touching. I could taste the exhale of her breath – it was cool and lovely and I wanted to savor it forever – but just before our lips could meet, I pulled my head away from hers. The tears came fast and unexpected. They stung my eyes and cascaded down my cheeks.

Lynne cradled my head in her arms, letting me cry into her shoulder, and, as she did this she spoke again of the spring. She told me she was taking me there and once more I heard those curious words slip from her lips – *it would show me the way.* There was an air of conviction in her voice. It was fervent in its confidence – religious even.

I dried my eyes on the sleeve of my shirt then lifted my face to meet her gaze. She watched me lovingly for a brief moment then nodded her head, gesturing for me to follow her deeper between the trees. Running was out of the question now. That southern August heat barely allowed us a slow saunter, but we continued our journey nonetheless, hand in hand, fingers entwined together like the souls of Orpheus and Eurydice.

I trusted Lynne with all my heart, but I needed to hear more about this mysterious spring that she was taking me to. After all, she had never once, in all the time I had known her, made any mention of it to me at all, and now we were travelling further into the woods than I'd ever been, away from the trails, far removed from any houses or roads, on our way to find it. I asked her to tell me about it, to explain what she meant when she said it could help me. She was hesitant to indulge me at first, but after I insisted, she told me her tale and as I listened, I found myself growing more and more enchanted by the fantastic things she was saying. This story is hers, just as much as it is mine and here is what she said....

Lynne was nine when she discovered the spring. She first stumbled upon it following an argument with her father. Her parents had recently separated and her mother had moved out of the house. She was just a little girl at the time and she didn't know how to deal with the sudden feelings of abandonment that her mother's departure had caused her, so she directed all of her frustrations towards her dad. One evening, following a nasty argument, she sprinted out the backdoor of her house and into the woods behind her home. These were the very same woods that she and I were currently trekking through. Her father had tried to chase after her, but he was a heavyset man and she was quick for her age, so she had no trouble losing him in the trees once she veered from the established hiking trails.

She ran until her legs were rubber, until she could no longer hear his voice calling out to her.

She ran until her heart thundered inside her chest, until her head grew light and woozy and her feet ached with every step.

When she finally stopped, she realized she was in a part of the forest she had never been before. A faint luminescence was radiating off the surrounding trees. Lynne followed the glow until she came to a clearing and it was here that she first laid eyes on it – glistening against the pitch black night, an enormous diamond flickering in the darkness – the clear, blue spring.

It beckoned her, she said. It commanded her to wade into its shimmering waters. This was an order she had no trouble obeying. From the moment she saw the spring, she had felt a strange, pressing urge to join it, so she stripped off her clothes and plunged herself into the glowing pool as quickly as she could.

She gushed about the experience so much that I nearly felt jealous. Hearing her talk, it almost seemed as if she was speaking about a lover. Her eyes twinkled like little stars as she reminisced about its cool, blue water. She confessed that she may not have had the strength to pull herself out of the spring that night, if not for a vivid image of her father that suddenly flashed through her mind.

He was writhing on the kitchen floor, clutching his chest, his face pale, his mouth gasping for air. A phone was in his hand, but he was too weak to dial out for help. Horror pierced Lynne's gut like an arrow because deep down, in her heart, she knew that what she was seeing was not a hallucination. It had been placed in her head by the spring, a vision of what was soon to come, a premonition of the future. The sparkling water whispered to her too, only she couldn't hear its words with her ears. Instead, they had been scorched across the surface of her brain, its message burned into her consciousness.

Go to your father, the spring had said. *You can save his life if you hurry.*

I studied her face as she explained this to me. Lynne had never been the type to tell tall tales, but I scanned her carefully anyway, searching for some kind of hint, anything that would suggest she was joking. She squeezed the palm of my hand and sent a knowing glance my way as if to say she understood my skepticism, but that she'd never lie to me.

I could tell the heat was beginning to press on me. It seemed to be affecting the rest of the forest too. All around us, tree branches bowed as if they were too exhausted to hold themselves up, their green leaves sagged under the weight of the thick humid air. They looked like mourning widows. We journeyed ever deeper into the forest as she continued on with her story. I listened intently. It helped me take my mind off the heat and off my troubles as well.

Lynne had exited the water as soon as she received the spring's warning about her father. She threw on her clothes on then took off running through the woods. She was not lost. The spring had shown her the fastest route back, and she made it home just in time to find her father in the early stages of cardiac arrest. She called an ambulance. Luckily, the EMT's were able to arrive at their house in time to help him. The doctors said that they just barely made it. A few minutes later and they might not have been able to save his life. Lynne's father was able to make a full recovery. His heart attack even served as the catalyst that drove her parents back together. After hearing about the incident, Lynne's mother had rushed to the hospital to be with them.

She said that she believed it was the spring that deserved all the credit. Had it not warned her about her father's heart attack, she wouldn't have been able to save him, and her family would not have had the opportunity to reunite. She stopped short after telling me that and began apologizing to me. I assured her that I knew she didn't mean any harm by what she said. You see, the reason I had been so upset, the reason she was taking me to the spring, was because my mother had died just three weeks prior. I did not have a father. He passed when I was a baby. I had no family of my own.

She went on to tell me more stories about the spring that day. Once it had helped her find her dog when he went missing. Another time, when she was feeling very lonely, it gave her hope when it told her she would meet a boy who would fill the empty space in her heart. That boy was me. I transferred into her school a couple days later.

Lynne loved the spring and its crystal blue waters, but she feared that if she overused it then its powers would cease to work, so she resolved to only call on it when she felt that it was absolutely necessary. She kept it secret too, to prevent others from mistreating it, and so it had always been there for her when she needed it.

It had always shown her the way.

I didn't know what to make of her tales. Of course I thought they sounded crazy, but I appreciated them because they allowed my mind to wander away from the fire that took my mother's life. As she spoke, I forgot about the heat from the flames that night. I forgot about how they licked at my heels and burned my legs as I crawled to safety. I forgot too, how my mother's screams slashed through the air – horrible screams; I could hear her cry my name.

The woods began to thin out into a clearing and I heard the sound of running of water. We pushed our way through the last of the brush and that's when I first saw it. The spring was bigger than I expected, maybe thirty feet across at its widest point. There was a blue tint to the water. It did not glow, but there was still a lot of daylight left. There was a strange electricity in the air and I swear the heat became less stifling as we moved closer to that pool. I could see all the way down to the bottom, an assortment of flat multi-colored pebbles lined its floor. Brown, white, green, red, and a thousand other colors – so many I couldn't keep track.

We approached the water together, fingers still interlocked, palms sweaty, but when we got near, Lynne put a hand on my chest to stop me. She told me that I no longer needed to worry, that the spring would show me the way just as it had shown her time and time again.

She peeled off her clothes in front of me. First her tank top, then her shorts. Lynne's body was firm and tight. Her stomach was as smooth and flat as stones laying at the floor of the spring. I couldn't take my eyes off her. She draped her arms around me. I could feel her soft breasts pressing against my chest and once again I could taste her cool, lovely breath.

I love you, she said.

And then she kissed me.

Her lips wrapped tightly around mine and her tongue swirled slowly inside my mouth. I ran my fingers over her bare body, exploring her curves, caressing her skin. She moaned softly and I could feel her voice in my throat.

It was she that broke our kiss – if it were up to me I would have never let it end.

She helped me out of my clothes, took me by the hand, and together we waded into the crystal pool. The water was cool and inviting. Lynne dove beneath the surface, and when she appeared again, she was on the opposite end of the spring. I paddled over to her. Swimming in those waters was truly like being born again. There are no other words to describe it. By the time I caught up to her, I knew that every word of her story had to be true. The spring had a very special aura. It was powerful and intense, and even though I had not been in its presence before, I could tell there was something extraordinary about it.

When I reached Lynne, I planted my feet on the floor. Those flat stones felt pleasant beneath my soles. I placed my hands on her hips. She was smiling at me. I can't recall if I was smiling too, but sometimes, when I reflect back on that day, I like to think that I was. I imagine that I was grinning ear to ear, laughing even. I imagine these things because I want to remember *that moment* in the spring as fondly as I possibly can. It was the last time in my life that I ever felt happiness.

The spring would snatch my joy away and instant later when it decided to show me everything I had been trying so hard to forget.

It showed me my mother, whom I had grown to resent so much over the years. It showed me the way she abused prescription pills and alcohol, the birthdays she had slept through, the parent teacher meetings she was too high to show up for. The spring showed me all the lonely, late night dinners I ate while she lay passed out on the couch in the living room. It showed me the petty jealousy I felt towards Lynne whenever I was around her and her parents, who seemed to genuinely care for her.

Then it showed me the night of the fire. It showed me how my mother fell asleep, sprawled out, facedown, her pants around her ankles on top of the bed in her room. The spring showed me how disgusted I was when I walked in and saw her like that. It showed me the blind rage I felt that night when I grabbed the can of gasoline from the garage. I used it to soak the walls of her bedroom and even the hallway. My mother was so passed out, so hopped up on pills, that the smell didn't even wake her. The spring showed me how I shoved the heavy oak bookcase from the study, all the way down the hall until it was in front of her door. She was barricaded inside her bedroom. Still she hadn't woken. I watched myself light a match then drop it to the gas sodden carpet.

The flames engulfed my home. It happened so fast that I nearly got caught in the inferno myself. The spring showed me how I escaped just in time. My mother was not so lucky. No longer asleep, she screamed my name out in the night, begging for me to help her, not knowing it had been I, who was responsible for the flames that were eating away at her flesh. Standing in that spring, I felt the same guilt that had consumed me when I heard her voice die out in that fire. The water Lynne and I were in felt as if it was warming up, but I wasn't sure if it was in my head.

I peered into her eyes, they no longer twinkled. Terror danced inside them now, as if she was gazing upon the face of a monster. I realized then that everything the spring had shown me Lynne had seen as well. She tried to leap from the pool, but I grabbed her by the ankle and pulled her back in.

The spring was showing me something else now. It was showing me what would happen if I let her go, how she would run home, call the police, and tell them everything. It showed me how the courts would try me as an adult, the horrors of prison, the life of an ex-convict. The water was definitely hotter now — like being inside a Jacuzzi. I was shaking her, pleading for her to understand, but she wouldn't listen — she refused. She beat on me with her fists and scratched at my eyes. She cried for help as loud as she could, but there was no one around for miles. The spring showed me even more after that. It showed me what I needed to do if I didn't want to be caught, how to get away and live free.

So I listened.

I dunked her head beneath the water. By now the spring was boiling; it bubbled and fizzed all around us. Hot steam drifted off its surface. I ignored the heat and squeezed her throat as tight as I could. She thrashed and kicked and tried to pry at my hands, but I was too strong for her. The spring was whispering to me, encouraging me on.

It's the only way to save yourself, it said to me.

I didn't want to hurt Lynne. I loved her, but I was terrified, and the spring's words made so much sense to me. I drowned her in that clear, blue water that day and took the first bus out of town that evening. There was nothing to leave behind. Most of my belongings had been destroyed in the fire, my entire family was dead, and now so was the only girl I ever cared for. I've been a drifter ever since. I wander the country like a nomad, begging for money, or working odd jobs whenever the opportunity presents itself.

We were both reported missing. The media spun our disappearance into a romantic story about two young lovers who ran away together. I wish that were the truth. I check the paper from time to time to see if she's been found, but I've never seen anything that would indicate that she or the spring has been located. Not a night goes by where I don't lay awake thinking of her. I often wonder if she's still out there, lying the bottom of the spring, atop those smooth flat stones that felt so good beneath my bare feet.

That was all many years ago, but lately thoughts of suicide have been growing stronger by the day. The spring is my last chance at salvation. I'm on my way back there now. It's only a couple hours walk from where I'm currently writing this. The directions have been burned into my brain ever since that hot August day, and I should make it by nightfall if I keep walking. I wonder if the water really does glow at night like it did in Lynne's story? I've only ever seen it in the daylight. When I get there, I want to stand in the spot where she kissed me and think back to how wonderful it felt. Then I'll get in the water, sink myself to the bottom, and wait for its command. Maybe there's nothing more the spring can really do for me. Maybe it will tell me to open my mouth and take as much water into my lungs as I can. If that's what it decides is best, then I will follow its instructions without question.

The clear, blue spring will show me the way.

THE EYE OF RA

J AY **Bennett hadn't noticed** the chubby man sitting alone in the corner booth until it was nearly time to close. He had been wiping down a couple of pub tables in the bar area when he spotted him, noshing on a plate of *Big Buck's En Fuego Jalapeño Poppers* and watching Division III college football highlights play on the television mounted on the wall. There was nothing particularly interesting about the chubby patron. His brown, argyle sweater vest and khaki trousers didn't exactly command attention and his plain unassuming features did nothing to accentuate his remarkably ordinary appearance. Yet still, there was something curious about the man that Jay couldn't quite put his finger on.

Closing time meant Jay would soon be spending the next hour and a half mopping puddles of urine off the bathroom floor and hand-drying dishes in the kitchen, while Trevor, his nineteen-year-old, zit-faced assistant manager, played Candy Crush and browsed Facebook on his phone. Jay hated closing the restaurant – mostly because he despised answering to a lazy, community college washout almost half his age. From where he was standing, he could see Trevor sitting in the office at the back of the restaurant, staring into his phone and giggling away like an acid-dropping rave bunny at Burning Man.

Any minute, Jay thought to himself. *Any minute the little shit's gonna stroll his pimply ass out here and force me to scrub the toilets 'till they shine. I just know it-*

"Um, excuse me?"

The voice that interrupted Jay's pity-party was soft and sophisticated. Right away he could sense an air of intelligence in its tone – something not commonly heard at *Big Buck's Wings & Beer,* the restaurant where he worked. Jay looked up to see the man in the brown argyle sweater vest waving him over to his booth.

"Yes, you sir. Excuse me, but may I speak to you for a moment?"

Jay glanced back towards the office. Trevor was busy furiously tapping away at the screen of his iPhone. He let out a sigh and sauntered over to the booth.

"You need the check? We're closing soon."

"Not necessary," replied the chubby man. "I already cleared my tab with the pretty young thing who works behind the bar."

Jay tossed the towel he was holding over his shoulder and folded his arms across his chest like a nightclub doorman. "Then what can I do for you, mister?"

"Well," the man paused briefly to collect his words. "You're Jay Bennett, correct?"

Hearing his name come out the mouth of a total stranger felt like an unexpected punch to the gut.

"I am," Jay said, doing his best to appear unmoved by the chubby man's inquiry. It was defense mechanism

98

he had developed during his stint in prison. Jay found out very fast while serving his time that the best reaction to an unforeseen predicament was typically having no reaction at all. "And you are?"

"Oh yes, where are my manners?" The man in the sweater vest extended a sweaty palm out towards Jay. "My name is Robert Wilkins. Uh, Dr. Robert Wilkins." Jay remained silent, causing the doctor to retract his hand. The chubby man studied the ex-con before continuing on. "FYI, I'm not the kind of doctor who went to *med school*. My degrees are cultural anthropology and archeology — Ancient Egyptian studies to be exact. My colleague and I have published hundreds of papers on the subject. Feel free to look me up if you don't believe me. A quick Google search should confirm my claims."

"Honestly, I don't really give a damn," grunted Jay. "What is it that you want, already?"

The doctor neatly folded his napkin and used it to dab his brow — Jay found the mannerism reminiscent of a 19th century plantation owner. "Right. I suppose there's no further need for introductions. Might as well get right down to it. Jay Bennett, I'm here tonight because I have a job for you."

"I already have a job, and if you're trying to hire me to do something illegal then look elsewhere. I'm on parole and I don't plan on going back to prison any time soon."

Jay snatched the towel from his shoulder and started towards the bathrooms.

"Wait! Please!" the doctor blurted out. "This job pays well! *I promise!*"

Jay spun around with every intent to tell him off, but

froze when he spotted the sly smile that had crawled its way across the chubby man's face. "Besides, it's a hell of a lot more fun than scrubbing toilets."

The doctor waved a hand, inviting Jay to sit across the table from him. With two pudgy fingers he nudged his plate of Jalapeño poppers aside then bent over to retrieve a black leather briefcase that had been sitting at his feet. Jay scooted into the other side of the booth. He swiveled his head to glance back at the office. Trevor was still gawking like an idiot into his phone.

"How do you know my name?" Jay asked.

"My associate gave me your information," replied the doctor nonchalantly. "Who you are, what you do, where to find you. He told me about your criminal record. Twelve counts of burglary, three counts of drug trafficking, and assault with a deadly weapon. He said you beat a man with a crowbar?"

"I was defending myself. The guy shot my partner."

"Yeah, after the two of you broke into the man's house. You're lucky he made a full recovery or else you'd probably still be locked up. I'm surprised you even found a gig at a hole like this."

Jay glared at the doctor, his lips twisted into a frustrated scowl.

"I'm not here to judge, though. After all," the chubby man popped the latches of his briefcase and lifted the lid, "I was hoping to encourage you to break the law one more time."

He removed a red envelope from his briefcase and placed it on the table, pinning it with his index finger. "What do you know about Egyptian mythology, Jay?"

100

"I know a little."

"Have you ever heard of Ra, the sun god?"

"I think so," answered Jay. "He's the one with the bird head, right?"

"Very good!" A proud light beamed in the doctor's eyes. "That is correct. Ra is the most important god in Egyptian mythology. He was believed to have ruled over the sky and earth. And his head wasn't just that of any bird. Most often, it was depicted as a falcon. Now, this was no accident. You see, birds of prey have the keenest of eyesight and legend has it, *the eye of Ra could see all.*"

He scooted the envelope across the table towards Jay, then lifted his pudgy finger, freeing it from his grasp before renewing his spiel.

"There's three thousand dollars cash, a photograph, an address, and a phone number in that envelope, Jay. The money is yours whether you take the job or not. If you do accept my offer, there will be an additional $7,000 in it for you. The photograph is of an artifact I'm asking you to steal for me. It's called the Eye of Ra. It's a very rare gold coin with an extremely special engraving in it. It was excavated during the University sponsored dig I helped oversee one year ago and I want it back."

"And the address is where I can find it?" Jay asked. He was already thumbing through the envelope's contents.

"Yes. It's the home of an ex-colleague of mine. He's the one who has taken it. It shouldn't be too difficult for a man like yourself to retrieve. He doesn't own a gun and I'm certain he never turns on his home security system. Plus, he's blind. All you have to do is keep your mouth shut and there's no way he could ever identify you. Call the phone number once you have the Eye of Ra in your possession. We will arrange a rendezvous point and I will gladly pay you the rest of the money when you hand it over to me."

"This artifact is worth a lot of money?" asked Jay.

The doctor laughed. "No monetary value other than the gold it's made from, which by the way, wouldn't get you as much as I'm willing to pay. However, for me the artifact is priceless."

"Why haven't you gone to the cops? You said this guy stole the coin from your dig. Why not just ask them to get it back for you? Sounds like the college should have a claim that it's their property."

The doctor snapped his briefcase shut, quickly securing the latches. "I don't plan on letting the University have the coin either."

He stood up from the table.

"Hold up, where are you going?" asked Jay. "I still have a lot of questions. Why me?"

"Every single one of your questions will be answered soon, Jay, but I'm afraid I don't have time to stick around right now. You're a skilled thief. This job will be a cinch for you. Call me tonight when you have the Eye of Ra."

"Tonight?"

The chubby man in the brown argyle sweater vest flashed him a haughty smile.

"Goodnight, Jay. Hope to hear from you soon."

Jay tucked the envelope into the waistband of his pants as he watched the peculiar patron amble out the door. A shrill high-pitched screech broke the silence of the now empty restaurant floor.

"Bennett!" Jay twisted around in his chair to see Trevor's lanky frame hovering in the office doorway. "Big Buck doesn't pay you to sit on your ass! Get in the bathroom before I call your PO! I want to be able to eat off those toilets!"

The rest of Jay's shift seemed to fly by as he mulled over the doctor's proposition. Every now and then he'd run his fingers across his waist, feeling for the contours of the envelope still stuffed inside his pants, just to make sure he hadn't dreamed the whole conversation up. The doctor had told him the gig paid $10,000 – more money than he made in three months wiping down tables and washing dishes. He thought about how degrading it was working under Trevor. There was only four months left on his parole and he had already decided he was going to quit his humiliating court-appointed job as soon as he was out from under the thumb of the justice system.

That kind of cash would really help out until I could find a new way to make some money, he thought to himself while puffing on his after work cigarette in the parking lot of *Big Buck's.*

Jay tugged the envelope from his jeans and searched through it until he found the photo of the artifact. An icy cold chill swept through him as he gazed down to the picture in his hand. The design etched into the face of the coin was breathtaking – a pattern so impossible and mesmerizing Jay didn't even notice the cigarette fall from his mouth as he ogled it. Staring at the coin was like being able to see in color for the very first time. All at once, he felt the urge to hold it – to grip it between his fingers.

"The Eye of Ra," Jay whispered.

His decision had been made. Not more than a minute later he was punching the address into his phone's GPS as he pulled his car out of the parking lot.

THE CLOCK ON JAY'S DASHBOARD flashed 2:00AM by the time he pulled up to his destination. The home was bigger than he was expecting. It was located in the quiet foothills, overlooking the noisy commotion of the city where he lived and worked. He had passed a couple houses on his way up, but now there were none in sight. Jay let out a satisfied sigh of relief. Because of the home's seclusion, the possibility of nosy neighbors and unexpected eyewitnesses was virtually off the table. It was the kind of place that a cat burglar dreamed of hitting.

He killed the engine and stared steadily out the window at his target, watching for signs of life. With any luck, the doctor's former colleague was out of town and Jay would be able to search the residence at his leisure. Jay slipped his hand into his sweatshirt pocket and gripped the handle of his butterfly knife – a safeguard he hoped he wouldn't need to use – then exited his vehicle and crept around the back searching for an open window.

He slinked his way through the shadowy yard towards a wide arched window in the back of the house. To his surprise, Jay found it was unlocked. With a gentle nudge of his hand against the glass it easily swung open, allowing him to slip inside.

The doc just might have been right about this being an easy gig, Jay thought.

He was now standing in a living room decorated with fancy furniture and ostentatious art. Hanging on the wall was an expensive looking painting. Jay examined it closely, trying to discern if it had any value, even going so far as to lift it from its hanger before seeing the $19.99 price tag stuck to the back of the frame.

"No need to hang it back up, Mr. Bennett, I never liked that piece anyways. My ex-wife decorated the place."

The voice stopped Jay dead in his tracks.

"Yes, Mr. Bennett. I know you're down there. Won't you please join me in my study?"

Jay leaned the painting against the wall, and scanned the room searching for the source of the voice.

"The study, Mr. Bennett! I'm in my study upstairs."

He located the staircase in the foyer. Without a word, Jay removed the knife from his pocket and tiptoed up the steps. The voice had identified him by name. A surge of panic washed over him. Visions of being thrown back behind bars were swimming through his head. "Second door on the right," the voice called out when he reached the top of the stairs.

The floorboards squealed under Jay's feet as stepped down the dark hallway towards the door the voice appeared to be emanating from. He paused when he reached it and squeezed the handle of his knife tight in his fist. There was no hint of light leaking out from underneath the door. Whoever was waiting for him in the room was doing so in pitch-blackness.

"No need to knock, Mr. Bennett," answered the voice. "I'm already expecting you."

Jay pushed down on the handle and cracked the door.

Its squeaky hinges tore through the silence as he opened it just wide enough to poke his head through. There was no visibility. With his free hand he yanked his cellphone free from his back pocket, turned on the screen, and waved it in front of him, bathing the room in a pale green light.

Floor to ceiling bookshelves lined both sides of what looked to be an office. At the wall directly opposite Jay was an elegant cherry wood desk. Sitting behind it in a leather office chair was an elderly man, his beard bedraggled, unkempt, crusted over with God knows what. Jay cringed when he looked closer to see the upper half of the man's face completely wrapped in bandages.

The strange man turned his head in Jay's direction. "Come on in, Mr. Bennett. I promise I don't bite."

Jay pushed the door all the way open and took a couple timid steps inside the room.

"I hear you're looking for the Eye of Ra," said the old man – a perverse smile warped his wrinkled face. "Well, it must be your lucky day because you've come to the right place."

"I don't want to hurt you," warned Jay, "but I'm prepared to. Just give me the coin and I'll be on my way."

The old man scoffed.

"Ha! You don't want to hurt me? Unfortunately, that's not for you to decide. Nothing is. We don't get to decide anything, didn't you know that?"

"Listen-"

"Quiet, Mr. Bennett!" the old man snapped. "You'll be leaving with the Eye of Ra tonight. There's no question in that, but I figured I'd at least disclose to you a little about the Hell you're about to unleash on yourself first.

My associate, Dr. Wilkins, already told you about the coin. We excavated it a year ago during a dig of an ancient unmarked tomb recently discovered 53 kilometers outside of Cairo."

"Dr. Wilkins?"

"Yes, Dr. Robert Wilkins, my associate — the man who hired you to steal the artifact. Who do you think requested him to seek you out? To put it plainly, you've been set up. I'm sorry that we had to lie to you to get you here, but eventually you'll come to understand that we had no choice. None of us do."

"You're full of it, old man," replied Jay.

The old man smirked.

"Oh, how I wish I was. Where was I? Ah yes, the dig. Wilkins and I were able to recover quite a bit from the tomb – most of which is currently touring the country, travelling from museum to museum. The exhibit is quite lovely and I'd advise you to give it a visit next time it stops back in town, but…" he paused and let out a bizarre titter, "that won't be necessary."

Jay darted towards the old man and swung his knife downwards, burying its blade in the desk's polished wooden face.

"That's enough of your crap! Just give me the coin or the next time I stick this knife in something it'll be your neck!"

The old man inhaled sharply in excitement.

"What a guess! You'll appreciate just how funny that threat was one day. I promise you that."

He opened the drawer of his desk and extracted a small leather pouch from it. Now that he was closer, Jay could make out brown splotches speckling the bandages that covered his eyes – dry crusty blood. It looked like the wraps hadn't been changed in ages.

"The coin is right here, Mr. Bennett, but I hope you don't think you've intimidated me into giving it to you. The fact of the matter is I'm turning it over because I have to. That's just the way it's supposed to go. But, before I do I will finish telling you my story."

"Listen I don't care about-"

"Not all of what we recovered from the tomb made it to the exhibit though," the old man continued. "You see, the coin in this bag conveniently went missing without anyone else even knowing it existed. I discovered it myself, in the hand of one of one of the mummified corpses we found in the tomb – a young priestess no older than sixteen when she was buried. It goes against my code of ethics to take *souvenirs* from an excavation, but the coin... well, just look for yourself."

He reached his fingers into the pouch drew out a gold coin about the same size as a fifty cent piece then placed it on the desk in front of him. Jay held his breath. The design etched into its face was hypnotic – far more captivating in person than it was in the photo.

"The Eye of Ra," the old man whispered. "Pretty, isn't it?"

Jay reached out an arm, but the old man snatched it up before he could grab it.

"Not yet!" he shouted. "I'm not done with my story! I discovered something fascinating about this artifact very soon after taking it in my hand. It passed on to me a strange ability – a sort of clairvoyance if you will. I could

108

sense things, Mr. Bennett. I knew what others were think-ing before they said it – what things would happen before they actually occurred. Soon after, these powers took on other attributes. I learned I could read minds, anyone's I wanted. I didn't even need to be in the same room as them – hell, the same continent even! That's how I discovered my wife was having an affair."

Jay tried to say something, but he couldn't find the words. His eyes remained glued to the coin in the old man's hand.

"Dr. Wilkins is the only other person I ever shared this secret with, but even he doesn't understand what my powers would eventually become. He thinks they're driving me mad, but he doesn't understand, Bennett. He doesn't understand this coin like I do, like you will. He doesn't understand that the Eye of Ra really does see all!"

"Give me the coin," muttered Jay. "I...I need it."

The old man laughed.

"Of course you do! I knew that the power was getting to be too much once I realized I couldn't turn it off. The thoughts of billions of people all streaming through my mind was maddening in its own right, but that was just the tip of the iceberg, really. The Eye of Ra's true power is much more horrifying. Imagine, Mr. Bennett. Imagine being able to see everything!"

It was only now that Jay was beginning to under-stand just how warped the strange man's psyche really was.

"Everything that ever did exist and everything that ever will exist! My eyes no longer perceived the world the way that you do. My mind no longer experienced time in a linear fashion. I've seen it all! All the good, and yes, Mr.

Bennett, all the evil as well. I witnessed Vikings rape and pillage villages in intimate detail. I watched countless genocides occur throughout the course of human history. I looked through the terrified eyes of a 12-year-old Pakistani girl in the year 2087, as the heat of a nuclear bomb engulfed her and her schoolmates in flames!"

The old man whipped his hand up to his face, and began tearing away at his bandages.

"I couldn't take it anymore, Bennett! I couldn't bear to see these things any longer! That's why I did something about it! That's why I dug my own eyes out of my face with my bare hands!"

Jay recoiled at the horrid sight now in front of him. Two gaping blood caked craters sat in place of eyes on the man's mutilated face.

"The coin is a curse, and Dr. Wilkins believed he was helping me con you into transferring it onto yourself, but he doesn't realize it won't work like that. The truth is, its power doesn't transfer to whoever holds the talisman next. It spreads. Even removing my eyes has only given me temporary relief. The visions are already starting to come back to me. Soon, they'll dominate my every thought again. The only way to be rid of it is to die!"

"You're nuts," Jay muttered.

"Oh, by this point I'm sure, but that doesn't matter. The curse is real, Mr. Bennett. I don't want you to have it. If I could break the chain, believe me I would, but our fates are set in stone. Free will is an illusion. There's no point trying to explain it to you anyway. You'll learn the truth soon enough. You're the next man to bear the burden of this power. I've already seen it. That's why I had

Wilkins convince you to come here. There is no escaping fate, Mr. Bennett. Tonight you will wield the Power of Ra just as I have and I…tonight I will die and finally be free of this damn curse!"

The old man jerked forward and ripped Jay's knife from the desk. Without warning, he then dove at him, slicing the blade wildly through the air. Jay grabbed ahold of his arm knocking the knife away, but dropped his cellphone as they wrestled to the ground. With Jay's only source of light gone, darkness once again enveloped the study. The old man was stronger than he had anticipated. Jay gagged as the blind lunatic wrapped a hand around his throat. It felt as though he was crushing his trachea. Jay reached his arm out, desperately searching in the blackness for something to strike his attacker with. A hard plastic object brushed up against his fingertips and instantly he knew what it was. Jay wrapped his hand around the handle of his knife then thrust it upwards until he felt it penetrate flesh.

The grip began to loosen around Jay's neck and with a thud the old man slumped to floor. Jay could feel the warmth of his blood begin to pool around both of their bodies. He pawed about on the ground for his cellphone, eventually finding it underneath the cherry wood desk. A pale green light swam back into the room when he powered the screen back on.

The old man's body lay motionless on the floor, the point of Jay's butterfly knife submerged deep within the side of throat. Jay leaned against the desk and gasped for air. Under the light from his cellphone the blood still spilling from the old man's neck took on a deep purple hue. Jay bent over, yanked the blade from his throat then wiped it down on a part of the carpet the old man hadn't gushed on.

In the dead man's hand Jay spotted the coin. He pried the artifact from the corpse's fingers and stumbled out the door. An ice-cold shiver ran up his spine, causing his body to tremble when he looked down to the bewitching artifact resting his palm. There was something strangely comforting about holding it.

When he made it outside to his car, Jay searched through the red envelope that the doctor had given him until he located the phone number. He dialed it into his keypad, but stopped before hitting send. Something was telling him the number was fake. It was such a strong sensation that he didn't feel the need to put it to the test. Jay put the phone back in his pocket and started up the engine.

He wasn't concerned about locating Wilkins. For some reason, he had a strange inclining as to where he could find him. Now that Jay had a homicide on his hands, he figured he'd pay the doctor a visit in order to tie up any loose ends. As he pulled away from the house, he reflected on what the crazy old man had said to him.

The Eye of Ra sees all. What a crock of shit.

A pair of headlights approached in the distance from the opposite direction. Ever so briefly, Jay felt his brain go numb as a static image appeared in his head – a picture he could see in his mind's eye.

"It's a blue Dodge Neon," he blurted out.

A 2005 marine blue Dodge Neon drove past his car.

A FAVOR FOR A FAVOR

I T MUST HAVE BEEN the most run-down, filth-ridden motel room I had ever seen — the kind of place where cockroaches didn't feel the need to scatter at the flash of a light bulb. I wouldn't be surprised if a whole civilization of the nasty things were living between the walls, laying their repulsive egg sacks wherever they pleased, and multiplying faster than an Asian kid on Adderall. I was seated at the edge of the bed, shifting uncomfortably atop its warped mattress while trying to ignore the rank funk radiating from a pile of unwashed sheets bundled up in the corner. It was the type of room people did everything but sleep in. That was fine by me — I didn't come there for shut-eye, anyway. In my left hand was a half-drunk bottle of Jack Daniels. In my right was a .32 caliber Smith & Wesson.

The extraordinarily depressing location was poetically fitting in a way — I was extraordinarily depressed after all. It was my wife who was the cause of my misery. She had broken my heart, leaving me with nothing but a vacant grief-stricken soul, like a teenager who listens to Fall Out Boy and writes poetry on Tumblr. For a while, suspicions of infidelity had loomed over our marriage, but I had always chalked up my conjectures as nothing more than paranoid delusions. They say denial is the best remedy for heartache. It wasn't until I stumbled across a series of implicitly sexual emails between her and the pastor of our church – a married man in his own right – that I was faced with the morbid reality of my wife's secret sexcapades.

Pastor Alonso was a slick, fast-talking, cut-throat, shark who dressed more like a U.S. senator than a man of the cloth. He pulled in a far bigger salary than one might expect a holy man to earn. A lot of people would be surprised to find out just how profitable the preaching business can be, especially when you head up the 2nd biggest mega-church in California. Alonso had a taste for life's opulent luxuries and wasn't afraid to flaunt it. It wasn't uncommon for him to drive a Mercedes Benz to church or show off his collection of Rolex watches during Sunday services. I guess that's why my wife gravitated towards him. She always did have a weak spot for material things.

There was one thing that all the pastor's money couldn't buy him though – kids of his own. His wife, Darcy's, on-again off-again battle with the big C had thrown a monkey wrench into his plans to start a family. Recently, her cancer had taken a turn for the worse and while she lied up in the hospital on her death-bed, the pastor and my wife were getting together for some *extra bible study sessions*.

When I confronted my wife about the emails, things got ugly. Names were called, expletives were hurled, and threats were thrown out (by her mostly). She explained to me that the pastor invited her and the kids to move in with him once Darcy passed – an offer my "better half" had accepted. She said she was going to give him the family he always wanted. It just so happened that family was mine. I didn't have the money to fight a long drawn out custody battle or hire big time lawyers, but Pastor Alonso did. Couple that with the fact women usually win these kinds of disputes (even if they don't always deserve it) and you can see why things were looking so bleak for me. Another man had stolen my wife, my children, my life, and there was nothing I could do about it.

The room slowly started spinning and I realized my good friend Jack was up to his old tricks again. Nausea was beginning to settle in and I didn't want to spend my last moments alive vomiting the Carl's Jr. cheeseburger I had wolfed down an hour earlier, so I decided to stop stalling and finish what I came there for.

I placed the revolver's barrel in my mouth and rested my finger on the trigger. In case you were wondering if my life flashed before my eyes, allow me to be perfectly blunt – *it didn't*. And I was thankful for that too. I could think of a million things I'd have rather been doing than reliving the agony that woman had put me through. I shut my eyes as tight as possible in preparation for the bullet to pass through my brain.

THEY SAY THAT HE WHO HESITATES IS LOST. In short, the proverb means that spending too much time deliberating on an important decision can ultimately lead to disastrous consequences. Although in my case, one tiny minute moment of pause may have actually prevented said consequences and saved my life. The cold metallic taste of the revolver's barrel on my tongue caused me to question my actions for only the briefest of seconds, but sometimes even that can be more than enough time to change a man's fortunes. As I sat there, trying to talk myself into pulling the trigger, the telephone in my motel room began to ring. I slid the gun out of my mouth, sat good old Jack down on the night-stand, and answered the phone.

"Hello?" I said in my best possible not-about-to-kill-myself voice.

"Jacob! I'm so glad you picked up!" I had no idea who the voice on the other line belonged to. I never heard it before, but whoever it was, they seemed to know me. "Listen, Jake," he continued, "before you go and...redec-orate the walls with the inside of your skull, we need to have a talk first."

I hadn't told anyone where I planned on being that evening, but this guy not only knew my name and loca-tion, but even the fact that I was contemplating punching my ticket to that big toga party in the sky. Had he been watching me? I needed some answers. Using every working brain cell in my head, I came up with the most rational, thought-out, intelligent question I could construct.

"Uhh...what?"

"I said we need to have a talk, Jacob. Now sit tight, I'm on my way over to your room right now." And with that, he hung up the phone.

I stared blankly at the wall, completely dumbfound-ed – my mind still trying to process what happened. I wondered for a moment if I had just been the victim of a prank call. It seemed from our short conversation, that the guy on the other end of the line had been watching me. My first inclination was that he might have been some sort of pervert. After all, the motel wasn't exactly a four star accommodation and I *did* notice that the place looked to be a magnet for weirdos, freaks, and other types of seedy characters when I checked in. I took a swig of liquid courage. For some reason I always felt braver when Jack was around.

Knock knock.

The knock on the door nearly caused me to lose control of my bowels (that Double Western Bacon Cheeseburger was coming out one way or the other). I tried to convince myself that I was being neurotic, but something about the call made me feel uneasy.

I had become aware of a dark inexplicable feeling that began bubbling from within the pit of my stomach the moment the phone first rang – an awful combination of dread, fear, hate, and a myriad of other terrible emotions all simmering together into some kind of unspeakable brew.

"Who is it?" I called out. No one answered. I waited for a response and then tried again, this time with a little more bass in my voice, "Who is it?"

Knock knock.

I stood up from the bed, tucked the gun into the waistband of my pants, and zipped up my jacket, making sure it was properly concealed before making my way towards the door.

Knock knock.

"I SAID WHO IS IT?"

"House keeping." The voice on the other side of the door sounded like it belonged to an elderly Hispanic woman.

"Oh," I chuckled at myself for letting a maid get me so riled up. "Please come back later. Thank you."

Knock knock.

"Housekeeping."

"I said come back later, please."

"You want sheets?" By this point, the woman was seriously trying my patience. Either she didn't speak English or she was a complete moron. "I come in, clean toilet?"

"There's a sign on the door knob! Can't you read!?" I swung open the door, ready to give the woman a piece of my mind. "It says do not dist- "

There was no one in the hallway. I leaned my head out of the room to see if the irritating maid wasn't bothering some other poor sap, but the corridor was completely barren. Convinced that I had officially lost my mind, I retreated back inside and closed the door behind me.

Knock knock.

Not a second later, the knocking started up again.

"Housekeeping."

"GO AWAY!" I shouted at the top of my lungs. Where had she come from? Just moments earlier I was alone in the halls.

Knock knock.

"I change towels?"

"Listen, please just leave me alone," I begged. "There's no way in hell I'm letting you in."

It was getting harder and harder to ignore that

strange dark sensation that was still stewing inside my stomach.

Knock knock.

"I SAID GO AWAY!"

Once more I opened the door and once more there was not a cleaning woman in sight. This time, however, I was not alone. Doubled over in laughter before me, was a teenage boy, no older than sixteen. He was wearing a forest green hoodie and a matching flat-billed baseball cap tilted off to the side – a fashion choice that made him look spectacularly douchey. His baggy jeans sagged halfway down his ass, exposing a pair of striped boxers and accenting his douchiness even further. A black bandanna hung out of his back pocket as if he was some kind of gangbanger. I found this to be particularly stupid since he appeared to be type of suburban white kid whose mom drove him to soccer practice in a minivan.

"Can I help you?!" I grunted. I was about ten seconds away from ringing the little twerps neck. By the way he was convulsing in laughter, it was clear that he was the mastermind behind my harassment.

"Ho-ho-ho man!" he managed to squeeze out between breaths, "You should have seen yourself. You look like you just got caught with your dick in the family goat!"

"What?"

The boy wiped a tear from his eye and took a deep exhale in an attempt to rein in his laughter, "Damn, did that go over your head? Sorry, now that I think about it, the expression is a little before your time. It originated in Scotland in the mid 1700's. A lot more people owned goats back then so I guess it used to be funnier. When you've been around as long as I have, it's hard to stay caught up with the latest lingo. What are all the kids saying these days, Jake? Is YOLO still a thing? You know what, never mind. I came here to talk to you about something else. May I come in?"

"No, you may not," I extended my arm across the door frame to block the entrance of my room, "Why don't you get the hell out of here, kid? I'm busy."

"Oh yes, I can see that, but I'll only take a minute of your time." The boy ducked under my arm, scrambling past me before I could stop him. Once inside he paused for a moment, surveying the room, and smiling snidely to himself. "Jeez Jake, this place is a dump! Why the blazes would you want to blow your brains out here? I personally would have chosen the Ritz Carlton uptown if I was going to off myself. Oh, but not before ordering some of those delicious sweet potato truffle fries from the bar in the lobby!"

"You've got about three seconds to get out of here, kid!"

"I'm shaking in my boots." He giggled briefly then continued, "Honestly man, intimidation isn't your forte. I promise I'll leave in a second, but as I said before, I wanted to have a little chat first."

"What do you want?"

"To help you out."

"You can help me by getting out of my room."

"A bit snippy aren't we? Jacob, I know you've had a rough day, but it doesn't have to end the way you think it does. So what if your wife hurt you? Buck up! There is a way to remedy this situation."

122

It was then that I realized the darkness inside me had never gone away. Instead it had been flourishing — spreading from my core as it pervaded throughout the rest of my body. How did this kid know so much about me? For a second time that evening I was so rattled I could hardly spit out a sentence.

"Wh-who are you?" I said. He leaned in and cupped his ear like an old man whose hearing had waned over time. "Were you w-w-watch — "

"Was I w-w-watching you? Is that what you were going to say? Learn to *ENUNCIATE*, man! Sorry to interrupt, but if I let you do all the talking we're going to be here all night and believe me when I tell you, I've got other places to be. Now then, why don't I answer your second question first? Yes, I was w-w-watching you, but not in a creepy staring at you through the window kind of way. You know, like Ryan Gosling in *Drive?* Did you ever see that movie? It's surprisingly good, and that Gosling, he's got chops I tell you! The guy is so damn handsome too! Some lucky bastards just hit jackpot in the genetic lottery, am I right?"

The kid was giving me a bad vibe. I slid my hand into my jacket pocket and felt through the fabric for the handle of my revolver. All the while, he continued to blabber senselessly about how *The Mickey Mouse Club* was the greatest thing to ever happen to the entertainment industry. I needed to somehow get control of the situation.

"Shut the hell up, kid!" I shouted. "You better give me some straight answers right now. Why were you watching me?"

The boy's smile quickly disappeared. He scanned me

up and down, probing me with his eyes as if he was examining every inch of my body, a look of utter disgust on his face. It was bizarre. His very stare made me feel ashamed and violated. "More questions, huh? First off, you should probably make sure the hammer isn't cocked on that little lemon squeezer of yours. You're going to shoot your dick off and then you'll really have a reason to kill yourself."

Somehow he knew about the gun I was hiding under my coat. I unzipped my jacket and pulled it out from my pants. He was right. I had left it cocked.

"I was watching you because I saw a doomed soul – a lost spirit so to speak – who was about to let the bad guys win and I just couldn't bring myself to allow you to do it." He moseyed over to the television and dragged his finger down the screen, leaving a spotless streak across the otherwise dust-covered glass. "Take it from a guy who's been there before. I know exactly how you're feeling right now. I too have been betrayed by someone I loved – cast down and thrown out in favor of another."

He paused for a moment, looking down at the dust that collected on his fingertip. "But I haven't answered your first inquiry yet, have I? Who am I? Well, that's a loaded question. I'm a man of many epithets. Over the years I've been known as The Bearer of Light, The Son of Perdition, even The Proud One. In a story he once wrote, Washington Irving referred to me as Old Nick. I have been anointed a prince, while at the same time branded a beast."

"You're telling me that you are The- "

"Please to meet you! Hope you guessed my name!"

"But that's impossible."

"Why? You go to church, don't you? Is it so hard

to believe that asinine little book – the one you people so arrogantly proclaim to be God's true word, actually got something right? Don't go patting yourself on the back for being a Christian, though. The Bible's filled with more half-truths and garbage than a supermarket tabloid."

I was completely taken aback by what the boy was saying. A couple minutes earlier I was getting ready to lodge a bullet in my brain, now I was talking to a teenager who had just declared himself to be the embodiment of evil.

"If you're the devil," I asked, "then why do you look like a kid?"

"Why not? I do as I please. I can appear as whatever or whoever I want. You think this is weird, once I made myself look like a snake just so I could talk to a hot naked chick."

"Yeah, but it doesn't make any sense."

"Neither did Carlos Mencia's comedy career, but it happened anyways. By the way, I assure you I had nothing to do with that." He shook his head, "I suppose it's proof you require, eh? I miss the old days where you people would blindly take me for my word. It made it so much easier to cheat at poker." The boy gave me a mischievous wink. "Alright, why don't you pick up the phone? There's someone who needs to speak with you."

Not a second later a shrill, earsplitting sound cut through the motel room. The telephone on the end table was ringing. I shot a skeptical look over to the teenager. He was holding his hand to his ear as if there was an invisible phone in it.

"Hello?" I said as I picked up the call.

"Housekeeping. I clean now?" As the boy's lips moved I could hear the cleaning woman's voice over the telephone. "No hablo Ingles. I come in?" He burst into a fit of laughter.

I was floored. I tried to play it cool, but I'm certain he could read the shock on my face.

"Check this one out." He cleared his throat. "I'm leaving you, Jacob." Now he sounded like my wife, "Pastor Alonso has a bigger house than you. As a matter of fact, that's not the *only* thing that's bigger." This sent him into another round of giggles. After he had his laugh, his voice returned to normal. "Not bad, right? I mean, I'm no Danny Gans, but I bet I could still play The Nugget."

And when he said that, he smiled, but it was just a little too wide – wider than a mouth should stretch. Ever so briefly I caught a glimpse of his teeth. It was as if hundreds of tiny daggers were protruding from his gums. He shifted his head ever so slightly and his peculiar facial features had disappeared. Once again he looked like a typical teenager.

"You can't have my soul," I said, "It's not for sale."

The boy scoffed, "Come now, do you really think I just go around *buying* people's souls from them? Ye have little faith in humanity, Jacob. Most people are too smart to fall for that kind of thing. What's a lifetime of happiness compared to an eternity in hell?"

"Then why are you here?"

"Like I said before, I do as I please, and it would please me very much to do a favor for you. No contracts or souls involved. Honest Injun!"

"What kind of a favor?" I asked.

He turned and started out the door. "Why don't you accompany me for a walk and I'll explain? Oh, and bring that little pistol with you."

As the boy exited my room, I picked up the phone again and held it to my ear. I didn't hear a dial tone, so I followed the cord only to find that it wasn't even plugged into the wall. Jack was still sitting on the nightstand, waiting to provide consultation for me if I needed it. He was going to have to wait just a little longer. I followed the boy out the door.

I CAUGHT UP TO HIM halfway down the hall and together we headed down the rusty metal stairs that lead to the parking lot.

"I see that you're in a bit of a bind, Jacob. Your wife of fifteen years is leaving you for that idiot pastor and taking the kiddies with her. What were their names again? Oh yes, Hunter and Elizabeth. Such darling children- "

"Leave my kids alone!" I blurted out. My unexpected outburst surprised even myself, but hearing him mention my kids by name had set me off.

He stopped halfway down the stairs and jabbed a bony finger into my chest.

"Listen here, tough guy. Just because I might happen to look like a boy band reject at the moment, doesn't mean I won't turn into some sort of ten-foot tall Lovecraftian monstrosity and bite your legs off if you continue to disrespect me, capiche?" I nodded my head. "Good, I don't know what all the fuss was about anyways. I love children.

I'd have one of my own, but it's so hard to find a suitable candidate to bare the antichrist. There's something about heralding in a millennium of Hell on Earth and bringing about the apocalypse that turns most women off. The only people whoever volunteer for the job are nut balls and whackos, and trust me Jake, I don't want no *baby mama drama* anymore than you do!"

I think he was making a joke because he paused for a second and glanced over to me as if he was expecting to hear laughs. He continued talking once he realized I didn't find him amusing.

"If you ask me, you have three options.

"Option number one. You go back to your room and blow your brains out. You never see your kids again, and your wife continues fucking the pastor.

"Option number two. You don't do anything, *like a pussy.* Go back to your boring and now *lonely* existence. You'll see your kids the second Saturday of every month, and your wife continues fucking the pastor."

"I suppose this is where you tell me about option three?"

When we made it to the base of the stairs, he gestured towards the parking lot indicating the direction he wanted to walk.

"Smart man," he chortled. "Option number three is this. You take that .32 caliber Smith & Wesson over to the pastor's McMansion tonight. Your wife's there right now, *discussing church business.*" He made a set of quotations in the air with his fingers when he said that. "I'm sure he's got her down on her knees, taking communion as we speak. You know? Accepting the Holy Body inside her mouth and all that- ”

“Ok, ok, I get it, but that's a terrible joke. We aren't even Catholic. What are you trying to say? You want me to kill Pastor Alonso?”

“Kill the pastor, kill your wife – hell – kill his annoying little shih tzu while you're at it. You have to kill them, Jacob. Don't let them take your children from you. End their lives for trying to ruin yours. I'd do it for you, but no killing is one of the few rules I'm bound by on this miserable plane of existence.”

I had to admit, it was an idea that had crossed my mind earlier that night – more of a fantasy than anything. I never actually considered going through with it.

“But that would be a sin,” I said. “Now that I know Hell exists, there's no way I'd do anything to risk damnation.”

“Look who you're talking to, Jacob. Don't you think I have a *little bit of pull* down there? For this one particular night I will absolve you of your sins. Think of it as a Get-Out-Of-Jail-Free card. And don't worry about the fuzz either. I have friends in high places! You won't even be considered a person of interest in the murder investigation.”

I couldn't believe I was even entertaining the idea. I had become so engrossed in what the satanic little douchebag was proposing that I didn't even realize he was leading us to my car until we were standing right in front of it.

“So if it's not my soul you want, what are you getting out of this?”

“Ah! I see my reputation precedes me! Like I said before, I'm just doing you a solid, man.” He stuck his fist out waiting for me to bump it. I left the devil hanging. “Maybe one day in the future, you'll repay the favor…or not. You certainly wouldn't be obligated to."

"What kind of favor?"

"I don't know, pick up my dry cleaning? I haven't thought of it yet. Who cares? I may never even bother you after tonight."

I reminisced back to when my wife and I were young. We were so in love and now I was standing in a parking lot, under the neon lights of the world's dirtiest roach motel, letting the baby faced demon talk me into murdering her. How did it come to this?

"She's my wife," I said. "Part of me still loves her. I don't know if I could do anything that would harm the mother of my children."

He rolled his eyes.

"Oh and clearly she loves you too! Why else would she be on her back right now letting that pastor plow her into next week?"

And when he said that his voice got deeper – a thousand octaves lower than anything I'd ever heard in my life. The sound was maddening. It made me want to bury my fingers into my ear canals until my eardrums burst.

"Your adulterous whore of a wife sins with that slimy, two-faced, sorry excuse for a human being as we speak! If that wasn't enough, she plans on taking *your children* and *half your money*! And for what? Because you don't have a big house or a fancy car? She used you until something better came along, and he did the same thing to his wife. Hell is filled with men and women like them! Send them where they belong." It felt as though his voice was microwaving my brain from the inside. I grabbed my head and fell to my knees. "That pastor sins in God's name with your wife and you want to let them get away with it?! Send them to hell, Jacob! Send them to me and I will make sure they suffer until the end of time!"

"OK!" I cried. "I'LL DO IT! I'LL DO IT!"

"Excellent!" his voice had conveniently reverted back to normal. "Let's get started, shall we? I'll meet you over at the pastor's house. I'd ride with you, but I'm The Lord of Fucking Darkness and you drive a Prius so...you know."

EVEN THOUGH HE WASN'T IN THE CAR WITH ME as I drove over to Pastor Alonso's home, I knew that I was far from alone. Every time I doubted my sanity, every time I started to question if what had transpired was even real, he was there. Standing on a street corner, waiting at a bus stop, even watching me from the windows of other cars as they passed me by. I realize now that he was keeping an eye on me, making sure I didn't get cold feet. It came as no surprise to find him already waiting for me on the front steps of the pastor's massive house when I pulled up.

He placed a hand on my shoulder when I got near and spoke some final words of encouragement to motivate me.

"You're doing the right thing, Jacob," he said. "Just remember, they had this coming."

From the moment I nudged open the pastor's gaudy, oversized, front door, I could hear him and my wife wailing away from the bedroom upstairs. I drew my gun and followed the moans up the steps. The little devil followed close behind.

"Jeez, Jake. It sounds like a couple of pigs getting slaughtered in there. Is that what it was like when you two used to bump uglies?"

I brushed off his inconsiderate quip and leaned against the bedroom door once I got upstairs. The boy was licking his lips in anticipation. It seemed as if he wanted them dead worse than I did. Doubt began to seep into my mind. I was no killer. The very thought of murdering the mother of my children was beginning to make me feel sick.

Perhaps sensing apprehension, he started whispering in my ear, "Do it Jake. Send them to hell."

His words were easy to ignore. My kids were all I could think about. Could I really take their mother away from them? Even though I had let the boy manipulate me that evening, I still had my free will. I knew that I had the power to walk out the front door if I wanted to. No one needed to die.

"He who hesitates is lost, Jake."

How could I even pull the trigger? For God sakes, I still loved the woman. That's when that dark inexplicable feeling that had been growing inside me started to dwindle. In its place I felt hope. Hope that maybe if I could talk to her, even hear her speak, I would come to my senses. Then, almost on cue, her voice rang out, resonating through the air like a magnificent melody plucked from the fingers of a master harpist.

"Fuck me, preacher man!"

I kicked in the door.

MY GUN HAD SIX BULLETS, but it only took me three. It would have been two, but I couldn't resist the opportunity to relieve the pastor of his Holy Scepter. It's strange how draining murder can be. All I did was point my gun and pull a trigger, yet my body felt like I had just run a marathon.

"I knew you had it in you, Jacob, but holy hell, I didn't expect you to blast off his pecker too!"

It wasn't his wisecrack that startled me. The boy's voice had suddenly changed. It was deeper than a teenager's now, more dignified too. Perhaps most alarming, it was a voice I knew very well — one I heard echo off the windows of my church every Sunday for years. Pastor Alonso's voice. I whirled around to see the man I just shot smiling at me from the doorway.

"Relax," he said as he entered the room, "It's just me, Lucifer, King of The Underworld, Father of Lies, yada yada yada."

I looked back to the bed. The real pastor's bullet riddled body still laid motionless next to my wife's corpse, their cadavers entwined within a set of tacky bloodstained bed sheets.

"Wh-why do you look like Pastor Alonso now?!" I asked.

"Why does it matter? I do as I please."

Before I had a chance at a follow up question, the thunderous sound of the pastor's front door being slammed shut carried through the house and up to the bedroom. My heart began to race as a bevy of heavy footsteps made their way up the stairs.

"What the hell is going on?!" I demanded, but the

trickster didn't answer me. There was a wicked grin painted across his face. It sent a wave of fright through my body.

"Do you know what they're going to do to you in prison, Jacob?" he said with a sneer. Two uniformed police officers strode into the room.

As the policemen made their way towards me, my panic began to intensify. All I could think about was wasting the rest of my life away in prison, forced to play housewife at the behest of my cellmate, a tattooed skinhead named Knife Face.

I still had three bullets left and I knew there was one way out of the situation. I raised the revolver to my temple as the cops marched towards me. I don't know if I really would have pulled the trigger had they attempted to arrest me. Thankfully I didn't get the chance to find out because instead of drawing their guns on me, they brushed right by without saying a word. I watched in awe as they started wrapping the pastor and my wife's bodies' in the soiled silk sheets. To my surprise, they appeared to be cleaning up my mess. You-Know-Who fell to the floor and began howling.

"HA! Now you really do look like you got caught with your dick in the family goat!" He thrust a finger into my bewildered face. "I'm just joshing you, Jake! These fine gentlemen are with me. Them, too." He thumbed over to the doorway. Two more men I hadn't noticed before wearing plain clothes but still brandishing badges were waiting in the doorway. "Jerry, come over here for a second!"

The older heavyset man sauntered towards us. His somber face and reluctant gait made him look like a kid who just got caught with his hand in the cookie jar. The no-longer-baby-faced-demon patted him on the back. "Do you know who this man is, Jacob?" I shook my head. "Jerry here is the head of the police department. That means he's very important."

"Pleased to meet you," I said. I really wasn't. At that point all I wanted to do was distance myself as far away from the pastor's house as possible and forget the whole night ever happened. The police chief remained silent. The shame and discomfort in his eyes told me the feeling was mutual.

The demon gestured over to the other man still standing at the door. "That guy over there just made detective." He turned his head towards him. "Hey, congratulations on your new promotion, Bill!" The detective looked away to avoid eye contact. Once again my partner for the evening focused his attention on me. "Guess who's going to be heading up your wife's murder case?"

"What about the pastor?" I asked, "Who's going to be looking into his murder?"

He stretched his arms out and twirled around as if he was showing off a brand new coat. "What are you talking about? Pastor Alonso wasn't murdered! He just suddenly decided to do missionary work in Africa. See? Everything wraps up neat and tidy and you get off scot-free. Now Jacob, before you leave tonight, I wanted to speak to you about that favor."

"What?"

"You know. We talked about this. I said that maybe one day I might ask you to return the favor I did for you, remember?"

"Yeah," I said, "I remember. I guess I didn't expect it

to come so soon."

"Well, life's funny like that sometimes. Don't worry though. It's really nothing you can't do in your sleep! I'm not going to ask you to pick up and dispose of dead bodies like these suckers."

"What do you want?"

He leaned in close and looked at me with a solemn expression on his face. "Listen to me, Jacob, because this is the only favor I will ever ask of you. It is imperative, that you never attempt to contact Darcy Alonso. Do you understand?"

"What?" his request had left me puzzled for numerous reasons. "But Darcy Alonso has terminal cancer. She's dying."

His lips curled into a devilish smirk. "Well, let's just say I did her a little favor."

"What are you going to do with her?"

"What's it matter to you? I do as I please."

I waved my finger in his face. "But you said I'm not obligated to listen to you, right? If I wanted to, I could go over to the hospital right now and tell her about everything that happened tonight."

"Of course you can, Jacob! Like I said, there's no binding agreement between us. Your soul is yours and you're free to do what you want with it. As a matter of fact, I stake no claim to any of these men's souls. They're just people who were kind enough to repay the favors I did for them!

"You see, I've done favors for a lot of people, Jacob – cops, judges, lawyers, even pedophiles who take pleasure in the rape and murder of children. Hey that reminds me, don't your kiddies walk home from school every day?"

And when he said that, he looked me right in the eye. It was as if his stare caused my mind to play out a thousand different scenarios, each one more heinous and vile than the last. Those eyes were like looking through a window into Hell.

"Darcy and I are going away," he continued. "All you have to do is forget about her. Forget about this entire night if you want! But don't forget that I'm always watching you, Jacob."

He didn't need to say another word. The message was clear. I turned and exited the pastor's house without looking back. The next few hours were a blur to me. I remember driving back to my home, vomiting in the kitchen sink (that Double Western Bacon Cheeseburger finally did make its escape), then passing out on the couch in my living room.

My wife's body was found 48 hours after I shot her inside of a liquor store dumpster. Just as he said, I was never even considered a suspect. Her murder was pinned on some 19-year-old kid from the hood who had never even met her. It took no more than a week for the jury to reach a guilty verdict. He was sentenced to death. The kid is currently incarcerated and trying to appeal the jury's decision, but something tells me he won't have any luck. I have a feeling that I'm not the only person who has a favor to repay.

Darcy Alonso checked out of the hospital that evening and was gone by morning. Word around the church was that she and the "pastor" had believed her miraculous recovery to be a sign from God, so they sold their house and set out across the globe to spread his message. If you ask me though, that story's a bigger load of bullshit than a politician making a campaign speech while rolling in a pile of fertilizer.

It was hard for my children to lose their mother at such a young age, but they've been learning to get along without her. I like to think I've been doing a hell of a job as a single parent, cooking, cleaning, and taking care of them. It took a while for things to get back to normal for us, but they're finally smiling and laughing again.

About a year after everything happened, I received a letter in the mail. I didn't think much about it at first. It was the middle of December, and I had already collected dozens of Christmas cards. It wasn't until I tore open the envelope that I realized that dark inexplicable sensation had made its presence known once again in the pit of my stomach.

The message inside the card was short, but it hit me like a punch to the gut.

Merry Christmas from the Alonsos!

The doctor says we're due to have the best Christmas ever!

Attached to the card was a picture of Darcy and the "pastor" wearing ugly Christmas sweaters and grinning from ear to ear. Darcy's sweater, however, was pulled up past her midsection, exposing her belly. She looked to be about nine months pregnant.

SCHIZO

ONNY POLK SAT UPRIGHT IN HIS BED, back against the headboard as terrible memories of his childhood began flooding back to him.

Memories about the Bird Woman – the creature his diseased mind had conjured up during his youth. The thirty-nine-year-old family man was no stranger to schizophrenia, though he hadn't felt its symptoms since he was a boy – before his doctors had put him on a plethora of anti-psychotic medication.

He remembered the way The Bird Woman would wake him in the dead of the night, her slippery, forked tongue sliding into his ear, wriggling and writhing like some sort of alien parasite attempting to invade his brain. He could still vividly recall the way her breath always smelled of rotten meat, how its stench would rape his mouth, leaving its rancid flavor in the back of his throat every time she leaned her face into his and whispered her awful secrets. Secrets that appalled him as a young boy, that terrified him even more than her hideous, warped face.

He glanced over to his wife, Gina, who was sound asleep next to him in bed. Donny hoped a familiar sight would somehow snap him back to reality. She looked so peaceful as she dozed, her tranquil slumber uninterrupted by the panic attack her husband was currently experiencing. He felt as though he was losing his grip on reality. Gina was real. That much he was sure. What he wasn't sure about was whether or not The Bird Woman hovering at the foot of his bed was real too.

It was the first time he had seen her in three decades, but she was just how he remembered her – pale white skin, stringy black hair, and a pair of mustard yellow eyes whose perverse stare made Donny feel both terrified and unclean at the same time. His old nightmare had finally found a key to the vault in his mind and now she was free – unleashed for the first time in years and back for vengeance.

The Bird Woman lifted her leg and placed a deformed foot on top of his bed. Her black, crust-covered toenails left grime and dirt on his white cotton sheets. Donny's heart skipped a beat as he watched the creature slide a second filthy, grotesque appendage on top of his mattress. She was coming for him – just like when he was a child. He considered waking Gina, who was still snoozing next to him. His wife knew about his history with hallucinations, but had never seen him have an actual breakdown. Donny wasn't sure how she'd react. The Bird Woman crouched on top of his legs like a hyena. Horrible whispers had begun to trickle out of her disfigured mouth.

His meds!

How could he have forgotten about them? Donny remembered that he always kept a bottle of Clozapine in his nightstand just in case his hallucinations ever returned while he was in bed. He opened the drawer and rummaged through the darkness, frantically searching for the anti-psychotics while the Bird Woman started to slink up the bed. The smell of rotten meat began to force its way up his nostrils. Donny held his breath in an effort to prevent the repugnant stench from entering his lungs.

The Bird Woman was halfway up his torso now. Her grubby claws nipped playfully at his crotch as Donny hunted for the drugs. The whispers had gotten louder even though the awful creature's lips weren't even moving. Donny tried to calm down by reminding himself that the monstrosity was just a product of his mental illness, but she seemed so real. The desperate man's fingers grazed up against a plastic cylinder inside the drawer. He had found what he was looking for!

Donny yanked the pill-bottle from the nightstand and unscrewed the cap. The creature's chin was resting on his chest. Her forked tongue hung from her mouth, snaking back and forth across the base of his neck as if it had a mind of its own. He poured a handful of pills, not bothering to worry about the recommended dosage as the Bird Woman's slimy tongue slithered its way up the side of his face. The smell of her putrid breath had become overpowering.

With one eye trained on the monstrous sight, Donny raised the fistful of pills to his mouth, but felt a tug on his arm, giving him pause before he had a chance to pop the drugs. He turned his head to see his wife, Gina, eyes wide and full of panic, looking back at him. She swatted at her husband's hand, causing the pills to scatter across the bedroom floor.

The Bird Woman's gaze stayed fixated on Donny as

she lapped at his cheek like a child with a melting Popsicle. Gina opened her mouth to speak, voice quivering between her lips. Her words would send a new wave of horror through her husband's body, the likes of which Donny Polk had never felt before.

"Donny," Gina whispered. "I see her too."

THE OLD HOUSE

S A CHILD, I always heard whispers about the old, run-down house in the woods outside of town. Rumors of ghosts, ritual murders, cults, and mass suicides float-ed between the mouths of chatty locals for as long as I can remember. Many believed the place to be abandoned, but there were those who told tales of strange shadows that sometimes danced in the windows. Others swore they heard voices echoing out from behind the walls of the di-lapidated structure when they passed by. The story I'm going to tell you is about my experience with that place. I never saw specters frolicking in the darkness or heard the ghastly wail of some menacing phantom, but the events that unfolded that sunny afternoon still scare me just the same.

It was warm that day. The sun broke through tree-tops above our heads, scattering down to the forest floor, glimmering like golden confetti. I was twelve at the time. Peter was only nine, but even at that age, my little brother seemed to be on a constant mission to prove his bravery to me — as if he felt it was the only way to validate himself in my eyes. We trudged through the last of the brush until we made our way into a clearing where the old house stood. We had both heard stories about the place before, but this was the first time either of us had ever actually visited it.

The derelict old building was an intimidating sight. Moldy rotten wood covered the face of the home like the diseased skin of a leper. Some of the windows had been smashed out while others were covered in a thick brown coat of dust. The house's entire frame crooked off to the left at an angle so sharp, it seemed as if it was going to collapse at any moment.

"There it is," I told him. We stood at the edge of the clearing for what felt like an eternity, the two of us just staring at the time-damaged relic. "You don't have to go in there, Peter."

My younger brother sent a frustrated scowl in my direction.

"I'm not afraid."

"I didn't say you were."

"I'm going in there – all the way in the basement," Peter said matter-of-factly. "And when I do, you're gonna tell all the kids at school tomorrow how brave I am."

He puffed out his chest and marched up the steps to the front door. I'll never forget the pride in Peter's eyes when he turned back around and waved to me just before disappearing through the slanted doorway. I took a seat on the grass and leaned my back against a tree to wait for him. An hour passed and still there was no sight of him. By the time the sun had started to set and Peter still hadn't returned, I could feel anxiety beginning to build inside of me.

What if the rumors were right?

What if a family of cannibals lived inside of that place and they were already preparing my brother for dinner? What if a monster was hiding in the basement, waiting to tear Peter to shreds as soon as he set foot inside? I wanted to check on him, but I was far too afraid to go into the old house myself.

So I waited.

My brother finally emerged from the broken-down building just before the sun had set for the evening. Needless to say, I was relieved. I couldn't help but notice the curious expression on his face when he approached me – almost as if he was sizing me up for the first time.

"What took so long, Peter?" I asked him. "I was worried you got hurt!"

"Sorry. I lost track of time." His voice was flat and expressionless. Its very tone made me scrunch my face.

I brushed it off and grabbed him around the arm. "Come on. We need to be home before it gets dark or Mom will ground both of us."

My mother gave us a stern lecture about staying out after dusk when we got back. The night went normally enough, but Peter's demeanor remained cold and distant. I had been curious to ask him about the house, but I didn't want to do it in front of my mother and father. We shared a room, so that evening when we were getting ready for bed, I decided to prod him.

"So, Peter?" I said when I walked into the bedroom after I finished brushing my teeth. "You were in the old house for a while."

"I told you. I lost track of time," he responded.

"How?" I asked.

Peter sat up in bed. The blank expression on his face didn't change, but somehow it felt even more removed than before.

"I was looking at stuff."

I let out a nervous laugh.

"Well, did you see any monsters in there?"

I'm not sure how long it took for him to answer me. It felt like the silence lasted forever and a day. When he finally spoke again his answer was short, succinct and to the point. He simply smiled at me, answered "yes," and then blinked his eyes.

I spent the evening in my parents' room after that, but I was too afraid to sleep.

In the morning, Peter was gone. My mom and dad called the police. By the end of the day, they had filed an official missing person's report. His face was on the milk cartons and billboards. There was a massive statewide manhunt for him. Investigators believe that he was abducted so of course the press had a field day with it – the little boy who was taken from his bed in the dead of night.

The thing is, I don't believe Peter was abducted that evening by a prowler. I think whatever happened to him in the old house is what really led to his disappearance. It was my conversation with him before bed that cemented that idea in my mind – specifically when I asked him if he'd seen any monsters. His reply had terrified me more than words could ever describe.

It wasn't the grin he flashed before he answered. Though I found his smile disturbing, it's not what had captured my attention, nor was it his response confirming that he had indeed seen a "monster" while in the house.

The Old House

The thing that truly frightened me, that sent me running to my mom and dad's room, was what happened when he blinked his eyes. It scared me because when they closed, his eyelids shut the wrong way.

TROLL BRIDGE

THE WAY THE WIND SOUNDED as it passed between the trees just beyond his grandmother's yard, Andrew could have sworn he heard the forest calling his name. For as long as the young boy could remember, the woods had instilled a sense of intrigue and wonder in him. Many a night, he lied in bed dreaming about what kinds of magical exploits took place underneath the forest's canopy. He was a child with an avid curiosity and a voracious appetite to explore, but his granny had instructed him never to wander between the towering redwoods mere footsteps beyond her property line. It was a rule that always frustrated the boy, especially now, as he stood in the yard so close to the trees he was yearning to journey through.

Good boys listen to their grannies, and Andrew always tried his very best to do just that, but the gusty call of the woodland sirens had grown too strong for him to ignore. He peered over his shoulder through the window of his granny's cottage. An old friend of hers from way back had stopped by and the two were busy laughing about their childhood adventures. Andrew knew just how wrapped up in conversation his grandmother could get when one of her old chums came to visit. It wasn't uncommon for her to lose track of time and gab the entire afternoon away. The young boy understood that his opportunity to explore the woods had finally arrived. With any luck, he could sneak off, play for a while, and return home before she even noticed he was gone. And so, Andrew took off from the yard, disappearing between the trees.

The forest was every bit as enchanting as he thought it could be. Under the cover of the woods, Andrew was free to let his imagination run wild. There, he could be anything he wanted: A brave warrior on the hunt for a fearsome ogre, the leader of a band of merry men lying in wait to ambush a malevolent king, even a noble knight rescuing a princess from the clutches of an evil dragon. The broken tree branch he discovered lying on the forest floor at the base of an old spruce became his sword – one that he wielded with pride and honor.

Deeper and deeper Andrew traveled into the forest, slaying imaginary banshees and engaging invisible orcs in mortal combat. The woods became alive with the sights and sounds of a child playing out his fantasies and having the time of his life. As his adventures rolled along, so too did the hours. The sun had already begun to take its nightly hiatus from the sky before the boy snapped out of his roleplay.

Time had escaped him and with the evening rapidly approaching, the young boy feared his grandmother might have already noticed he was missing so Andrew threw down his "sword" and began his quest back to home.

As dusk turned to nightfall and the stars took their places in the sky, the young boy became disoriented navigating his way through the forest. The trees looked different in the moonlight and finding his way back was proving to be a more difficult task than the child originally anticipated.

Shadows danced across the forest floor as Andrew wandered aimlessly through the backwoods, teasing him like mischievous little imps. The flora had taken on sinister feel as well. Shrubs and bushes seemed to bend and twist like freakish circus performers, contorting their bodies into revolting shapes in the darkness. The air had grown more frigid. Andrew crossed his arms over his chest and rubbed his shoulders in an attempt to relieve himself from the awful chill. In the distance, an unsettling noise, shrouded under the nighttime veil that had befallen the forest, sent his imagination into a tailspin.

He began to picture bloodthirsty savages covered head to toe in tattoos, swarming him from the shadows, and surrounding him on all sides. Andrew could envision their faces riddled with piercings, wide-mouthed crocodile smiles full of teeth filed into points, and necks adorned with jewelry carved from human bones. Grotesque images of the savages closing in and tearing Andrew apart piece by piece like a pack of ravenous wolves ripped through his mind. A shiver ran up his spine at the thought of these wild men peeling sheets of skin off his chest, back, and thighs, exposing the tender muscle underneath to the cold forest air. He wondered if he'd remain conscious while the cannibals chewed through his abdomen in pursuance of his internal organs.

The child realized how isolated he was out in the woods. His cries for help would fall on deaf ears as the cannibals dug out his eyes with their dirty, grimy nails. A morbid question entered his head. Would he be able to feel their tongues as they lapped away at the fluids spilling from the gaping sockets in his face? He pictured the savages sucking on his ocular nerves, slurping and smacking them between their lips like pasta as he screamed in agony.

Finally, a sliver of hope arrived in the form of running water off in the distance. He tracked the noise until he came to a large creek flowing through the forest. Although he had never been that deep in the woods, he knew that if he followed the water, there was a chance it would eventually open up into the lake near his grandmother's house. From there he'd be able to find his way home. With a renewed sense of confidence, the child traveled along the stream, hoping to make it back before his granny sent a search party looking for him.

The unnerving sound arose from the abyss between the trees again and Andrew hastened his pace, praying that he'd come across the lake soon. The forest had gotten thicker, and the child was now climbing through bushes and over boulders on his way down the creek. He was a prisoner of the trees – the redwoods looming up from the forest floor looked down on the boy like domineering turnkeys, laughing at him while he tried in vain to escape his wooded jail.

Further downstream, Andrew noticed the water becoming choppier and the stream bed widening further apart. It was now big enough for a small boat to float down – if one were capable of navigating the quickly intensifying rapids that were tearing through the once tranquil waters. Another strange noise emanated from the shadows and thoughts of cannibals noshing on his liver broke free from his mind once more. He started running – not from any one thing specifically, but from the forest itself.

With tears rolling down his round face, Andrew sprinted beside the creek as fast as his feet would take him. Low hanging tree branches scraped against the skin of the young boy's arms, slicing and dicing him with their prickly appendages. It felt like he was running in quicksand. The mud along the creek bed was thick and gooey. Every step Andrew took was more challenging than the one before it. His chest burned. The cold forest air filled his lungs, stinging them as if he had inhaled thousands of angry bees. Eventually the child's legs began to weaken, stiff and sore from plowing through the muck.

Completely exhausted, Andrew finally collapsed to the ground and conceded defeat to his tall, woody jailers. He stared up to the trees dejectedly, awaiting whatever grisly fate the forest had in store for him. Seconds turned to minutes while he lied atop the blanket of fallen pine needles covering the earth below him, but nothing ever came – not one savage in sight. Eventually, Andrew rose to his feet, feeling slightly ashamed for falling victim to his imagination. The boy quickly dusted himself off and prepared to continue his journey, but paused when he noticed the curious sight up ahead of him.

A strange clearing in the middle of the forest had caught the boy's attention. Under moonlight, the field had the look of a charming oil painting. None of the forest's normal plant life had made its way into the beautiful oasis. Instead, bright orange and purple flowers the boy had never seen before populated the meadow in dense, colorful clusters. The fearsome redwoods that had been tormenting the boy all night boycotted the area. Not a single sapling had made an attempt to germinate in the field's lush, rich soil. The creek Andrew was following had opened up even more as it entered the mesmerizing sanctuary and was now as wide as a river. It roared through the clearing with the ferocity of a leviathan — an astonishing vision, yet a picture eclipsed by something even more breathtaking. In the center of the meadow, standing proudly over the raging waters, was an extraordinary bridge.

Andrew marveled at the majestic wooden masterpiece. The bridge was broad and sturdy. Large arches jutted out from either end, earmarking either side. The boy stumbled through the last thicket of bushes and into the meadow, moving towards the spectacle. Thoughts of cannibals and eyeless cadavers fell to the wayside, supplanted by his strong desire to investigate the glorious structure spanning the waterway.

From up close it was even more impressive. Once he was near enough to touch it, Andrew ran his fingers along the bizarre runes engraved into the bridge's archway. Remarkably, the entire construct appeared to be cut from a single piece of wood — one not native to the forest. Andrew recognized that the tree required to carve such a monument would need a trunk more massive than any redwood in the forest. Captivated by the brilliant work of artistry, the boy ventured onto the bridge in order to admire more of its craftsmanship. Another set of runes lined the railings, forming different patterns and arrangements, each design unique and spellbinding in its own way. The bridge's deck was solid and durable, yet yielded slightly to his footsteps.

It felt as if Andrew was walking over freshly cut grass.

The redwoods formed a perfect circle around the clearing. Beyond them lay more darkness and uncertainty – more opportunities for his imagination to send him into a hysterical frenzy like it had before. On the bridge he felt safe. He pondered over the thought of waiting out the night in the clearing, but remembered his granny and how worried she would be if he didn't make it back that evening.

Again that terrible noise seeped into the air – the very same one that had sent Andrew sprinting through the forest in panic, but this time every muscle in the young boy's body tensed. His palms immediately began to perspire; his body quivered with fear. It sounded like the death rattle of a hundred dying men – a sickening groan, louder than ever, drowning out even the roar of the river. Worst of all, it had risen up from beneath the bridge he was standing on.

Andrew prayed his mind was just playing tricks on him again – that the noises he was hearing were some sort of auditory hallucination, but deep within the pit of his stomach he knew that unlike the cannibals, whatever had made the sound was no figment of his imagination. A moment later and his fears were confirmed. A colossal hand reached up from below the deck and wrapped five brawny fingers around the railing. A second hand just as massive as the first followed suit and soon Andrew could see the dreadful face of a monstrous creature as it pulled itself onto bridge.

It towered over the boy, the beast's thick, burly body nearly as wide as the overpass itself. River water fell from its dark matted hair, splattering the deck as it lurched towards him. Its skin was the color of stomach bile, an inhuman putrid shade of yellow that made Andrew's brain turn over in his skull. The stink radiating from the monstrous thing was unlike anything he had ever smelled before. It leaned down, bringing its humongous face just inches from the child's, the rotten smell of its breath so foul Andrew began to feel light-headed.

"What are you doing on my bridge, boy?" Its voice grinded inside Andrew's ear like rusty, metal gears.

The young boy was at a loss for words. "I...I..."

"Hmmm? Speak up." The behemoth turned its head and pulled its hair back, revealing a long pointed ear. "Can you not talk?"

Andrew tried to speak again, but fear had gripped hold of his tongue. The creature looked as if it belonged in a nightmare. The pair of tusks jutting out from its gums were more horrid than any terrors the young boy had dared to dream while running through the forest that night. Its beady orange eyes, set far too close together on its face, glowed brightly against the darkness.

"I was lost," Andrew finally managed to squeak out. "I followed the creek and it lead me here."

The beast reared its head back and released thunderous cackle so booming it shook the surrounding trees.

"Do you know what I am, youngling?"

"I think so," said Andrew.

"Well? Out with it then."

The boy swallowed the lump in his throat. Ever so timidly he replied, "Are you a troll?"

The troll's lips curled into a harrowing smile. "That is correct, and I take it you are afraid of trolls, no?"

Andrew nodded his head in agreement.

"Ha!" The enormous beast scrunched its nose. "Why do you fear trolls, youngling? Speak the truth. We trolls have no patience for tall-tales, for it is a known fact that we cannot lie, ourselves."

Andrew had heard before that trolls were not capable of lying. It was something his granny had once mentioned off-hand. All of his knowledge about them had come from her. The creature seemed to be growing impatient so he decided to answer him.

"M-my granny told me that all trolls f-feed on children."

"Your granny told you this?" responded the troll. "What does your granny know about my kind? Not much, if these are the types of things she fills your head with."

Andrew looked up curiously at the beast.

"Never judge a book by its cover," the troll continued. "My species is a vegetarian one. We can easily sustain ourselves on the nectar from the flowers you see in this meadow." It waved a hand and gestured towards beautiful plants that grew in the clearing.

The troll pointed a finger towards the trees. Not a moment later, a white owl came soaring out of the shadows towards the bridge. It perched atop the troll's index finger. With its free hand, the gargantuan gently caressed the owl's snow colored feathers. The bird hooted peacefully as Andrew watched on in awe. The troll smiled and lowered its arm so that Andrew could pet it.

"It's okay, child," gurgled the beast. "This bird of prey will not hurt you."

Andrew extended his hand out, and carefully stroked

its head like one might do a cat, prompting yet another satisfied hoot from the bird. The young boy then put his hands in his pocket and hung his head indignantly.

"What worries you, little one?" asked the troll.

"I'm upset with my granny. I don't know why she would say such bad things about your kind."

"Don't be cross with her," replied the enormous, yellow being.

"But it's not fair! Trolls don't even eat children! They eat flowers like you said, right?"

The troll pouted and a deep sigh emerged from its mouth.

"As I said before, we trolls are incapable of lying. Your grandmother is wrong about most of my species being carnivorous, but there was one bad apple. His name was Lillifoot and my race is very ashamed of his existence."

"Lillifoot?" repeated the boy.

"Yes, we trolls have funny names. My father was known as Prissypants. My eldest brother's name is Mookiepie."

Andrew giggled and the beast chuckled too. Even the owl cooed out into the night, but the troll halted his laugh abruptly and his face grew somber. There was a great sadness in its orange eyes.

"Lillifoot wasn't like the rest of my species. Flowers didn't satiate his hunger. He began to feed on the animals in the forest, but after a while, even that wasn't enough for him. After savoring human flesh for the first time, he developed a taste for it, and yes, little one, children were his favorite."

Andrew gasped at the thought.

"So some trolls do eat children?"

"Just Lillifoot," the beast answered back. "Once word got out of what he was doing, the other trolls banned him from their territory so that he could never harm the humans they shared their land with. He was ostracized, young one — forced to live out the rest of his life as a hermit."

Andrew watched as the troll raised the owl to its face and gazed tenderly into its wise eyes.

"Is your name silly?" asked Andrew.

"Pardon?"

"Your name? You said all trolls have silly names. That means you do too, right?"

"I suppose," the beast responded, never breaking eye contact with the owl resting on his finger.

"So what is it?"

"What is what?" asked the troll, clearly distracted by the bird.

"Your name," said Andrew. "What is your silly name?"

"Oh, my name!" the troll chortled. "Forgive me. I fear this gorgeous creature may have caused me to lose focus of our conversation.

And with that the troll violently snatched the bird around the neck causing it to let out a terrified squawk. Andrew watched in horror as the monstrosity standing before him opened its massive maw. The owl's head crunched under its ferocious bite. Blood-stained feathers casually fell from the troll's mouth like crumbs. The beast turned its head towards Andrew and smiled at him again, only this time bits of brain were dripping from its lips.

The troll's voice rumbled over the bridge like an

earthquake. "My name is Lillifoot."

IMMORTAL

WHAT YOU SEEK is just beyond this door, young man."
Young man.

No one had called David young in a decade. Those were words that harkened back to a simpler time for him – before his obsession with immortality began to consume his life. Before he had wasted his physical prime locked away in his den, poring through archaic texts and studying ancient hymns. Before he devoted his life to investigating the validity of age-old legends from bygone cultures around the world.

From the Philosopher's Stone to the Fountain of Youth, David had researched tales of eternal life stemming out of every corner of the globe. He had even focused his efforts on more obscure, lesser-known lore, like the Owanu Frog of Ghana's Sisaala tribe and the disturbing story out of Slunj, Croatia that had come to be known regionally as *the night of the Star Child.*

It wasn't until he reached his mid-forties that he was able to piece together a trail of evidence that gave his quest direction. He had begun to recognize patterns throughout his studies of history – tiny consistencies buried in long-forgotten writings, reoccurring symbols carved into timeworn relics, peculiar regularities that had no right turning up in the places and times that they did. Now, after more than two decades, all of his findings had led him to one place – a lone monastery sitting atop an icy mountain in Eastern Tibet.

David had braved the conditions in order to speak to the wise holy men he believed held the secret he had spent most of his adult life searching for, but when he arrived he found the temple mostly empty, save for one old monk with tired eyes. Pangs of disappointment surged inside the gut of the frustrated traveler when he first laid eyes on the elderly hermit. After all, he had come so far and been so sure that the monastery housed the key to his deepest desire, but the deep age-lines in the old monk's face told him a different story. It told the story of muscle atrophy, the story of cognizance withering away, of bones becoming brittle. The old monk's face told the story of aging – the story of impending, unstoppable death.

With a pair of wrinkled, weathered hands, the hermit seized David by the arm, and led him inside, away from of the cold. The entrance hall of the temple was barren. A row of torches lined the interiors' gray stone walls providing only just enough light to illuminate the path ahead of them. The old monk, still clutching tight to his new guest's arm, began to hobble down the dim corridor. Together, the two navigated through the darkness in silence until they reached a winding staircase plunging downward into the monastery's shadowy depths. With his free hand, the elderly man removed the last torch off the wall and gestured towards the stairway.

"What exactly is this place?" David had asked the holy man as they began their descent.

But the old monk said nothing. Instead, he directed his gaze ahead, his tired eyes focusing on nothing but the twisting steps in front of him. David felt alone as they snaked their way into the abyss – like a tiny rock floating by itself in the vacuum of empty space, millions of miles removed from the closest celestial body. The pangs of disappointment he had been feeling just minutes earlier had begun to mutate into something else entirely. Paranoia, angst, and dread were now running rampant inside of his head, weaving themselves into an indescribable terror.

Just when he thought the black void he had found himself in would drive him mad, a golden radiance caught David's eye. As the two proceeded closer to it, the source of the glow became clear and David realized that his research had not been in vain. The base of the stairs came into sight. They appeared to open up into a small chamber with nothing but a large red door built into the wall. Beautiful ornate symbols were inscribed into the face of it. Egyptian hieroglyphics, Sumerian designs, and a variety of other ancient multicultural characters lined the perimeter of the impressive structure. By the time they reached the bottom step, the old monk's torch was no longer necessary. A brilliant light was seeping out of every crack in the door, flooding the chamber in a golden hue.

The old monk released David's arm and raised a wrinkled weathered hand towards the shining spectacle before them. It was here that he uttered those words – those words that had harkened back to a simpler time for the explorer.

"What you seek is just beyond this door, *young man.*"

"Just beyond this door," David repeated.

A rush of excitement swelled through him. He had found it. He had succeeded where Ponce de Leon and thousands of others like him had failed. He had located the secret to immortality.

David reached for the handle of the door, and with a quick tug, jerked it open. A blinding light burst forth, enveloping the room, swallowing David and the elderly holy man. He fell to the floor clutching at his chest. As the light intensified, so too did a searing pain he could feel in his heart. It was as though the entire core of his body had caught fire. The pain was unbearable – the most excruciating thing he had ever experienced in his life.

Questions started whirling through his head. *What is going on? How could it feel so horrible?* He had never once read, in all of his studies, that the youth rejuvenation process would be a painful one. Something had to be wrong.

Summoning every last ounce of strength, David crawled along the ground until he reached the door. He propped his shoulder up against it and drove his feet as hard as he could into the ground in an attempt to force it shut.

With a *THUD,* the door snapped closed causing the blinding light to disappear behind it, and leaving only a golden glow to wash over the room once more. Down on the floor again, David rubbed his eyes while he waited for the pain in his chest to subside. When his vision had regained focus, he looked up to scan his surroundings. What he saw ignited an inferno of terror that burned mercilessly inside of his body, spreading like wildfire.

Looking down on him was a familiar face – one he

Immortal

had watched age in the mirror every single day of his life. *His face* – and it was sporting a satisfied smirk. He was somehow staring up at himself as if another person was wearing his skin like a costume. Shock and confusion overran his mind. No longer able to gaze upon the imposter he attempted to bury his face in his palms, but when he peered down, the sight sent pulse after pulse of panic through his very essence. His hands were no longer his, but he knew he recognized them. They were wrinkled and weathered. Hands he had seen before – hands that once belonged to an old monk with tired eyes.

NEPTUNE'S FANCY

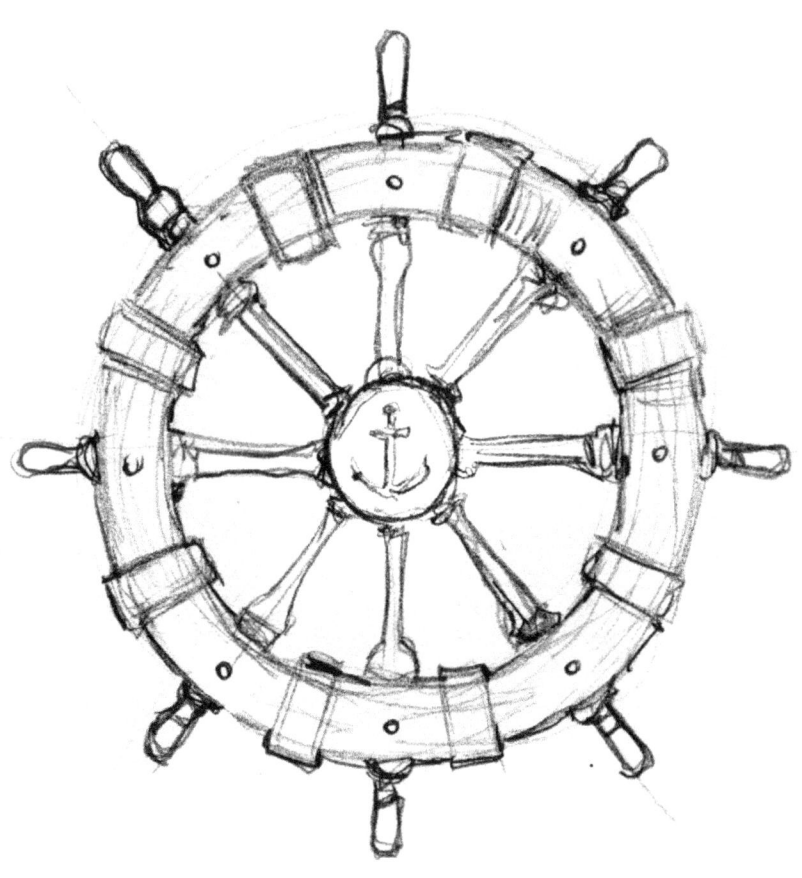

U PON MY SOUL, she was a lovely thing, pale skinned, dark hair entwined with the green weeds of the sea. A pity she looked dead. We hauled her up in the tuna nets, along with dolphin heads and fins. Those warm-blooded bastards would trail the fishing fleet and try to steal our catch when they could. Cunning they were too, but the dead ones 're not as smart as they might be since the razor edges of our nets would slice them up if they weren't quick enough.

Aye, but she was whole I saw, as we laid her on the deck. Perhaps she'd fallen from some rich man's pleasure vessel in a drinking party out at sea. A whore more likely than not, and naked she was as on her born'in day. But as I leaned over to touch those blue-tipped breasts, I was surprised to feel her move beneath me hands.

"Hai! Cap!" I yelled, "She be not altogether dead, I think!" And the others came closer then to take a look. Those turquoise lips, they parted in a gasp and she opened up her eyes, as red as blood.

Of a sudden, she sprang up and dashed across the deck! She crouched amongst some boxes there and we could see she weren't no human girl at all. How lithe she was! How lean! Her lips drew back to show her teeth, small, white, and sharp like a barracuda's. Moisture beaded, shining on her face and arms. The muscles in her thighs were taut, but scratched deep by our razored nets. Her breasts were large and pointed. Her fingers and toes were webbed. Rainbow-colored scales speckled her body in places, growing over her skin like the heavenly sores of some angelic leper. She was an apparition of a sailor's blackest, sweetest dreams.

Antony, our ship's first mate, was the first to break the trance induced by them round red eyes. Cautiously, he gazed about as he forced himself to venture closer to the thing we'd just caught by chance. Antony was the most respected sailor on our boat — a Scot, tall, red, and broad at the shoulders, who had once served in the Queen's Navy. The monster girl was silent as she eyed him from her fortress-nest of boxes. Then she made some sounds down in her throat — a seal or dolphin maybe like was how it rang inside my ears.

The cap clutched his brother's arm and shook his sister's son and roused the rest of us to wakening. The shock of our first finding her then dripped away like spindrift against a boat's hull. Now we was all just curious as hell, and Antony was standin' closest to the girl. He took another step and held his hands out so as to let her get the scent of him by way of introduction. She didn't seem to take too much to that cause soon as he was near enough she bit off a piece of his finger.

"Ayeii!! Ya poor, dumb animal!" Antony hollered and waved his damaged finger in the air — it was bleedn' horrible. He pulled a kerchief from his pocket and wrapped it tight 'round the tip of it. "Ya needn't a' be afraid, gal!" he called out. Antony was a godly man and wouldn't curse the devil himself. "I did not intend ta harm ya!" The rest of us set up a general roar, but the mate said "Quiet down ya fools, or else you'll frighten the girl, or fish, or whatever that thing is! And ya wouldn't be wanting to scare a wild animal when it's cornered and hurtin' and female ta boot!"

"Aye," the cap agreed in a soft voice, parroting Antony, as was his wont. "And I'm bettin' if she's scared enough to dash for it, she's primed and able to tear the insides out of anything that's got in her way!"

That's when some sailor said he feared she'd slaughter us all!

"Kill her, Cap," another cried, "Before she comes at us with that shark-toothed mouth of hers!"

Then Antony, who had the most reason to wish her harm, raised up his bandaged hand and bade us to relent. "Ya gents're being hasty here," said he in a peaceful voice. "Mayhap she's not so vicious as we might suppose." And he hid his bloody hand behind his back. "Mayhap she be a gentle thing when she's at home beneath the sea."

"Aye," the captain interrupted, a gleam came to his eye. "She's not a monster come into our midst lads, but a treasure rare! And beautiful she is too! A valuable oddity! A priceless curiosity! Boys, we could peddle her in any port for coins enough to last us years to come!" He put his arms around the shoulders of those men closest to him, and went on. "Fellow sailors! Brother merchants! Relatives and friends! If we handle this thing correctly here, we'll all come out as rich as kings!"

And then the eyes of all of us glistened with that golden light. The cap had hit upon the thought that each of us had been afraid to see. A treasure trove indeed, she was.

But what to do? How to proceed? Once caught, how did ye keep such a ken of the sea? It was my thought then to give her tuna. Why else would she pursue the nets? A poor, dumb thing I thought her to be. Human in form mayhap she was, but without a soul she were no more than a beast. And beasts were such that man was commanded to rule in those first days of the creation of the world.

She would'na take the tuna from the deck where I'd tossed it, but she took it soon enough from the bleed'n hand of Antony. And when she made her noises then again, a light struck up across the first mate's face.

"I hear her, brothers! She speaks the Queen's English!" He sputtered and looked around at each of us, but seeing that we did not hear nor understand the words of the female gave him pause. "But it's as plain as milk!" he offered toward the cap. "As clear as me mother's words when I sat upon her knee!"

"Are ya daft, man?" the cap inquired. "Ya say there's words inside them chirps and whistles?"

Antony turned around, gazing wide-eyed at the creature as she went on with them noises, those blood red eyes of hers staring back at him just the same.

"She says it was me blood that done it. The bit of me flesh that she consumed," he turned to look at the cap. "She says that's why I can hear her in me head."

He pulled the rag from his torn finger and we could see the white tip of the bone as he dripped his own blood

onto a piece of tuna in his other hand. The girl-thing spar-
kled her bloodshot eyes at him, but reached for his injured
digit instead of the fish. Gently, slowly, she seemed to move
as she raised the bloodied finger to her lips and nipped at
his damaged flesh.

"Have ya gone mad?!" cried the cap. "Feedin' ye'self
to this sea beast?!"

The creature pulled Antony's finger, which by now
had been gnawed halfway to the second knuckle, from her
mouth and began to yammer once more. We stood in awe
while he nodded his head as if he were understandin' her
yips and yaps.

"She be tryn' ta get back to her home, gents," he said
with certainty.

"And where would that be?" laughed the captain. "A
thousand leagues below the ocean's surface?"

"Nay, it be off the coast of an isle 'bout a week's sail
west of here," Antony replied. "She told me so herself. She
said she was makin' her way home when our nets snatched
her up. This jewel of the ocean be royalty, Cap'n. Her king
rules the sea and she's his favorite wife."

"You sayn' this thing, this fish-woman, this web-toed
female, be Neptune's fancy?" asked the cap.

But Antony kept right along as if he hadn't heard
him. "Our nets've done too much harm ta her legs." And
he gestured towards the gashes running up and down the
merwoman's thighs. "Now she's ask'n for our help. Her
kingdom's built of gold and pearls and precious rubies.
And she swore to me, on the sanctity of her husband's
throne, that if we return her home, then we'd be paid in
all the priceless gemstones this barge can haul."

"Aye," responded the cap. "Why be as rich as kings when we can be as wealthy as gods?"

There was a low rumble from the crew when he said that. Visions of golden underwater towers jutting up from the ocean's rocky floor danced and twirled through our heads like barmaids in a tavern when the grog is flow'n heavy and the music be merry and the drunks be clapp'n along, encouraging 'em.

"Bah!"

From amidst the crowd arose a voice – hoarse and graveled it was – that broke us from our fantasies. It was Old Man Job – a half-blind, half-drunk scoundrel that had joined our crew 'bout three years prior. Job wasn't much use for sail'n and he wasn't much use for whalin' or fish'n either, but the captain kept him around cause he mopped the deck and cleaned the heads for a bottle of rum, a place to sleep at night, and a little bit of food to go in his belly. When we wasn't out at sea, Job slept under the stars and begged for his meals. I'd have felt sorry for the old vagabond if it wasn't for his nasty demeanor – cold and hostile, calloused from years of livin' in the gutters with rats. Couple that with the fact that he'd been caught a number of times stealing from the crew, and you can see why I thought so little of the wretched bastard. Truth be told, none of us cared for him, but we tolerated Old Job 'cause he took on the duties nobody wanted.

Every sailor on the ship then turned his head towards the elderly old man. He was sneering at the girl still crouching amidst the stack of crates, a trail of Antony's blood trickling from her turquoise lips.

"A fool's errand ya be suggest'n, Antony!" said he. He

snorted like a pig then spit a thick wad of phlegm from his mouth. It landed at the first mate's feet and a bit of it caught the toe of his boot. "And a dangerous one at that! We haven't the rations fer such a voyage, and what've Salle rovers? Have ya not considered such things?"

"We can restock off the coast of Portugal," Antony replied. "From there our destination is only three or four days out depend'n on the wind," and he once again began to bandage his bloody finger. "As for pirates, my vote says the risk is worth the reward."

Job pulled a flask from his coat and took a swig, then fired an eye at the fish-girl so sharp it could've pierced her scaly skin. "I don't like that thing, Cap'n," he said, his voice grinding like a stone pestle being put to work. "It's an abomination of God, and we shouldn't be a' trustn' it."

And then the cap's voice erupted into fire. "Shut your vile trap, old man!" he shouted. "Did you forget your place on my ship? Next time you think to instruct me on anything, I'd suggest you bite your tongue 'less I'll be cutting it out with the blade I keep in me boot! Antony, set course for the port of Lisbon so we can restock. Friends and brothers, I aim to get rich. In a week's time we'll never be need'n to pluck another fish from the briny blue again!"

And with that, we raised the main sail and changed course, setting off west towards our dreams of wealth and fortune.

MORALE WAS HIGH AMONGST THE CREW three days into our voyage. The men sang shanties 'bout mermaids and treasure when we was work'n, and when we weren't, they talked of the extravagant things they aimed to purchase with their share of the loot. You could feel a buzz throughout the ship as every sailor was excited to see what treasure lay at the end of our journey – every sailor 'cept Job, that is. He hadn't spouted off since the cap had put him in his place, but I could see – even with me bad eye – that the old man's heart had yet to thaw when it came to the web-toed female.

Antony, on the other hand, had grown as close as heat to a flame with the girl. She was moved to the first mate's private quarters, away from the curious eyes of the men on our vessel. The door was kept closed for privacy, but remained unlocked as per the captain's orders. Periodically, Cap would send a sailor down to check on 'em so as to make sure the Scot and the fish-girl weren't engaging in any perverse, ungodly acts onboard his ship, but as I said before, Antony was a man of the book and I have my doubts that a deviant thought ever crossed his mind.

That isn't to say our first mate wasn't actin' strange 'round the girl, though. He took to feed'n pieces of himself to her nightly and I had the dubious honor of assisting him on those first couple evenings when the cap had ordered me to pay them a visit.

First, Antony would instruct me to fetch a tuna from the deck – a big one – as it turned out the girl had an appetite on par with a that of a horse. When I returned, he would unsheathe the knife he wore on his belt and roll the sleeve of his shirt up around his elbow. Much to the displeasure of my eyes, Antony would then dig the blade's edge into his forearm and carve free small sliver of flesh. Inside the mouth of the tuna is where he'd place the lump of skin and muscle so that she could eat it with her supper.

The girl devoured her fish raw, like I hear the heathens of the Orient do – head, bone, and tail, all with the bit of Antony's flesh inside it! I'd watch her eat it while I helped him dress his wound. The smacking of her lips as she savored the uncooked tuna in her mouth was difficult on my ears – every bite, accompanied by an abundance of nauseating noises. Slurp'n and suck'n sounds would fill the first mate's cabin while she licked at the poor dead fish's eyes and grinded its bones between her pointed teeth. A gruesome sight it was indeed, but I came to reason that Antony was lett'n the she-thing consume him for a purpose. It was explained to me through my discussions with the first mate, however limited they might've been, that over the course of each day Antony lost the ability to understand the fish-girl's tongue. Only when his flesh was inside the merwoman's stomach could he make heads or tails of her high-pitched whistles. And how clever of him it was, I did believe, to continue their discussions and gain her trust, so as to ensure she did not go back against her word.

I was glad that it was he and not I that had bonded with the creature. She appeared almost human at passing glance, but moved and acted like a wild animal. Gaze into her eyes and all you'd see was a feral beast staring back at you. This I found to be unsettling. I wondered too how the Scot felt safe sharing his cabin with her, but alas, men have done far stranger things for the promise of wealth.

On the final night before Lisbon, the she-thing even managed to bite me hand as I was offering her a fish. An accident is what I believed it to be. Mayhap I should've paid more mind when delivering a hungry animal its meal.

Nevertheless, her teeth had broken the skin and drawn blood enough that I needed to bandage myself. Happy to oblige I was, when Antony dismissed me from his quarters for the evening following that encounter.

By the time we docked in the port of Lisbon the next day, our rations had run bone-dry. The cap sent only his most trusted men out for supplies and ordered the rest of us to stay onboard. He feared that turning us loose in the city might've lead to some unwanted queries from locals 'bout the special cargo we was haul'n. When sailors reach dock, sailors tend to drink. Now, a boozed up sailor can still be of use to a captain in a lot of ways, but keep'n a secret ain't one of 'em. All this was for the best as I was not wanting to take on any extra responsibilities that day anyhow. From the moment I had woken that morning, my joints had ached terribly and my head had felt misty and muddled.

Antony had locked the girl away inside his room while he was out leading the cap's chosen few through Lisbon. I, along with most of the crew, stayed on the ship and waited for he and the rest of the men to return with provisions so we could be on our way. Without the freedom to leave the boat, there wasn't much to do 'cept drink myself to sleep and hope my joint pain passed, so that's exactly what I aimed to accomplish that afternoon.

I was takin' a catnap in me hammock when I felt a cold, clammy hand wrap around my forearm. The sensation shocked me something fierce, but a sudden feeling of dread kept me from opening my eyes right away. For ya see, I was sure as birth and death it was the fish-girl that had snagged me. With Antony out acquiring rations, my groggy mind reasoned she had come to me looking for a meal. After all, it had been I alone who was assisting the first mate during her grisly suppers. Those icy fingers were gripping me tight and the damp hand had me certain I was 'bout to wake and find her stand'n over me, grinning down with that mouth full of daggers, and staring through me with those blood red eyes.

But when I finally mustered the courage to look I saw that it was Job who had stirred me back to the waking world. I sat up in me hammock and readied myself to crack 'em with the back of my hand for rousing me from my nap. There weren't a lot of men on the boat that I would strike, but Job was the lowest in the pecking order, and a known thief at that, so I had no qualms with belting the old bastard, especially after catch'n him sneaking around the berth when he should'a been topside scrubbing the ship's heads. To top it off, the pain in me joints was throbbing worse than ever and I had attributed that to my sudden wakening, but the look of distress on his face gave me pause long enough for him to speak, and I lost the urge to strike him once he opened his yellow-toothed mouth.

"Ya needn' a' be upset 'bout me risin' ya from yer slumb'r," he said. Even the sound of his whisper'n grinded awful-like inside my ears. "I came ta talk 'bout that monster we pulled from tha drink a few days back. Tha thing that's got our first mate wrapped 'round 'er scale-y finger and our cap'n fantasiz'n 'bout a treasure that may 'r may not be real. There be not someth'n altogether right 'bout the journey we're embark'n on. Ta me, it stinks ta Hell and back! Last eve' I hid behind the Scot's door an' listened to tha things he was say'n to tha creature. Well, he weren't talk'n of no jewels or kingdoms, I can tell ya that! I can't say fer sure, cause I could'na understand the monster's tongue, but his words, they sounded treacherous! She put a spell on him, I be think'n — one that somehow gives 'er tha key ta his mind. Mayhap, her power lies in tha fact that she be eat'n little bits of him nightly. I watched ya help 'em feed her and that's the only reason me head can fathom why he'd collude with such a beast in tha first place. Witchcraft it is! Now, I be think'n he and she may be lead'n us ta our deaths! We must be wary, you and I. For ta blindly trust a soulless creature such as she is as mad as takin' the Devil for his word!"

I yanked my arm free from his grasp and told him he was lucky I wasn't the type to rat him out to Antony 'bout his eavesdropping. He tried to plead with me, but my bleary mind had been made up and I was in no mood to listen to the ramblings of a dirty old thief.

"Ta hell with ya!" he shouted at me. "Yer just like tha rest of 'em then! Just like the cap'n! So blinded by yer greed ya can't see tha danger right b'fore ya eyes! Well, if ya don't believe me, then I'll prove it to ya!"

Job then stormed from the berth with the fury of a tempest while I strained to forget the old man's warnings long enough to fall back to sleep. We was puttin' a lot of trust in Antony to lead us to the Promised Land. True it was, the first mate had never given any of us a reason to doubt him, but I wondered then, as I lay in my hammock, if that was *cause enough* to follow his lead without question.

We raised anchor and set off from the dock the next morning. Once the shore had disappeared behind the horizon, the cap called every able-bodied sailor up to the deck for a meeting. When I arrived I was surprised to see the fish-girl stand'n beside Antony and the cap. It was the first time she had been topside since we caught her. She was dressed in a garment so as to cover up her lady parts. More animal than woman she might've been, but the cap had insisted that keep'n her covered was the Christian thing to do, so he made sure to have her garbed in front of the crew. It was the first mate's sleeping shirt she was wearing, and it hung from her thin frame, swallow'n up her figure – like a young boy sport'n his father's coat.

"Friends and brothers," the cap sang out. "Our stern is to the coast so there'll be no turning back now. The next time we drop anchor we'll be doing it the bay of this fair sea queen's kingdom." He waved a hand towards the girl, but she paid him no mind. She was still act'n skittish and feral – just the same as she'd been since I first laid eyes on her. "Our first mate, Antony," continued the cap, "has been communicating with the female. It is he and only he who she has trusted with the coordinates to her kingdom so follow his orders, sailors, and we'll all be wealthy men by the week's end."

Antony took a step forward to address the crew. He may not've been the captain, but he had the ship's reverence just the same – maybe more. "Ahoy, fellow sailors. When we set off on this vessel four days ago, we did so as fisherman, and whalers, but when this voyage is over we'll be returnin' home as men with influence, men of means."

"Hear, hear!" cheered the crew.

"In a few days we'll be a' reach'n our destination," he explained. "The entrance ta this girl's kingdom lies within a place her people call the Golden Grotto." And when he said that, I saw an eager smile stretch across the captain's face. "It's a place plucked straight from the fables we read as children. A cavern where the water's liquid gold and the walls are encrusted with diamonds. When we find the Golden Grotto, we'll be so close to the treasure we'll be able ta reach out and touch it." He pulled a piece of paper from his jacket. "I've takin' the liberty of drawing us a map based on me conversations with tha girl. Now if ya be needn' me, don't hesitate to call down ta my quarters. I'll be in there with the lass discussing the customs and diplomacy of her people. Such things will come in handy upon our first encounter with the royal party."

Antony and the she-thing then departed from the group. Most of us went back to crack'n jollies and laugh'n bout our good fortune after that, but not Job. I spotted him hovering in the back of the crowd all by his lonesome. He just kept right on starin' at the Scot and the girl until they disappeared below the ship's deck. Only now do I think I know what he was gapin' at.

He had spotted something wrong regard'n those two, something I believe that I had spotted as well, but had been too afraid to admit. And now that these events are behind me, I can permit meself to recognize the signs that I had so willfully ignored. It wasn't Antony that had broken free from the group first once the meeting had adjourned, it was the girl. He had followed her all the way below deck and not the other way around – like a child tail'n his mother on an afternoon stroll through the marketplace.

Job saw it then and I see it now.

ILLNESS WOULD BEFALL ME not long after the meeting. By that very evening I had come down with a sudden fever that set my skin ablaze, sent throbs of pain coursing through my muscles, and left me confined to me hammock. And so I slept, soaked in sweat and shivering from the chill running through my veins as the crew carried on their duties top-side without me. It was during my malaise that I began to experience horrific nightmares – visions that buried themselves so deep inside my head they torture me to this day.

I dreamt of a city beneath the ocean, looming up from the seabed like the unholy mecca of Lucifer. So real these visions seemed throughout the duration of my delirium, that I could'na tell the difference between reality onboard the ship and the fabrications of my ailing mind. There were castles built of black jagged coral, so razor-sharp that the barbs and spines jutting from their immense bastions would rip a man's skin open upon contact. Spires standing hundreds of feet high, erected from the bones of sea-crea-tures more massive than any whale were scattered about the place. Each underwater structure was enormous and intricately decorated, adorned with thousands of sea-shells or draped in colossal curtains of kelp. I had no body during these bizarre fever dreams, instead I moved about the sunken city like an ethereal specter.

In the center of the district was a church with point-ed steeples. Its walls were sculpted from one large piece of smooth black rock, extending upwards from the earth. Its roof, a dark, sea-green mass of repulsive projections, wriggled as if it consisted of millions of monstrous worms.

At first I thought it was made of seaweed and the moving parts were a simply a product of the ocean's influence, but as I ventured closer to the wicked house of worship I found this not to be the case. Nay, I fear the truth is far more unsettling. For, to my dismay, I discovered that the thing draped over top the church was in fact alive and conscious!

It was like no creature I'd seen b'fore – at sea or on land. It had no head or tail and I could not for the life of me tell you where the beast ended or began, but it writhed about and moaned loud and deep as though it were suffer'n horrible. The moving bits were tentacles of some kind, the tips of which were flat and white, each as long as a full-grown man. An enormous green slug covered with feelers is how I'd describe the unfortunate thing. Foolish it may sound, but I could'na help but feel sorry for the monstrosity. To my eyes it seemed as though the slug was a prisoner of that church. The unhallowed cathedral's steeples rose up through the beast's flesh, skewering it alive so that it could not swim away.

Closer to the terrible place I journeyed, unable to stop myself. I realized then that I was not in control of my actions. A chanting arose from the black church, drowning out even the cries of its monstrous captive. The voices were not human. They sounded of singing dolphins, but unlike the girl, there was some semblance of language in their words, albeit ones I could not understand.

Through the doors I traveled, ever nearer to the chants, and there I witnessed horrors that could warp a sane man's mind. The underside of the slug-thing above the church was now visible. The creature had no eyes or ears, at least none that I could recognize, but its enormous oval maw, large enough to swallow a merchant ship whole, spanned half its body. Every one of its teeth was as big as a baby humpback and as sharp as the devil's tongue. Columns arranged in a circle ascended up, piercing the creature's pink spongy belly so as to pin it in place.

The interior walls were carved in runes the likes of which I'm certain no man has seen since before the time of Christ. There were no pews inside the structure, and aside from the pulpit and the columns, the chamber was completely bare, but I was not alone inside the church. There were hooded figures in black robes as well. They floated between the pillars in the center of the room and I knew then that they were the origin of the strange chants I'd been following. The shrouded beings were busy performing their depraved religious ritual and did not acknowledge my presence so I watched in silence as they worshiped and sang their ominous incantations. In response, the immense slug above cried and moaned throughout the strange ceremony, but never did the dark monks react to its bellowing.

When the chanting came to an end, all but one of the worshipers removed their robes and dropped them to the floor. They were males the same race as the fish-girl and bore the same sharp teeth and webbed fingers as she. Colorful scales even speckled their bodies in a similar fashion. They formed a circle 'round the one figure still cloaked and lowered their heads in what I assumed to be prayer. This monk was bigger than the lot of 'em – at least twice as large. I had'na noticed 'till the others removed their garments, but now the size difference was palpable.

It was their leader – the Archbishop of their ungodly congregation. It turned to face me and I realized then that I wasn't as invisible to these things as I had thought. From the sleeves of the high priest's robe emerged a pair of gigantic webbed hands, though they were unlike those of the merpeople surrounding it. More monstrous in appearance were these, with grayish-green skin and talons in place of nails. On its wrist it wore a golden bracelet of a strange unearthly design. Mesmerizing I found it to be – both stunning and frightening at the same time, and unique to any piece of jewelry I've ever seen in my life. I feared with all my soul to look upon the face of the horrible being, but as I said before my actions were not mine to control. The thing then raised its claws and removed its cowl, revealing its awful features to me.

There would be no mistaking the priest for human as one might the girl or the other worshipers of that sinful underwater temple. Nay, this creature was no more man than the beast imprisoned on the church's roof. Its head was a swollen, misshapen mass of blue-gray scales and I'm not ashamed to say that I still shudder when I think of it. A dark green fin ran down the middle of its skull, disappearing into its robe. I found meself somehow grateful that it was still wrapped in its ceremonial garments 'cause the sight of its naked, bloated body may have been enough to break my psyche. Nevertheless, so hideous was the priest's face – froggish and fishlike in appearance – that I'm sure even the most courageous men would scream aloud if they were to lay their eyes on it. A series of gills flapped on the sides of creature's neck and tusks extended from between its flabby gray lips. Its glassy eyes, yellow and unblinking, sat too far apart on its face, protruding outwards like a pair of rotten cabbages as they studied me.

Without doubt, the unhallowed congregation was the most appalling vision I've ever seen. I attempted a scream, but alas I could not, though the slug expressed enough displeasure for the two of us. It started to thrash above our heads and cry at a deafening pitch. The other worshipers then started up their dolphin chants again, but this only seemed to trouble the sea monster more. It shook the foundation of the building, yet even that did little to cause the priest to break its awful stare from me. My mind was swirling with the horrid sights and sounds occurring inside the submerged church, but just as I started to believe that they would drive me mad, my vision began to darken and the blare of the creature's screams faded away to nothingness.

When my sight had returned, I was again lying in my hammock on the ship. I had my body back and no longer did my skin burn to the touch. For the first time since Lisbon, the fog that had settled inside my head had started to disperse. My fever had recessed, and with it the visions of that wicked temple and the city beneath the sea, though the images I bore witness to managed to stay with me, as I could still recall those terrible dreams whenever I closed my eyes.

I WOULD COME TO LEARN that I had been laid up for three days and in that time things had changed aboard the ship. The merriment that'd been buzzing through the crew just days prior had vanished only to be replaced by nervous whispers and a sense of trepidation. Out at open sea, surrounded by nothing but the deep blue depths, sailors tend to gossip just as females do, and once my strength had returned to me, a few of the fisherman made it their duty to catch me up on what I'd missed while I was wrought with fever.

The recent trouble seemed to be stemming from an altercation that occurred the night the illness took me. As I slept – so sick that I was well-nigh dead to the world – an incident occurred that had rattled many of the men on the boat, and not surprisingly it was regarding Job and the girl.

The story as it was told to me is that Antony had been topside that evening, navigating the ship through a patch of stormy weather so as to ensure the winds did not blow us off course. When the sea had calmed, he returned to his cabin to find the old man, dagger in hand, harassing the fish-girl and declaring that he aimed to kill her. The old man was bleedin' awful from the side of his neck. The merwoman had taken a bite out of him after he'd made an earlier pass at her with his blade. Gushing his wound was too! A crimson pool had collected at his feet, but despite the loss of blood, Job had a fire burning so bright inside him that night he had moved beyond all reason.

Antony ordered him to halt, but the old man refused to yield to his commands. He wanted only to bury his dagger into the merwoman's heart and there was no threat the Scot could make that would deter him from his mission. Aye, all else had become trivial to the old man. Job backed the girl into a corner, raised the knife over his head and readied himself to come down on her with the point of his blade. But the Scot was quicker and stronger than he.

B'fore the silver-haired beggar could drive his dagger into her chest, Antony dashed across the room and sunk a knife of his own between the blades of his shoulders. The men who had witnessed this said Job then folded like a book, crumpling to the floor an instant later. As it turned out, the first mate's knife had delivered a fatal blow, but the old man did not pass quietly into the afterlife. He groaned and howled for minutes. Some of the crew tried to tend to him, but the beggar's injuries were too severe. Antony's knife was buried down to the hilt. In time, Job's breathing shallowed and his eyes began to dim, but just b'fore his soul would leave his body and travel to the heavens – or down to Hell, where I believe it may've been destined – he raised a finger towards the first mate and uttered his final words.

"She's *his* master now."

The cap did not reprimand Antony for killing Job. After all, he was only a beggar and as I said b'fore, the old man did not have many friends aboard the ship. Nevertheless, he was given a proper eulogy the next morning and his body was buried at sea. The Scot, however, was absent from the ceremony and it was then that the rumors began. Those who witnessed what happened, did not believe that lethal force had been necessary. Antony was one of the strongest sailors on our ship and could've easily subdued the frail old man without the use of his knife.

The girl we was harboring was an unnatural, frightful thing – strangely beautiful though she was – and with the death of Job, much of the crew was beginning to grow nervous 'bout her presence on our vessel. Mayhap the old man's final words was getting to 'em. This is something I cannot say for sure, but a bit of mild panic had broken out amongst the men, and it seemed to have spread like a plague while I was ill.

The lot of 'em knew little 'bout the feeding practices I'd been assisting Antony with in secret b'fore my fever struck. I'm sure their fears would've swelled considerably if privy to that information so I thought it best to keep me mouth closed when they started prodding me about such things during our discussions. No need to fan the flames, I thought, especially when we were so close to our destination.

Antony might've been able to quell concerns himself had he appeared on the deck now and again following Job's death, but for much the time I was sick, he'd been cooped up in his quarters, battling an apparent fever of his own. Word amongst the men was that the cap had checked on him and upon seeing his condition, feared for his first mate's health. He ordered Antony to relinquish the girl so another sailor could mind her while he recovered, but the Scot had somehow talked him out of it. Ill he may have been, but Antony was still a persuasive and powerful speaker. He managed to convince the cap to send him a hand instead, so as to help him feed the girl since I was too delirious from fever to offer my assistance.

The man's name was Jacob. He was a young fisherman from a poor village, who had learned everything he knew 'bout sailing while working aboard the ship. He too had been questioned by the others 'bout Antony and the girl, but refused to talk of them. However, once he heard that my fever had passed, he sought me out to converse about our shared experiences. Jacob approached me the afternoon I woke from my watery nightmares and requested that we speak in private. We found an isolated spot at the hull of the boat. It was only there, where he knew others would not hear our discussion, that he felt secure enough to open up to me. The young fisherman spoke in a hushed tone and I knew from the cadence of his voice and the way his hands gripped me tight around my shoulders that he was very troubled.

"Antony has mandated that I do not speak of my chores outside of his cabin," Jacob whispered to me. His silky blonde hair had fallen over his face and for a moment, he looked almost mad. "He knows his practices are unconventional and he fears it would upset the crew if they were told how he goes about the girl's feedings." I nodded in agreement, for in the many years I've walked this Earth I've come to recognize that even a fool alone in distress is far more rational than a collection of great thinkers when danger's hanging over their heads. "But you've been present for them too," he continued. "You were helping feed the girl before the illness fell upon you. Before I was chosen to take your place."

I remained silent as it was not yet my turn to speak. Something was weighing heavy on the young man's heart – a secret he felt a need to disclose.

"The only thing that kept me sane during the time I spent with the Scot was knowing you had not run screaming from his cabin after witnessing those horrors." Jacob paused for a moment and bit his bottom lip. His face was rife with terror. I bade him to carry on so he took a deep breath and glanced over his shoulder. Once he saw no one was in earshot he resumed his account. "The things he did. The way he fed himself to her..."

His voice trailed off again and his dark brown eyes fell to his boots. It was difficult for him to relive those moments. I placed my hand atop his shoulder to soothe the young man's worries.

"Aye, friend," I replied with a smile. "It is a dreadful habit he's developed."

I assumed that Jacob was speaking of the very same practice I had witnessed Antony partake in with the merwoman. His disgust was something I found reasonable. Watching the Scot carve the flesh from his arm was a sickening sight to behold, but Jacob was acting as if he'd just crossed paths with the devil himself. When he spoke, his voice quaked with fright and his lips quivered like the plucked strings of a lute. I thought mayhap his fears were overstated, but when the young man opened his mouth again, I began to reconsider that notion.

"Dreadful?!" he cried. "If only one could describe such things with a word as modest as dreadful! Nay, there is no way to express the horrors I witnessed inside of that man's chamber. Tell me how you managed to keep your sanity?! I saw you those first few days. When you weren't assisting him, you walked about the ship as if nothing were the matter. How did you keep your conscience clear, knowing full well what he was allowing that creature to do to him?!"

I shrugged my shoulders, but b'fore I could answer him Jacob started up again.

"He said it was for the good of the ship, but I won't be a part of it anymore! Now that you're well, I'll be informing Antony that I no longer wish to aid him while he feeds himself to that terrible thing. If it doesn't frighten you, then I beg you to take my place. *God,* how he allowed her to eat him alive! The way she sank her teeth into his chest and stomach! The awful hymns he would recite! They burned my ears! He sang them aloud with a smile on his face as she devoured him – as she sucked the blood from his veins!"

I tried my best to calm him, but Jacob had worked himself into a frenzy. His face bore the desperate look of an injured animal and all of my words appeared to fall on deaf ears. It seemed as if he was losing his mind b'fore my very eyes. Of a sudden the young fisherman spun around and ran off. He stormed below the deck and I knew he was heading to the first mate's quarters. I didn't try to follow him though. The last few things he'd been yammering on about had made me hesitate.

From what I could gather, Jacob's time with Antony sounded far different than my own. Never did he let the girl bite directly into his flesh while I assisted him, and the part 'bout her drinkin' his blood sent a chill through my body. I pondered too about the hymns the young man spoke of and found myself thinking back to the dark monks of my dreams, wondering if they and the first mate's songs were one in the same.

Moments later I would hear a scream rise up from the berth and I knew at once that it came from Jacob.

BY THE TIME I ARRIVED BELOW DECK, a dozen men had already gathered around the first mate's quarters. Jacob was shout'n and holding his arm, and I could see the sleeve of his shirt was stained a deep red.

"Ya blasted beast!" he shouted. "Ya Godforsaken animal!"

Antony was in the doorway. He had put himself between the crew and the girl. Blood was smeared across her face and it looked as if she was still chewin' a piece of the young man in her mouth. I peered back at Jacob and realized then just how much muscle she had torn from his arm. Jacob's wound was spilling like a waterfall. I could see the bone of his forearm; a flap of his flesh, attached by only a single piece of skin, dangled loosely from the mangled limb. The young man screamed again – harsh and shrill it sounded echoing off the walls.

"Ahhh! It burns! Like fire! Like a flame to my flesh!"

The men were trying to console him, but the young sailor had fallen into full panic. The captain had entered the berth by now, having been lured by all the commotion. He instructed some of the crew to take Jacob topside and help him dress his injury. It took four men to pull him away, kicking and screaming, from the first mate's door. I stayed behind. Jacob was bucking like a wild horse, and though my health had improved, I was still weak from my fever's lingering effects. Once he was gone, Antony stepped outside his cabin and closed the door behind him to address the cap.

"He burst in like a madman, Cap'n," Antony explained. "No fair warning at all. Not even a single knock. It startled the girl."

This was the first time in days that I'd gotten a look at the Scot and I understood then why the cap had been so worried 'bout his well-being. Antony looked to still be suffering from what had been ailing him. His face was as pallid as a phantom floating through the fog, and it seemed as if he'd lost considerable weight. His movements were sluggish. Each of his steps demanded the will of the world. Even his curly hair that had been such a vibrant, fiery red just days before had dulled to a drab orange. Antony gazed out at the remaining men through a pair of glossy, tired eyes set deep in the sunken sockets of his face and a strange thought then crossed me head that he had the look of a man waiting for death to take him.

"How much further, Antony?" asked the cap. "The crew is restless and I can't be having anymore of this nonsense on my ship."

"We'll be a' reach'n the grotto b'fore next eve, Cap'n," the Scot mustered out.

And when he said that the cap's eyes glimmered for the briefest of moments. Driven by the promise of riches, he was. So much so that he'd begun to let the treasure consume his every waking thought. The cap scratched at his beard while he contemplated the first mate's answer.

"Good then," he finally responded. "And how're you feeling?"

"Aye, strong 'nuff ta make the journey, but I need me rest."

The cap turned to face the rest of us.

"Well, you heard him," he barked. "Let him rest! Tomorrow we drop anchor and there'll be no more disturbing him 'till then!"

Fever struck Jacob that night, just after dusk had begun to settle in – and – by the time the sun had fully sunk below the edge of the sea, the young fisherman had been reduced to an unconscious, babbling, sweat-soaked mess of a man. The crew was in an uproar. Their fears had more than doubled once word of poor Jacob's condition had travelled through the ship. I pitied him, knowing full well how terrible my own illness had been and prayed that he made a swift recovery. I believed that our fevers had been connected. After all, the only three men who had fallen ill on the ship had each felt the merwoman's teeth pierce their flesh. Mayhap her bite was venomous. This is something I now know to be true, though I would have no idea just how potent her poisonous mouth could be until a good deal later.

The cap himself stood guard outside of Antony's door that night so as to prevent a repeat of the Job incident from earlier. This worked well enough to suppress any budding unrest. The night passed along without a skirmish, and before I knew it, the sun had begun to reappear over the Eastern horizon.

The morning passed by easily enough. Though tensions throughout the ship were still high, I found myself sharing laughs with a few of the men as we waited to hear word from the cap. It wasn't until mid-day that he made his way up topside to speak to us. His eyes were red and swollen from lack of sleep and his arms hung loose and heavy like pendulums from his shoulders. When he spoke I could hear the fatigue in his voice, but his eagerness for adventure and hunger for wealth was still apparent.

"Today is the day we make our fortune, men," he said to us. "Today we become rich."

And then, in a moment so timely that it must've been

orchestrated by The Fates themselves, the excited shouts of a crewmate called down from the crows nest above our heads.

"I see it! I see it! Land ho!"'

BY THE TIME WE DRIFTED INTO THE BAY, the late afternoon sky was beginin' to rust, and it looked as if the heavens were cast from copper. The island was so small, a man could set out on foot at dawn, explore every nook and crevice of its terrain, and still return back to where he started b'fore evening came about. The beach was littered with palms. Birds with bright feathers and hooked beaks grazed its sandy shores. Beyond that was a lush garden full of ferns, colorful flowers, and exotic trees.

Antony appeared topside with the girl shortly after the beaches first came into sight. He navigated the ship to a cove tucked away in a rocky corner of the isle. Here is where we were told we could expect to find the Golden Grotto. The mouth of the cove was too narrow for our ship, so we lowered three whalers into the water and rowed out. There were six of us to a boat. Mine brought up the rear while the boat with Cap, Antony, and the fish-girl lead our modest procession. Most of the crew stayed onboard the ship and I'm not ashamed to admit that I envied them for it as my trust in the Scot had been waning since the prior day's incident with Jacob. The other men in my whaler must've felt the same way for their faces were grim and cheerless. There was gloom hangn' in the air and I felt less like a treasure hunter and more like a doomed soul embarkn' on a one-way voyage down the River Styx. Our boats were rigged with harpoons, but we were fisherman not soldiers, and the cap was the only one among our three vessels carrying a pistol.

At a glance, the grotto was by no means remarkable. After hearing Antony talk of it, I had been expecting marble statues and jewel encrusted archways, but the mouth of the cave was small and ordinary and our heads nearly touched the ceiling as we paddled inside it. We used torches to light our way through the darkness. I thought my nose had grown numb to the stench of fish, but the smell inside that cave was so harsh and overpowering that it caused my eyes to water. Black rock formations rose out from the water's surface like tentacles of the kraken, and our voices bounced hollow off the walls.

Aye, the grotto was a peculiar place indeed, but peculiar for all the wrong reasons. The Scot had promised us a wondrous vault full of precious emeralds and rubies, but the deeper into the cave we travelled, the more I felt my dreams of riches drift away. The walls were made of stone, not diamonds, and even the slightest hint of gold was absent from its murky waters.

A steady unease was growin' throughout the group as we snaked our way down the grotto's narrow canal. So deep we had journeyed into the treacherous cavern that the mouth of the cave was no longer in sight. The flames from our torches were casting strange shadows on the walls. They danced and frolicked across the rocks like ghastly spirits. A feelin' of dread was beginning to swell inside me like a rising, black tide and I feared I might never again gaze upon the sky. Eventually, our party came upon a dead-end, but this only gave my worries even more reason to flourish. Now the promise of treasure seemed farther away than ever. I know that I was not alone in this thought because after some time it was the cap himself who turned to Antony and began to question him.

"Where are the rubies, Antony?" he demanded. "Where are the pearls and the emeralds you spoke of?" His words were full of rage, but the Scot said nothing. His only response to the captain's interrogation was a stare so cold and distant that I briefly thought he might've been dead. "Answer me!" shouted the cap, and when he said this, he lowered the barrel of his pistol between the first mate's eyes. "Where is the gold? Where are the diamonds?!"

The girl leaned over the edge of the boat and dipped her webbed fingers into the water. Aloof and childlike was her demeanor, as if completely oblivious to the ruckus the cap was raising. The torchlight reflected red off her scaly skin and I remember thinking she looked like Hell incarnate. The captain cocked his pistol so as to impress his point upon the Scot, but Antony sat in silence, never flinching, only breathing.

"Captain!" one of the men called out. "There be somethin' in the water!"

The lot of us then spun around and saw six heads breach the water's surface. Now I know you may think me mad, but I recognized the creatures from my night-mares. I was now face to face with the very same wretched monks that had tormented me during my fever-dreams. A chill ran through my body once this realization came to pass. That fishy smell had somehow grown more potent, so much so that it left its foul flavor in my throat every time I drew a breath. Time seemed to stop as we stared in awe at the horrid things treading water before us.

A scream rose up from behind me, sharp and jarring, it pierced the moment like the tip of a dagger, and when I turned in its direction I saw that it was coming from the cap. The fish-girl had ambushed him from behind while his attention had been diverted. Her arms were wrapped tight around his shoulders and those shark teeth of hers had burrowed themselves into the side of his neck. He fired a desperate shot, but alas, the cap was too far-gone. The bullet missed completely, and when he tried to cock his pistol again, his fingers betrayed him, and he dropped his weapon into the dark waters. The blood running down his throat looked black against the glow of the torchlight. Again and again, she tore away at his flesh, opening his wound larger with each bite. Antony did nothing to stop her. The other men in the boat pulled at her arms and legs, but the girl's grip was strong and they couldn't pry her loose.

I glanced back towards the mermen just in time to see the last of 'em dive out of sight. Seconds later our boats were rocking back and forth and I knew then they intended to tip us over. Out of instinct I snatched a harpoon and jabbed it into the water, though I could'na see a thing beneath the surface and my spear came up empty each time. A mate in the second boat did the same, but the mermen lunged up and grabbed hold of his harpoon's shaft, then pulled the poor bastard overboard. He breached just long enough to let out a horrible cry before the creatures pulled him back under.

The girl continued to feast on the captain, but his screaming had sunk to a pitiful groan. No longer did he have the strength to struggle. His throat was red and gnarled. It looked like raw meat.

My boat was the last to capsize, and by the time I hit the water, the wicked things were already swarming the sunken sailors just as piranhas do. They glided through the water with incredible speed and grace, attacking from every angle, and tearing into the men with ease. The cave was pitch-dark now. The torches had been extinguished, but I could feel the creatures moving all about me. My crewmates' garbled cries told me just how deadly those waters were, but even the sounds of the slaughter didn't disturb me as much as Antony's voice when I heard it chanting out amidst the madness. Flat and colorless it sounded, as if the first mate was under the influence of a spell. He recited those blasphemous prayers – the very same I had heard in my nightmares – as the creatures massacred our friends and brothers all around us.

I shut my eyes and began to swim. The fish-people were faster than I – this I knew – but I reasoned that fleeing was my only chance to survive. I couldn'a see a thing in the darkness so I used the screams of my fellow sailors as my guide. I swam from the carnage as fast as my arms and legs would allow me. So sure was I that I'd soon be meeting my death, that I had already begun to make my peace with the thought of their teeth shredding my flesh. I could hear the blood soaked cries of my crewmates even after I emerged from the cave.

I gazed out over the cove as my eyes adjusted to the twilight and saw the ship still anchored in the bay. The sight was indeed a relief, but I knew I was far from safe. As long as I was in those waters, I was nothing more than prey.

I felt myself growing weary. My heart was pounding inside my chest like the stampeding hooves of a hundred horses. My muscles were aching terribly and my vision was growin' blacker by the minute. Once or twice, as I made my escape, I thought I caught the fishy stench of that cave, but every time I peered over my shoulder expecting to see those things chasing me down, I found that I was still alone.

My mind was fading fast and I feared if the fish-people didn't kill me then the cove's warm, tropical waters would, but just before darkness grabbed me, I felt myself plucked from the sea, as if by an angel, and pulled aboard a boat. When I opened my eyes I saw the worried faces of my crewmates staring down on me. One of them attempted to ask me questions, but I'm afraid to say, my memory completely leaves me after that.

NEXT THING I RECALL, I was back in my hammock aboard the ship. I had awoken from yet another deep sleep. So long I napped, that we were already more than half way home. Many days had passed since that bloody afternoon.

I was told by the crew that they had lowered a rescue boat into the water when they heard the crack of the captain's pistol, but the screams pouring from the grotto had deterred them from entering the cove, and so they waited until they spotted me making my escape. The men said that my eyes were wild when they pulled me from the drink, and that I yelled and blathered like a madman, but my warnings had frightened them enough to turn back and leave the rest for dead. I passed out by the time they brought me aboard the ship. Not long after, they raised the mainsail and decided to make a hasty departure.

I spoke to Jacob while I recovered below the deck. His fever had left him and he was eager to talk about the nightmares he suffered through. When I told him of the grotto, he said the scene I described unfolded just the way he experienced it in his dreams. He saw that awful city as well, and witnessed those monks and that wicked high-priest performing the same depraved rituals that I observed.

THAT WAS ALL MANY YEARS AGO. I left the fishing business and moved as far inland as I could. Jacob, too, retired early. He travelled back home to live and care for his elderly mother, but even though we went our separate ways, the two of us made sure to keep a correspondence. Ya see, we shared a mutual bond. Those awful dreams still haunted us and they were often the main topic of conversation in our letters. We believed it was the fish-girl's bite that induced it, and that mayhap her venom still flowed inside our veins.

I looked forward to hearing from him because he was the one person I felt I could speak freely to about my nightmares. Through our discussions, we tried to decipher hidden meanings in our dreams. We researched the ancient runes we saw carved inside the dark church and tried our best to translate the monks' language, though we made little progress in this endeavor. In his letters, Jacob often spoke of a book that he was searching for – an ancient tome written by a mad Arab that he believed would hold the answers to our questions. To my knowledge he never tracked it down, but I wonder if the book could have helped him once things took a turn for the worse.

I started to worry for my friend a little over a year ago. His words began to sound paranoid and I noticed a rapid decline in his penmanship. He told me his dreams were now unbearable and that they had been weighing heavy on his thoughts. This concerned me greatly. A few months later, I stopped receiving letters from him altogether. I wrote him many times, inquiring 'bout his well-being, but never received a response. And so, after some while, I decided to pay him a visit.

His village was out on the coast. It was the first time in years that I had seen the ocean and I was surprised to find myself undisturbed by the sight of it. Nay, in fact, I found comfort in its rolling blue waves. His mother answered the door when I arrived at Jacob's home. I introduced myself as an old friend, but a look of grief struck her face when I uttered his name, and right away I knew my fears had been confirmed.

She said that a terrible tragedy had occurred. It seems as though Jacob's final letters only revealed a small sliver of his tormented soul. His mother told me just how much he'd changed over the past year. He had become detached and standoffish. She said he was full of angst and that he often woke up screaming in the night. The man I knew was a devout Christian, but she said he had renounced the church, and when she asked him why, he would only talk of crazy things – as she would say – like ancient beings and sleeping gods. His behavior too had begun to scare her, but she was old and feeble, and feared if she spoke out then he might strike her.

And then, early one morning while his mother still slept, he stripped himself bare, walked naked through the village, and threw himself from a pier. He fell like a stone into the sea. A few fisherman setting out for the day witnessed the whole thing unfold. They said he was ranting and speaking in tongues, and it seemed as though he was talking to the ocean itself. His body was recovered and a memorial service was held in his honor. At the time I felt pity for him. I thought mayhap his dreams had worn away at his mind like waves do against the face of a cliff, but this I now know is not entirely true.

Mayhap it was my proximity to the coast, but soon I too began to have new, vivid dreams and they haven't stopped since I ventured out to Jacob's village. Each nightmare seems more real and frightening than the one that came before it. In them, I see more underwater cities filled with monstrous creatures like the high-priest from my fever dreams, but now their history is told to me as I sleep. These Deep Ones have lived for millennia below the ocean's surface. It is they who rule the fish-girl and her carnivorous brethren. They view these merpeople as abominations – an early failed attempt to breed with the human race – but they tolerate their existence and let them worship in their sunken temples. They are used in religious rituals, sometimes given up as a sacrifice to Father Dagon or Mother Hydra. Other times they are utilized by the Deep Ones to manipulate man.

I am sure now that there never was a Golden Grotto, nor was the girl really a queen of the sea, but the venom of her bite was powerful, and I think I can feel it taking effect even to-day. The thought of land now repulses me. For a week I've been in this village on the coast and have not been able to peel myself away. I want to go home, but the ocean won't allow it. It beckons me. I can hear its voice calling in the wind, gusting over the water, begging me to take the plunge just as Jacob did. It wants a sacrifice.

The more I dream, the harder it is for me to fight these urges. There is a realm of wonders that is unknown to man, dark cyclopean cities beneath the sea – magnificent, unconceivable spectacles. The Deep Ones build churches there and worship all-powerful gods – sleeping gods that will return, and when they do, it will mean the end of the world.

I used to think man ruled the sea – that the creatures dwelling in its depths were ours to hunt and kill, but the venom in me blood has pulled the veil from my eyes and revealed the harrowing truth. We are nothing in this world. Its true kings will show themselves soon enough. I can hear the prayers of those monks now, even when I'm awake. They haunt me and remind me of this fact. *He sleeps*, they tell me, *he sleeps*, but I know that he will not sleep forever for the day will eventually come when he rises from his slumber!

Ph'nglui mglw'nafh Cthulhu R'lyeh wgah'nagl fhtagn!

THE WENDALL LANE DIARIES

Disclaimer: I am not a paranormal investigator. I am an author. While looking for inspiration for a book, I came across a series of stories surrounding a home in the American Pacific Northwest. It is an extremely ordinary looking house in an extremely ordinary looking residential neighborhood, but the stories that have emanated from its former residents and the people who lived in the town that it's located in are quite extraordinary.

Through my research of the house on Wendall Lane, I have come across accounts that range from the supernatural to just plain bizarre. In order to protect the privacy of the people in the town and the current inhabitants of the house on Wendall Lane, I have not only changed the name of everyone in these stories, but the name of the street as well. Wendall Lane is just an alias for the true location of these accounts.

YOU SHOULDN'T

Alan Palmer lived in the house on Wendall Lane from September 2002 to July 2003. After months of trying to contact him about his time there, I finally received an e-mail agreeing to set up a meeting. Quite a few of the house's prior residents had turned down my requests for face to face interviews so I jumped at the chance to talk to him in person once the opportunity presented itself.

Palmer, who worked as a socioeconomics professor at a university in Washington, arranged to meet and talk over drinks at a place of his choosing in downtown Seattle. The bar was called Oliver's Lounge and was located in the historic Mayflower Park Hotel. Upon arriving, I was surprised to see just how crowded it was for 3:00 PM on a Tuesday. There were people seated at nearly every table while food runners and waiters dressed in white servers' jackets and black bowties hustled and bustled about the room bringing people their orders. Windows stretching from floor to ceiling allowed for an ample amount of sunlight to illuminate the space, giving it a genuinely open and inviting ambience. I spotted Palmer in the corner sitting at a small high table and sipping on a glass of scotch.

He greeted me with a hearty handshake and a bright smile after I introduced myself to him. The man was graying a little around the ears, and I could tell shortly after meeting him that he was incredibly intelligent, but aside from that he seemed to have the demeanor of a fellow 20 years his junior. Palmer was a light-hearted gentleman who loved a good joke and he insisted on telling me a few of his favorites before I turned my tape recorder on.

Once he had his fun, we started the interview.

B ELIEVE IT OR NOT, you're not the first person who's tried to contact me about the time I spent living on Wendall Lane. Apparently there are all kinds of ghost enthusiasts out there who've heard about the house through the various online forums these types of people tend to frequent. Nerds and losers – you know the type – they spend their time sifting through thread after thread on the Internet, pretending that they're doing something productive with their lives. Hell, most of them are probably overweight man-children sitting in their parents' basement and conducting their "research" in between anime cartoons.

Palmer let out a laugh, pleased with his depiction of the Internet paranormal research community. I decided to omit the fact that I first heard about him through one of the online forums he was talking about. He took a sip of scotch and continued on.

So naturally I ignored your e-mails, thinking you were another one of those 'ghost geeks.' It's strange. I probably wouldn't have agreed to meet, but I came across one of your books by complete accident. My nephew mentioned your work in passing when I was over at my brother's house for dinner a few weeks ago. I put two and two together and realized you were the same author who had been e-mailing me so I figured why the hell not? I'm game to talk about it if you are, although I must admit my story probably isn't as interesting as the demons or monsters or whatever the hell it is you write about. Not a whole lot happened while I was living there. In fact, the only reason I lived in the house for such a short period of time was because an old colleague of mine offered me a full professorship up here not long after I purchased it, and the commute was just too far. My workplace at the time had no job security, I was on the chopping block every year, so there was no way I could turn down the offer. This was before the housing bust in '07. It was a sellers' market. Banks were giving away loans like there was no tomorrow, so it wasn't difficult to turn right back around and flip the place. Hell, I even made thirty grand! Plus, I love Seattle. The weather sucks, but this city has culture!

We made small talk for a bit. He told some stories about work, his travels to Europe, and even asked me about some of the upcoming books that I've been working on. I was beginning to wonder if flying all the way out to Seattle to speak to him had been a waste of time. After all, Palmer appeared almost completely uninterested in discussing any and all aspects of the house. I directed his attention back towards the reason why we had met when I asked him to describe the most bizarre encounter he could remember having in the short time he lived on Wendall Lane.

(Laughing) Now you're starting to sound like the ghost geeks! Fine, fine, let me think. Like I said, nothing really strange ever happened, that's why I —

He paused for a moment and looked out the window towards the street.

There was one thing. I had almost forgotten about it — the TV incident. It was a Friday night in June, about a month before the house sold. There was nothing on. You know how crappy television programming can be on the weekends, especially in the summertime. I was scrolling through channels on my TV's menu looking for something to turn my brain off to when the title of a show caught my eye. It was called *You Shouldn't Watch*. I figured with a name like that, how could I not give it a go? Also, the show was on a channel I had never seen before — Channel 732. No name on the menu guide, just numbers. That was all the channel was listed as. To be honest, I don't watch much TV and when I do, I don't usually venture out of the HD channels so I wasn't even sure if it was covered under my cable package.

Now, I don't know what yours looks like, but the way my cable provider's menu was set up, different colors were used to distinguish between different types of shows. You'd get green for sports, purple for movies, and blue for everything else. However, the menu color for this particular show was black. The text was yellow, which was also unusual since the show's title is always written in white. Even the font was different. Don't ask me to describe what it looked like because I really can't recall. All I can say is I had never seen letters written in that way before. I know that sounds odd, but the best description I can give you is that even though the lettering looked completely alien in appearance, my mind could somehow interpret what it said – **YOU SHOULDN'T WATCH.** (Laughing) Now I'm starting to sound like the Internet weirdos.

Palmer polished off his glass and called the waitress over to order another drink.

Anyway, from the very second I turned on the program, I knew I was watching something very strange – very strange indeed. The black and white picture on my television was of a mostly empty room. There were no visible windows or doors. The place seemed cold and uninviting – like how I'd imagine a jail cell in a third world country would look.

Palmer laughed again, but this time I detected a hint of nervousness.

Not dead center, but slightly off to the left of the frame was a man sitting at an old rusty table. He was shirtless and looked to be very malnourished. It reminded me of those old photos you see of the Jews who suffered through German concentration camps during World War II. I remember wondering if he was a prisoner there. The man wore a torn and ragged pair of slacks, but had on no belt or shoes. His mouth hung agape as if his jaw was too heavy to close. There was no music or dialogue; the only noise coming from my speakers was the sound of his wheezy, raspy breath. God! It sounded like he was suffering from emphysema or something. I followed his gaze down to an old rotary phone sitting on the tabletop. He gawked at the thing like a buffoon while I stared back at the screen, mesmerized by the odd scene taking place on my television.

I hit the info button on my remote, hoping to read

a synopsis of what the show was about, but of course there was nothing, so I just kept watching. For minutes he didn't move. I remember chuckling to myself. You know, the way you do when something makes you uncomfortable and your brain thinks laughing will ease the tension? The whole time I was waiting, hoping for something that resembled dialogue. Anything to prove that I was just watching some weird movie and had simply turned it on at the wrong time, but nothing ever happened. Perplexed and a little bit bored, I stood up from my couch and headed over to the kitchen to rummage through the fridge for a little late night snack. I was about halfway done making myself a sandwich when I heard the most terrible noise.

Palmer paused briefly. At first I thought he had stopped his story because of the waitress returning from the bar with his drink, but he barely acknowledged her presence. The man was caught up in deep thought as though he had just remembered something important. When he finally began speaking again the tone of his voice had completely changed. Gone was the chipper upbeat persona I had come to know him by. Palmer was clearly distraught.

It sounded horrible – like a dying animal. I remember an awful nausea washing over me. It was the strangest thing. There was an ominous feeling in the air too – death, ruin, calamity all hanging over my head. Once I realized that the noise was coming from the television, I put down my sandwich and hurried back towards the living room. The scene on the TV was essentially the same except now the sickly looking man had turned his head up towards the ceiling and was howling and groaning in the most unpleasant of ways. The longer I watched the more it made me feel like I was going to retch. The whole thing was utterly abhorrent. The man would moan for 30 maybe 40 seconds at a time before stopping suddenly, then he would take another deep wheezy breath and the terrible sounds would begin anew. I cringed as I took it all in. It felt as if my visual and auditory senses were being assaulted and I was still fighting off the urge to vomit all over my living room carpet. Just when I thought things couldn't get worse, the man still groaning mind you, turned his head in the direction of the screen and stared straight into the camera. The thing is, I was certain he was looking directly at me. That's what it felt like. It was almost as if we were in the same room. I probably should have turned off the show, but after minutes of nothing, something was finally going on and I felt compelled to keep watching even though I was suffering immensely.

I stared into the glazed over eyes of the sickly looking man until he turned his attention down towards the phone sitting on the table –

Palmer hunched over in his seat and removed his glasses. He seemed visibly shaken. The 52-year-old econ professor clasped the bridge of his nose between his thumb and index finger and let out a deep sigh. Beads of sweat had begun to form on his forehead.

I'm sorry, forgive me. I haven't thought about this night in a long time. I suppose it's possible that my mind pushed this episode to the back of my consciousness and I forgot all about it – kind of a defense mechanism type of thing. I've read about case studies where army veterans who witnessed horrific events develop amnesia about their time in the military. It seems as though I may be going through something similar, except as I sit here and talk to you, everything begins to come back to me.

I asked him if he wanted to continue. He assured me he did, then resumed his story.

His hand quaked violently as he lifted the phone to his ear. His arms were rail thin and it looked as though he was struggling to hold it in place. With his other hand, he clumsily started spinning the rotary dial. Seconds later, my cell phone started ringing.

A chill ran down my spine, my nausea grew even worse, that ominous feeling in the air was now full-blown terror. I prayed with every fiber in my being that it was a coincidence as I looked at my phone's caller ID. You have no idea how bad I wanted the number to be one that I recognized. I didn't recognize it of course. Hell, it wasn't even a number. It was something else entirely. In that same strange, alien text from the TV's menu were the words You Shouldn't Listen written where the caller's number should have been.

That was enough for me. I hung up the phone and reached for the remote on the coffee table. I must have pressed the channel button a dozen times, but the picture never changed. I tried the power button and still nothing happened. The man began to dial the phone again. Once more my cell started to ring.

Palmer had gone pale. He looked completely different from when I first met him – the polar opposite of the smiling man who shook my hand earlier.

I tried to turn off the TV manually, I even unplugged it from the wall, but by this time I knew it would do nothing. The man continued to stare at me – his horrible, empty gaze was tearing me to pieces. Stomach bile slowly started to crawl its way up my esophagus. I'm not sure why I answered the phone, I couldn't help myself. Maybe I thought it was the only way to end the nightmare. My finger trembled as I pressed the answer button.

I didn't even need to say, "hello." He began speaking as if he was watching me through the television screen — and perhaps he was.

Tears began to well up in Palmer's eyes. I tried to tell him that he didn't need to go into further detail if he was uncomfortable, but he kept talking as though he never even heard me. By that point, he would have finished his story even if there was no one sitting across the table from him.

He spoke to me in a terrible voice — like he was gargling shards of glass. His words weren't in English, but somehow, some way, I could understand him. I could hear the man clearly over the phone as his lips moved on my TV screen. He said...he said, *you shouldn't tell.* Then, with an incredible burst of speed, he leapt out of the frame and the screen went to black.

Jesus Christ! He said, *you shouldn't tell.* Did I just tell? Vincent please, does that mean I just told?

Palmer fell silent and stared awkwardly into his glass for a moment. He then apologized and excused himself from the table. It was the last I saw of him that night. He sent me a text message fifteen minutes later explaining that he had to go home and instructing me to charge the bill to his tab. I tried to contact him once I got back to California, but he never answered my calls or e-mails. A few weeks later I found out what happened to him after performing a simple Google search of his name.

Pastel Colored Dreams & Human Flavored Nightmares

Twelve days after Alan Palmer and I met to talk about the house on Wendall Lane, he was found dead in his Seattle home. There was no sign of a struggle or forced entry, however, due to the horrific nature of his death, Seattle PD does believe that he was murdered.

Palmer's body was discovered in front of the television on his living room couch missing ears, eyes, and tongue.

THE PHONE IN THE KITCHEN

In June of 2016 I received an e-mail from a source that did not wish to be identified by name. This is what I read:

Mr. Cava,

First of all, I'd like to say that I enjoy your work and am happy to hear that you're thinking about writing a book about the house on Wendall Lane. The reason I am messaging you is because I know that you've been researching the house and I believe I have some information that you might be interested in. I am sending you a journal entry written by David Porter, a man who lived in the home between the years of 1984 and 1987. I will, of course also be providing you with all the necessary documents to back my claim.

Attached to the e-mail were scans of journal entries, written by David Porter that were later verified to be authentic. Many of these accounts are fairly mundane, some make refer-

ences to phone conversations he would often have with family and friends. *The nature of these discussions aren't outright odd, but they are noteworthy due to one peculiar entry from the winter of 1986, titled, "The Phone in The Kitchen." I have transcribed and published it below in its entirety.*

THE CALLS WOULD COME from the phone in the kitchen – always the phone in the kitchen. If the other phones rang, I could expect to speak to someone who was alive, but if it was just the kitchen phone then I knew the caller would be dead.

They came at odd hours too – always early morning before the dawn would break. I had known them all when they were alive. They were relatives and friends, coworkers and neighbors – each and everyone of them, people in my life who had passed on to the other side.

My grandmother was one of the first calls I received. She died before I turned twelve so the two of us had a lot of catching up to do. Nana became one of my closest confidants. I shared everything with her during our talks, all of my secrets, all of my hopes and aspirations.

It felt like a blessing to have such a gift bestowed on me – a telephone line to the afterlife, and though I couldn't dial out, someone always seemed to call when I needed them to.

I was never given an explicit set of guidelines, but there were rules that all the callers followed. Never did our conversations last until daybreak. It didn't matter if one of us was in mid-sentence, the caller always hung up the moment the sun would begin to peek out over the horizon.

They also refused to speak of the afterlife. It was something I often asked about during our discussions, but each and every caller was a master at pivoting the conversation away from the topic. Lastly, I was sworn to never tell another soul about the phone in the kitchen – even my brother Danny, whom I was closest in the world with – or else, I was told, the calls would cease. These were small prices to pay of course. A phone line to the afterlife meant I would never truly lose anyone. I would never have to feel alone.

Then my brother's accident happened and everything changed. Danny's car hit a patch of black ice on the freeway and he lost control. By the time I got to the hospital, his wife and children were already there. My brother was in critical condition. His chance of survival slim to none. I looked into the terrified faces of his family I felt shame. I knew there was no chance I would be losing Danny that night, not as long as I had the phone in the kitchen, but for his wife and kids, he'd be gone forever.

I needed to speak about it with someone who would understand, so I excused myself for a little while after the kids had fallen asleep, and drove home to wait for a call. Right on cue, the phone rang almost as soon as I walked through the door. I'd been expecting my grandmother – it always seemed to be her who called when things got serious – but when I heard the voice in the receiver on my ear, my heart sank in my chest. It was Danny, which of course could only mean one thing - my brother had passed on.

By the sound of his voice, he appeared to be in a pleasant mood for someone who had just died. Believe it or not, Danny was more interested in counseling me than grieving over himself and his family. We spoke for an hour, and during our conversation his words washed away my guilt. By the time our talk was over, I felt much better about myself.

I thought about Danny's family as I drove back over to the hospital. His wife was one of the most resilient people I knew, and his children were sharp as tacks. Deep down in my heart, I knew they would persevere through the tragedy, and I vowed to myself that I would be there for them if they needed me, just as my callers from the afterlife had been there for me. Still, a small part of me wanted to tell them about the phone. *If only*, I thought, *I could connect them to their father one last time.*

When I got back to the hospital, I was surprised to see Danny's children were all smiles. His wife was chipper too. I asked her what happened, and she said that shortly after I had left, my brother came out of his coma. He was doing so well in fact, that the doctors had already downgraded his status from critical to fair.

I was relieved to hear he was still alive, but Danny's recovery had raised a very disturbing question. If my brother wasn't dead, then how had I been talking to him on the phone in the kitchen? According to the doctors, he even regained consciousness before I had made it home.

They told us my brother would make a full recovery, and by the afternoon we were allowed into his hospital room to talk to him. I was happy for him and his family, but the mystery of who I had been talking to during my phone conversation was still weighing heavy on me.

After I got home from the hospital, I stayed up late, waiting for the phone in the kitchen to ring. I had questions that needed answers, and this time, I wasn't going to let the my caller pivot away from them. I had been waiting for hours when the phone finally rang.

It was my brother again – or at least someone who sounded just like him. I let the voice speak for a little while before I cut it off. I then explained to the caller that my brother hadn't died in his car accident, and that I no longer believed my phone line to the afterlife to be genuine. The voice on the other end of the line tried to continue its charade for a bit, but conceded when it realized it had been caught in a lie.

"I'm just so lonely," the caller whined. "Please, won't you still talk to me?" Now the voice sounded just like my grandmother's. "I can be anyone you want me to be."

The revelation made me feel sick. Whoever – whatever – I had been talking to all this time had been impersonating my dead relatives and friends in order to get closer to me. I disconnected the phone from the wall and tossed it in the garbage bin. Part of me was terrified that the phone would continue to ring, that whoever I had hung up on would begin to bombard me with call after call until I picked the receiver back up, but the calls never came, and I thank God for that, because I don't know what I'd do if they had. It's been years since that phone call, and even today I feel violated just writing about it. I wonder sometimes, what I was actually speaking to on the other end of that phone line, but the more I think about all the intimate phone calls we shared, the more I reflect on its strange attachment to me, the more I believe that I'd rather not know.

BIG F'N ROACH

I visited the town that the house was located in during the summer of this past year. I thought that meeting people face to face would be a good opportunity to learn more about the house on Wendall Lane, but I noticed quickly that my inquiries were met with a strange resistance from most of the locals I questioned. Many were not interested in speaking to me. Others were standoffish whenever I brought up the house. I did get a few people to agree to sit down with me, but my interviews with them yielded little to nothing in regards to the information I wanted to hear. I was almost ready to give up when I received a voicemail on my phone. I have transcribed it below.

You're the writer that's been asking about the house on Wendall Lane,
right? Your number's been floating around town. Not a lot of people like to talk to outsiders about
that place. Now me personally, I
don't mind you poking around town,
but there are people here who want
you gone. If I were you, I'd start
thinking about wrapping up your in-

```
vestigation soon, before some of
the locals begin causing you prob-
lems. There's a guy who might be
able to give you a juicy story be-
fore you go, though. His name's Bill
Huckley. We got to talk'n when we
heard you were in town, and he said
he wanted to meet with you. You can
find him at AJ's tonight. It's a
bar just off Exit 31. He comes in
every Friday night and gets ham-
mered. Bill's pal, Jim Baker, used
to live in the house. Make sure
you ask him about the guy. I'll be
at the bar too, but you won't know
it. We ain't gonna meet. Some of
the people who don't like you might
also stop through so be careful.
```

I arrived at *AJ's* that night around 10 PM. The bar was a total dive, low light, neon signs, and air that reeked of stale beer and sweat. I couldn't help but wonder if the anonymous caller was watching me as I scanned the room. I also wondered if anyone the caller had warned me about was there as well. I asked the bartender if she knew whether or not Bill Huckley was in the establishment that evening, and she pointed me to a middle-aged man with salt-and-pepper hair and a 5 o'clock shadow shooting pool in the back of the bar. It was Bill. I made my way over and introduced myself to him. Just as the voicemail had promised, Bill was more than willing to talk about the house, and when I asked him about Jim Baker his face lit up with an empathetic eagerness. We picked out a table, and sat down. I turned my tape-recorder on, and that's *when his story began.*

YEAH, I KNEW JIM BAKER – Jimbo's what I called him. Played in my fantasy football league last year. Good guy, but the dude was a total fish. Drafted a kicker in the 3rd round – easy money. Haven't been doing too well this season, but I just picked up Buffalo's 2nd string running back and now I'm one blown ACL away from riding that horse to the playoffs, baby. You see, the key is to snag the guys who back up the guys with brittle bones and tendons that snap like Kit Kat Bars. Then it's really just about playing the waiting game. What were we talking about again? Oh yeah, Jimbo!

He was a real mousy-looking cat. Short and skinny. Had a beard, but he kept the thing so neatly trimmed that it looked like he painted it on his face before he left the house every morning. Wore thick glasses. One of the smartest guys you've ever met unless he was talking football. I think he was one of those – not hippy – but what do they call them now? Hipsters! Yeah that's it. Anyways, I ain't saying he was a fairy, but Jimbo came in this bar every weekend and not once did I ever see him with a woman. You'd think he'd be cleaning up too 'cause he was pretty well-off for a guy in his early thirties. Drove a Benz. Made a bunch of money in tech then decided he wanted to take a break from the fast life. Apparently, he had a public freak out a ways back while he was running some dot-com up in the city. Said the stress had been building in him for years. S'pose that's why he moved out here and bought the house.

Speaking of the house, I guess you've heard the stories, huh? You must take 'em pretty seriously if you came all the way from California just to follow up on the place. As for me, I never believed the rumors. Every town's got its silly urban legends and ours was no different. Every time something happened in that house, this community would work themselves into an uproar, which meant I would have to hear people ramble about the place for weeks on end. All the while, I'm the guy going, maybe the only reason Old Lady McNealy suddenly dropped dead in her living room was because Old Lady McNealy was one hundred and two years old. Seriously, that geriatric bag of bones was so ancient, when she farted sawdust would come out her ass, and people actually wanted to call in an exorcist the day she finally up and croaked!

Now have no fear, buddy. You ain't leaving here empty handed. I know you flew up here for a story and – trust me when I tell you this – have I got a story for you. But before I tell it I'm gonna need a drink. I'll grab this round. You get the next.

HEY BARTENDER! FOUR SHOTS OF JACK... and... uh... what'll you be having?

It all started 'bout six months back. I was here at the bar when Jimbo walked in. He sat down right there at that table, if I remember correctly, then Trashy Tammy came over and took his order. The guy looked like hell. He was sweating bullets and his face was whiter than a Klan meeting at the North Pole. At this point, we had grown to be pretty good acquaintances. You know? Drinking buddies. So I could tell something was really bugging him when he didn't come up and say "hi."

He was just sittin', staring off into space, not even

touching his cheese fries so I decided to mosey on over to see how he was doing. I sit down at the table and start pickin' at his food and before I even get to ask him what his deal is, it all comes pouring out of him. Tells me he saw a cockroach in his kitchen earlier that night. Says he can't stand the thought of being under the same roof with the thing. I ask him why he didn't just kill it – and get this – he tells me he tried and just about burned his house down in the process. Good Ole' Jimbo tried to roast the roach with one of those fancy blowtorches people use to brown the tops of crème brûlée, but the sucker darted away and his wallpaper caught instead.

Now I'm laughing so hard at the guy I nearly fall out my chair. Can you imagine almost setting your house on fire 'cause you're too chicken to mush a bug? It was even funnier to me 'cause I run a pest control company – second biggest privately owned in the region thank you very much – so killing bugs is something that comes naturally to me.

Once I catch my breath, I tell him that I'd send one of my guys over to his place in the morning if he needed somebody to take care of it. That cheers him up right away. He hires me on the spot, I buy him a beer, and he doesn't mention the cockroach again for the rest of the night.

Next morning, I tell Miguel – my most trusted soldier – to spray Jimbo's house down. Once he finishes Miguel shoots me a text to let me know everything was copacetic, but *that afternoon* I get a call from Jimbo. His voice is trembling on the phone. He says the cockroach isn't dead. His voice is real jumpy and he's asking me how long it takes before the poison starts working.

Now, I'm not sure how much you understand about the delicate science of pest control, but my guys aren't messing around with the wimpy junk you get over the counter. We only use the very finest insecticides on the market. Any roach exposed to the powerful poisons employed in our arsenal should be belly up within a matter of minutes so the fact that Jimbo was saying we didn't get the job done was really starting to bug me – pardon the pun. I ask him if he's sure the cockroach is still alive and he tells me that he's looking at it on the wall in his bathroom and that it's even bigger than before. At least four inches long, not including the antennas!

That's a big F'n roach!

As a matter of fact, the only cockroach that's even known to grow that large is the *Blaberus Giganteus*. Otherwise known to a layman like yourself as The Giant Burrowing Cockroach of Australia and those are only native to...well...Australia. So I tell Jimbo that I'm coming down myself to scope the situation out.

When I get there, the guy opens the door and he's shaking like a meth-head coming down from a three-day bender. On top of that, he's nursing a pretty nasty lump on the back of his head. He tells me that after we got off the phone, he cornered the thing in his bathroom and swatted at it with a rolled up magazine. Nailed it dead-on and it didn't budge one inch. When he reared back to whack it again the cockroach went on the offensive. It fluttered its wings, then launched itself at him and buzzed around in his face. He tells me he let out a yelp in all the excitement and in that moment, that second or two his lips had involuntarily parted, the bug manages to somehow force its way

242

into his mouth. Said its back end was sticking out of his lips like a cigar. So ole' Jimbo panics, stumbles backwards, trips over the bathtub, and damn near knocks himself out when he bangs his melon against the wall. After it does its damage, the roach just casually crawls out of his mouth and buzzes away.

Now, *Blaberus Giganteus* can't fly, so Jimbo's story ruled out that possibility, but I've never heard of any other type of roach growing even half that size, so I figured he must've been exaggerating.

While I'm at his place, I check the pantry for droppings and egg cases – anything that I can use to identify his unwelcomed guest – but I can't find a thing. Most people would be relieved to hear that because it would mean they most likely weren't dealing with an infestation, but most people aren't as high-strung as Jimbo was.

He asks if we could tent the place. Normally, I'd strongly advise against fumigating a house for one solitary roach. Why pay thousands of dollars to accomplish the same job I can do with the sole of my boot? It's kinda like dropping a live hand grenade down your pants to scratch your ass.

But as I look into his eyes, I can see just how hot and bothered that bug has him so I reluctantly agree and schedule him in my next earliest appointment. Two days later, the tent goes up over his house. Hey, don't look at me like that! It's not like he couldn't afford it. I was just helping out a pal! So what if I made a little money on the side? I'm a good guy, okay? I even let him sleep on my couch while we gassed the place.

Once the tent goes up, he shows up at my place with

a duffle bag full of clothes and a smile on his face so big you would've thought he just hit the *Super Lotto Jackpot*. My wife made meatloaf that night. It tasted like dog chow, but Jimbo gobbled it up like he hadn't eaten in days.

After dinner, me and Jimbo go down to the den to have a beer. I ask him if he had seen the roach again since his run-in with it in the bathroom. He tells me things had been quiet as of late, but he caught a glimpse of it that morning before my guys showed up to fumigate his house. He was walking to the front door, when it scuttled past him in the foyer. Said he almost jumped out of his skin when he saw it. According to Jimbo, the roach was about a foot long now and maybe six inches tall.

Have you ever heard of a cockroach that big? Me neither, buddy, and I've pretty much seen it all in my line of work. In fact, I hadn't found any signs of a roach at his place at all and neither had Miguel. So then I get to thinking about how anxious Jimbo is all the time, and I remember he told me about the nervous breakdown he had that prompted him to retire early and move away from the city, so I start to wonder if the whole cockroach thing is just a figment of his imagination.

The roach is all the guy can talk about while he's staying with me. He's obsessed. For the next two days, it's *cockroach this* and *cockroach that*. My wife has the patience of a saint – she better if she's gonna stay married to me – but even she was starting to get annoyed with his blabbering. I could tell she was relieved a couple days later when we took the tent down and told Jimbo it was safe to move back in.

You know, I really hoped that would be the end of

it, but that evening after dinner I get a knock on my door and when I open it, it's Jimbo. He's an absolute wreck. He's standing on my doorstep in his PJ's with one house slipper on and I can tell he's been crying. I ask him what happened.

He tells me he was reading a book in bed when he heard a hissing sound. The noise was coming from directly over his head, so he looked up and there on the ceiling was the roach. *As big as a dog,* he tells me! Said it was staring at him and fluttering its wings like it was about to strike again, so he rolled himself out of bed and sprinted out the bedroom like it was on fire. He had phoned the cops, but they reprimanded him for calling 911 just to complain about a cockroach and that's why he had come to me.

At this point, I'm positive Jimbo's lost it, and I know my wife is gonna kill me if I let him spend another night on the couch so I invite him in, I give him a beer, and I tell him to relax while I take care of his roach situation myself. Sometimes, when a person is so caught up in fantasy that they can't tell the difference between what's real and what isn't, the only thing you can do is indulge them. My crazy Aunt Laura taught me that. She was convinced the government was secretly run by lizard people from the Sirius Star System.

Anyways, I ask him for his key, then I head out to his place. When I get there, I let myself in the front door. I look around Jimbo's house and just as I expected, the place is empty – even the bedroom. So I send a text to Jimbo, and it reads something like this:

Whoa! You were right! That's the

245

```
biggest sucker I've ever seen! Got
it though! Nailed it point-blank in
its face with enough insecticide
to kill a horse! Executed the bas-
tard just in time too 'cause it
looks like it was getting ready to
lay eggs. Gonna dispose of the body
properly before the larvae hatches.
Be back in 15 minutes.
```

After I'm done I leave my hat on his kitchen counter just in case he had any doubts that I had actually come by.

I thought I was being pretty crafty, but Jimbo didn't buy my ruse. No matter what I said, he refused to go back inside the house until I showed him the corpse. Couldn't help but feel guilty when I told him he couldn't spend the night at my place anymore, but he seemed to understand.

Heard he crashed at Richie Hooper's for about a week before Richie's wife kicked him out. Then he spent a couple days at Pete Duhn's. After he had exhausted all his friends he started shacking up at the budget motel just off the Interstate. Didn't see him around much after that. Stopped coming into the bar.

Then, all of a sudden cops show up and start asking questions. Turns out he went missing. Melanie Swan was the last to see him. She lived across the street. Said she watched him head inside his house with a brand-new hunting rifle. He walked in, but never walked out. Weird, huh?

It gets weirder.

Remember how I left my hat over at his place? Well, I had forgotten all about it and when I finally remembered where it was, Jimbo was already long-gone, but I still have the spare key he gave me, so I drive on over there after work one day and let myself in the front door.

The house is a mess; chairs are knocked over, the glass coffee table in his living room is broken, the place stinks to hell and back, and I'm thinking it's pretty obvious Jimbo must've gone off the deep-end. I'm feeling really sorry for the guy, but then I start to hear a noise coming from the kitchen. It sounds like someone is in there shuffling around. I'm thinking maybe Jimbo came back. I call out his name, but all I hear is more shuffling, then some kind of crunching sound like someone biting into an apple. I wonder if there's a burglar in there.

I'm against the wall right next to the kitchen door now, and I can hear that there's definitely someone in there, so as quietly as I can, I peer around the corner and that's when I see it. Jimbo's cockroach, just as real as you and me.

It's enormous. If I had to guess, I'd say close to seven feet long. Standing next to you it would come up to about your hip. Its antennas are as long as my legs. The thing's eyes are like two black softballs and its mandibles look like industrial size pruning shears. Right away, I recognize the stench in the house is coming from it. It doesn't smell like an ordinary roach infestation. I would have been able to pick that up immediately. No, this is way more pungent. There's really no describing it. Took two days to get the stink out of my nostrils and it still comes back to me from time to time like an acid flashback.

The thing is eating something. For a second I think it's a loaf of bread from Jimbo's pantry, but as it spins in its mouth, I see a face – *Jimbo's face.* I hear another sickening crunch and realize that noise is the sound of my old pal's skull cracking inside the giant cockroach's maw.

I try to back away slowly, but the thing spots me and flutters its wings. The sound is horrific – like a thousand angry bees getting ready to swarm me. Each beat of its wings hits me with wave after wave of the noxious stink it produces. I'm pretty sure it wants to attack, but lucky for me, it's too big to take off in Jimbo's tiny kitchen so it settles down and goes back to chewing on the poor guy's head.

I take that as my cue to hightail it out of there. I book it out the door, hop in my car, then put the pedal to the metal. When I get far enough away, I make an anonymous call to the cops and tell them I saw armed gunman breaking into Jimbo's house. What was I supposed to say? That there was a giant cockroach eating my missing friend's head? By the time the police arrived, the roach was gone. Never did find Jimbo's body, but I don't think anybody ever will.

I believe the stories about that house now – *all of them*. I keep wondering if I'm gonna get a call one day from the next people who buy that place. If I do, I'll tell them to give *Orkin* a ring because I'll never step foot in there again. There's something wicked about that house.

Now...

It's your turn to buy the round, and don't be cheap. Make mine a double this time!

BY YOUR BOOTSTRAPS

Wendy Hope has been missing for nearly a year. Since her disappearance, the only piece of evidence police have been able to uncover is a typed manifesto, signed in her handwriting and dated the day she vanished. It was discovered in her car two blocks away from the house on Wendall Lane. She had driven her sedan 75 miles from her home in upstate Washington before abandoning it. The contents of the letter are bizarre, its prose so desultory so chaotic that investigators who've examined it now question the status of Wendy's mental health on the day she went missing. It is believed that her disappearance was at least in part driven by a sudden mania – possibly an extreme bout of Paranoid Personality Disorder (PPD). The letter was leaked to the press and published online a few weeks after it was recovered. Since then, many theories have formed in respect to what actually took place that day, although none have been corroborated. Printed below in its entirety is the extraordinary and strange manifesto of Wendy Hope.

'D LIKE TO CONDUCT A LITTLE EXPERIMENT. Please follow along with my step-by-step instructions and I promise we'll get into the story very shortly.

Sᴛᴇᴘ 1: Stand up. Get out of your chair.

Sᴛᴇᴘ 2: Now bend over and, with your fingers, secure the laces of both your shoes. If you're not wearing shoes, grab ahold of your socks. If you don't have socks on, grip your toes. If you don't have toes, I can't help you.

Sᴛᴇᴘ 3: Once your laces or socks or toes are secure, begin to pull them upwards. Pull as hard as you can. Put all your strength into it. Try to see if you can lift both feet simultaneously off the ground until your soles are floating in the air.

Did it work?

If so, then congratulations. You have successfully pulled yourself up by your bootstraps.

If not, then don't fret. They say this feat is an impossible one. I've yet to pull *myself* up by my bootstraps and I've tried many, many times before.

There is this silly book I read when I was in high school called *The Surprising Adventures of Baron Munchausen*. It was written by 18th century author, Rudolph Elrich Raspe. The book was about a fictional German nobleman named Baron Munchausen who would often find himself caught in ridiculous, sticky situations. Just when you thought he was done for, he would always come up with some miraculous way to escape.

One time, the baron was riding through a swamp when his horse's hooves suddenly became stuck in quicksand. To his horror, he soon realized that both he and his steed were sinking into the muck and that if he didn't do something fast, the swamp would swallow both of them whole. So this is how the baron escaped – he grabbed a hand full of his own hair and began to tug on it. He pulled and pulled and pulled until both he and his horse were free of the dangerous terrain. If you think that sounds absurd, then you'd be correct. Baron Munchausen evaded death by performing an impossible feat. He pulled himself up by his bootstraps – so to speak.

Now let's get into the story.

Imagine a little girl. She's nine years old. She lives in a nice house on a quiet street with her mommy and daddy and her little brother too. The date is Friday, October 22, 1954. It's early evening and the little girl is upstairs in her room playing with dolls. From the corner of her eye she detects a hint of movement outside her bedroom window, so this little girl, she turns her head and peers down into the back yard and that's when she sees something that steals her breath.

There is an elderly woman standing in the doorway of her parents' garden shed, staring up at her. She is holding a hand shovel - one that the little girl's mother had used to plant violets in the backyard just earlier that day. This old woman, she wears a long, black dress. On her lapel is a circular green brooch with a gold trim. Her hair is white and thinning, and her skin the texture of newspaper that's been wadded and crumpled into a tight ball, then unwadded and uncrumpled and plastered over her face – a mask of wrinkles, creases and folds. It's close to Halloween, and thoughts of ghosts, goblins, and things of that nature have been prowling about inside the little girl's mind for days. She thinks the old lady is a witch.

So this is what the little girl does — she runs to Mommy and Daddy's room to tell them about the mean old witch she saw hiding in the garden shed.

When she gets there, Mommy is in front of her vanity putting on the finishing touches of her makeup and Daddy is fixing his tie in the mirror. The little girl's parents are getting ready for a big night out. They had arranged for a babysitter to watch the kids that evening so they could grab dinner and catch a movie. The little girl cries and cries about the witch, but Mommy and Daddy aren't having it. They have waited a long time to have a night to themselves and aren't about to let their daughter's *overactive imagination* spoil their plans.

A little bit later, the babysitter shows up and the little girl's parents are out the door. The babysitter is a young woman in her early twenties. She's watched the little girl and her younger brother before. Both the kids like her very much. They've always had so much fun with this babysitter and tonight is no different. As a matter of fact, the little girl ends up having such a good time that thoughts of that old witch lady in the garden shed drift away from her mind like morning mist. Drift away that is, until the doorbell rings.

It's far too late to be expecting visitors, but too early for the little girl's mommy and daddy to come home from their big night out. The babysitter stands up from the kitchen table, where she and the children had been playing a game of Candy Land, and answers the front door. Neither child can tell who the babysitter is talking to, but the little girl suddenly feels a terrible tightening in her tummy— *this my friends is called intuition.* Intuition is when – for one reason or another – we're allowed to peer through the veil of the universe and see the strings that shepherd us through time.

There's a short struggle. A moment later the babysitter falls to the floor like a ragdoll. She's gasping for breath and clutching her throat. There's a gash running lengthwise down the front of it. Blood fills her mouth like a birdbath, bubbling and spilling down the sides of her pink, rosy cheeks.

Standing in the doorway is the old witch – that wicked, nasty lady the little girl spotted in her parents' garden shed. The evil woman is still holding that hand shovel.

The spade is now coated in blood – blood that just seconds earlier had been flowing unobstructed through the veins of the children's babysitter. Now, it drips to the floor, staining the white carpet a deep crimson. A ridiculous thought pops into the little girl's mind. She thinks her daddy will be mad when he sees the stain. This is because he once sent her to her room for spilling grape juice on that very same rug.

The babysitter is dead. Her chest no longer heaves up and down. Her birdbath mouth is no longer gargling blood. Her pink, rosy cheeks have dulled to a stone white. In the dim living room light the old lady looks more like a witch than ever. The circular, green brooch on her lapel glistens in the darkness – it's the only thing about her that seems pretty – *well, almost pretty.* She steps inside and closes the door. This old witch, she does not smile or laugh in some deranged or twisted way. No, her face looks sober, determined, even-keeled – and perhaps this frightens the little girl even more.

The horrible old lady then slithers towards the children. They're far too scared to run, too scared to scream, too scared to do anything but sit in their chairs and watch the sinful scene play out before them. Yes, *scene* is exactly the right word. I hadn't intended to use it in that context, but it does fit perfectly. *Like a scene in a play*, the children and witch merely actors following a set of blocking instructions from some cosmic script.

The little girl's brother is scared stiff, but seeing him so helpless wakes her up from her near vegetative state. She lets out a cry then begins to scratch at the old lady, smacking at her arms and legs, tearing at her dress. She manages to rip the brooch from the witch's lapel, but try as she might she can't best the evil old lady. The witch might be an ancient old bag, but she's still far stronger than the little girl. So like all the other actors of this play, she follows along with the script, and right now the script is calling for her to concede, to sit in her chair, and to pray for her mommy and daddy come home early from their date.

Now the children are in a tight spot – just as tight of a spot Baron Munchausen was in when his horse got stuck in quicksand. The little girl is still holding the brooch she tore from the witch's lapel. She clenches it tightly in her fist, hoping that maybe if she squeezes it hard enough she'll crush it into powder and the old lady will wither away like the witch in *The Wizard of Oz*.

The old woman stands before the children, and, with both hands gripping the handle tight, raises the hand shovel over her head. The little girl is certain that she'll never see her parents again. She wants to comfort her younger brother, let him know he'll be okay, but her pastor told her that lying is a sin and she doesn't want to tell a fib mere moments before facing St. Peter in front of Heaven's Pearly Gates.

A movement behind the old witch stops the little girl mid-thought. There's another woman, a younger one creeping up on the old lady. She had let herself in the side door when the little girl was kicking and screaming. At first the little girl thinks it's her mommy, but she quickly realizes this new woman is much too young. No, this is a stranger – and a beautiful one at that. Her hair is walnut brown, her skin as smooth as milk. Even in that terrible, awful moment, the little girl can appreciate how pretty the mystery woman is.

This beautiful stranger, she inches slowly across the kitchen until she's only a few feet away. The witch doesn't seem to notice her presence. She stands still like an evil old statue, hand shovel still raised above her head, its pointed tip angled down towards the children. It's almost as if time has stopped, as if all the actors have been instructed by the director to freeze in their places.

Then, just like that, the stranger launches herself at the witch and for a moment the little girl thinks that the day is saved. This unfortunately is not to be. The old lady side-steps her easily, almost as if she had anticipated the stranger, almost as if she had read ahead in the script and knew what was supposed to happen next. The young woman, goes flying headfirst into the corner of a cabinet. The little girl's last hope is now laying on the kitchen floor, half unconscious, a massive knot swelling on her forehead.

The old witch wastes no more time. She raises the hand shovel over her head once more then drives it down, down, down into the little girl's brother. He does not scream — he hasn't made a peep since the old lady first appeared — but the little girl yells and cries enough for the both of them. She begs the witch to stop, but of course she doesn't listen. Again and again the wicked old lady thrusts the shovel into the young boy's body. The little girl can only watch as the light fades from her poor brother's eyes, as his breathing becomes more shallow, more erratic, as blood begins to seep through the dozens of new puncture wounds in his chest, stomach, and neck. Eventually, mercifully, he's dead.

And then this despicable old lady does something very peculiar. She puts the hand shovel down and takes a seat at the table across from the little girl and her brother's corpse. She looks tired.

The stranger has finally gotten her bearings back. She stands up and sees that she was too late to save the boy and this sends her into a fit. Tears well up in her eyes, her mouth twists into an angry sneer, and suddenly the little girl doesn't think the beautiful stranger looks very beautiful anymore.

This no-longer-beautiful-stranger, she picks up the murder instrument and stands before the nasty old witch, just as the nasty old witch had stood before the children. With one arm she lifts the spade over her head, angling the tip towards the ancient hag. This old lady, she makes no attempt to stop her. Instead she seems to be waiting for the stranger to take her revenge, but the younger woman hesitates before driving the point of the shovel into the witch's heart.

The little girl watches on in silence. She doesn't realize it, but she's rubbing the old lady's brooch between her thumb and forefinger. She can't explain it, but it brings her comfort. For a second it seems as if the stranger will miss her cue, but soon the spell is lifted, and whatever it was that was giving her pause vanishes from the room. No longer hesitant, she jabs the witch with the point of the shovel over and over again until the old woman slumps to the floor, dead as a doornail.

This heroic stranger, she starts towards the little girl. Perhaps she intended to comfort her, but when she sees the brooch in the little girl's hand an odd expression washes over the young woman — like she's just looked upon the face of a ghost. She backs away in a daze and stumbles out the side door without saying a word. The little girl watches her from the kitchen window as the stranger wanders around the backyard mumbling to herself as though she's lost her mind. She exits stage left, disappearing into the garden shed where the little girl had first spotted the witch. She would not see the stranger come back out of that shed, even though she'd keep her eyes glued to its door until the police arrived. Somehow, someway, the stranger had vanished.

I WOULD LIKE TO INTERRUPT MYSELF FOR A MOMENT. I have not

finished telling the little girl's story, but before I continue I feel that it may be important to tell you another one first.

Here it goes.

Imagine the distant future, hundreds of years removed from the time you and I are currently living in. In this distant future there is a man perusing the library. Yes, even in the distant future libraries still exist. This future man, he sees the spine of a book sticking out a little further than the rest of the books on one of the shelves. Curiosity gets the better of him so he pulls it out and looks at the cover. The book is called *The Surprising Adventures of Baron Munchausen*. He thinks the title sounds interesting so this future man sits down and reads the book and laughs out loud at all of the Baron's ridiculous exploits. He finds the book so hilarious in fact that he decides he just has to meet the author.

As I've told you before, the book was published in the 18th century by Rudolph Elrich Raspe, a man who has been dead for a good long time. Now, this would present a problem for you or I if we wanted to meet him, but remember, this man is from the future! He has access to amazing technology which grants him abilities that would be considered impossible by today's standards – as impossible as pulling yourself up by your bootstraps.

One such piece of technology is a time machine. So this future man, he hops in his time machine and travels back to the mid 18th century, and, once in the past, he tracks down Rudolph Elrich Raspe. The two share a drink at a tavern where the time traveler gushes to his new favorite author over how much he enjoys his work. Just before going back to his own time, he decides to leave Raspe with a little gift as a token of his appreciation – his copy of *The Surprising Adventures of Baron Munchausen!* A keepsake from the future!

But wait!

The future man has committed a huge blunder. You see, unbeknownst to him, he had accidentally traveled too far back in time. When he gave Raspe a copy of the book, the young author hadn't even begun to pen *The Surprising Adventures of Baron Munchausen* yet, but with the hard work now already done for him, Raspe then publishes the manuscript, making himself a very rich and famous man.

Now, I know what you're thinking. Why does it matter? Raspe might not have actually written the book, but it's not like he took credit for anyone else's work.

That's not the point.

I told that story so I could ask you this question: If Raspe didn't actually write *The Surprising Adventures of Baron Munchausen* and neither did the future man, or anyone else for that matter, then how, pray tell, did the book come into existence in the first place?

Ok, back to the little girl.

THE OLD WITCH WAS NEVER IDENTIFIED. Oh, rumors about her hung about for years and years and years, but it was all gossip, based mostly on local superstitions and urban legends. The stranger was never located either. It really was as if she vanished inside that old garden shed. Eventually the little girl's parents sold their home and moved away in order to distance themselves from that awful night.

Years have gone by and that little girl isn't so little anymore. She's twenty-two years old now, a college graduate – the first woman in her family to get a degree. She has a bright future in front of her, but still she hangs on to those scarlet memories of her past. The date is October 22, 1967. Thirteen years to the day that her brother and babysitter were murdered by an evil old witch.

It's early afternoon. The sun is shining high in a pale blue sky. This no longer little girl, this young woman, she's driving up the Interstate on her way to visit friends when she sees an exit sign for the town she used to live in. She hadn't even realized her former home would be along the route she was taking upstate. If she had, then she might have driven a different way. It gets her thinking – thinking about that evil old witch, that beautiful stranger, that terrible evening. She decides that she needs closure, that she needs to face her demons. She doesn't really come to this conclusion herself of course. In reality she's simply following along with script of that cosmic play, but she *feels* like the decision was hers and that's what matters. So she plays her role, just as it was written, and takes the exit on the highway. A few minutes later she's parked in front of the house where it all happened.

Nobody lives there. Whoever her parents had sold the place to must have moved out. A sign is spiked in the front lawn declaring the home is for sale. The young woman gets out of her car and takes it all in. Aside from some overgrown bushes and a lawn in desperate need of mowing, the house looks just how it did thirteen years prior. There's something compelling her, driving her forward, an invisible force of some sort. It draws her onto the property. She unfastens the latch on the side gate and lets herself into the backyard. It's surreal being there again. She gazes up to the second story window where her bedroom used to be and once more memories of that night come flooding back to her. She remembers glancing down from that window and seeing that nasty old witch staring back at her from the garden shed.

The shed is still there after all those years. The young woman steps cautiously towards it. She doesn't know why, perhaps it's just another irrational thought, but she half expects the evil old woman to burst out the door, arm cocked, ready to drive that hand shovel into her chest. But the witch is dead and in the back of her mind she knows that. She watched the stranger kill her herself. She watched the coroners scoop her cold, white corpse off the floor.

The young woman opens the shed's door. Of course there's no old woman in it. Again, that invisible force drives her forward. She feels a strange need to step inside the shed and close the door behind her.

Darkness swallows her when she does this, but she's not frightened. Why should she be? After all, it's just an old garden shed. She stands there in the blackness for a moment, thinking about the witch and the stranger, reminiscing again about that terrible night. She tells herself that she'll be able to find the closure she's been seeking inside that shed. But closure never comes. Frustrated, she opens the door, but when she looks outside she immediately realizes that something is very wrong.

It's night now. There are no hints of twilight – the afternoon isn't just deepening into dusk. No, the stars are out. The moon is shining high in a pale black sky. It seems as if the sun has been down for hours. It makes no sense. It had been broad daylight just minutes before.

The young woman steps out into the night and that's when she sees the violets – the very same violets her mother had planted in the yard thirteen years earlier. There is a terrible tightening in her stomach – *this my friends, once again, is intuition*. The young woman has reached a strange level of awareness. Her mind understands what has happened, but doesn't believe it. It's not until she sees lights on inside the house that she can even accept where she is – or more importantly when she is.

She moves unconsciously across the yard and peers through the window of the door that opens up into the kitchen. There she finds those scarlet memories waiting for her in corporeal form. The old witch is inside the kitchen, so is her younger brother, and so is she. Somehow, she's travelled back in time.

She watches in awe at the sight – herself when she was just a little girl struggling with the old witch, crying and tearing at her dress. It's so uncanny to relive that night from the vantage point of an outside observer.

A sudden series of thoughts ignite like fireworks inside her mind. Maybe she's not just meant to observe. Maybe she's been sent back because she's supposed to intervene – prevent her brother from dying at the hands of that evil old woman. Maybe she's been given the chance to do what the beautiful stranger couldn't. Why not? Everything up until this point has seemed so impossible. Maybe this is her opportunity to face her demons and change the past. Maybe this is her opportunity to pull herself up by her bootstraps.

So this young woman, this is what she does – she slides quietly inside the kitchen as the old witch wrestles with her younger self. She stalks behind her, doing everything in her power not to be noticed. The witch raises the hand shovel above her head and as she does this the young woman looks into the petrified face of her younger brother. She wants so badly to save him.

It's now or never, the young woman dives forward in an attempt to tackle the nasty old hag to the ground, but the witch moves too quickly. *Deja vu!* The hag pirouettes around her like a Pamplona bullfighter – like she read ahead in the script – and the young woman flies headfirst into the cabinet.

Pain shoots through her skull. Her vision gets fuzzy. She writhes across the floor not knowing which way is up and which way is down. Her head is throbbing. Even her ears are ringing.

Slowly, the young woman's vision returns and she's finally able to orient herself. When she gets back to her feet, she's horrified by the sight before her. The young woman was too late. Her brother's fresh corpse slumps to the floor just the same as it did thirteen years ago.

A realization comes to her as she stares at him. The stranger who had failed to save her brother when she was a little girl wasn't a stranger at all. *It was her.* Somehow, someway, it was her, and once again she's failed him. Tears begin to sting her eyes, her lips twist into an angry sneer, and thoughts of vengeance now dominate her mind.

She turns to the old woman and picks the blood-stained murder instrument up off the ground. This not-a-stranger, this no-longer-a-little-girl, can think of nothing other than slaying that evil old witch. The witch sits calmly in her chair, as if she has accepted her death is imminent. The young woman raises the hand shovel over her head and readies herself to drive the point into the old lady's body, but once their eyes make contact she finds she has trouble pulling the trigger. Now, she's face to face with the witch for the first time since she was a little girl, and the sight has stopped her cold. Something is off, something that makes young woman almost miss her cue. *Almost* is the key word here because eventually she's able to shake it off and break away from the witch's hypnotic gaze. It does the trick. A moment later, she comes down, down, on her, driving the shovel into the witch's chest, abdomen, even her throat.

When she's sure the witch is dead, she stumbles back across the kitchen and that's when she sees the little girl – this little girl, who only thirteen years earlier had been her. She tries to think of something to say. Back when she was the child, her older self hadn't offered any comfort, but this time, she wants things to be different. She wants to help. As the young woman attempts to come up with something to say, her eyes trail down to the little girl's hands. That's when she remembers how she had torn the brooch from the lapel of the old lady's dress.

She feels a terrible tightening in her stomach – *yes friends, again I am speaking of intuition* – and once more those invisible strings reveal themselves to her.

It sends her mind into a tailspin. The young woman feels an overbearing urge to run as far away from that place as possible. That invisible force pushes her out the door and into the backyard. Her head feels like it's on fire, but she isn't sure if it's from the knock she took or from the horrible thoughts stirring inside of it. Words are spilling out of her mouth, but she doesn't even know what she's saying.

The young woman heads for the shed. It seems like the safest place in the world so she throws herself into its darkness and slams the door behind her. She shuts her eyes.

When she opens them again daylight is trickling through the crack in the door and she knows she's back in the year 1967. Of course she is – that's what the script says after all. This young woman, this failed hero, still feels that terrible tightening in her gut. She leaves the shed, moves briskly to her car, then begins to search through her luggage. Her heart drops when she finds what she is looking for. It didn't suddenly appear; she had remembered packing it, but still she hoped it had somehow gone away.

It's the green brooch. The very one she had torn from the old lady's dress when she was just a little girl. The young woman takes the brooch in her fist and rears her arm back. She has every intention to chuck it as far as she can, but something won't allow her – a bizarre impulse to keep the piece of jewelry that she doesn't yet understand. And so she gives in to her desire, places the brooch back into her bag, gets in her car, and sets off again, back on route to her friends' place. She'll treat the bump on her head when she gets there. That's what it says in the script anyway.

YOU COULD SAY THAT THIS IS THE END OF THE STORY, but you would be wrong. This story has no real end. It has no real beginning either. Its narrative is just as circular, just as round as the brooch I wear on the lapel of my dress.

Decades passed since that day, and now I'm no longer a young woman. My walnut brown hair has gone white. My face is now a mask of wrinkles and folds. Anything about me that could have been considered beautiful has long since withered away. If a little girl were to see me now, she might even mistake me for a witch. I'm not a witch, of course. I'm not wicked or nasty or mean. I'm just an old lady who has peered through the veil of the universe and seen the strings that shepherd us through time

There is an invisible force. It compels us to move forward and sometimes – as in my case – it compels us to move backwards too. Maybe this invisible force is the will of God, and maybe it isn't. All I know is that deviating from the path that is set out for you is as impossible as pulling yourself up by your bootstraps.

The date today is October 22, 2015, over sixty years removed from the night I murdered my younger brother and the babysitter whom I adored so much when I was a child. I'm going back to that house now. I don't want to relive that night for a third time, but my part in this cosmic play has already been written.

I gaze down at this brooch and I know that soon my younger self will tear it from my dress. I also know that for some macabre reason I will feel compelled to keep it as a memento for years and years and years. Part of me has always wanted to get rid of it, but of course I've never been able to. It would be out of character for me and nobody deviates from the script. This I've come to accept.

However, there is one thing that I don't understand.

The Wendall Lane Diaries

It's a question I've pondered ever since I started to understand my role in this cosmic play, although I doubt I'll ever come up with a suitable answer.

Where, pray tell, did the brooch come from in the first place?

THE CURIOUS CASE OF STEPHEN HAIM

Dr. Sandy Rieve (now deceased) was a clinical psychologist who had over thirty years of experience working with patients suffering from extreme psychological disorders. She was renowned and respected in her field. After retirement, Sandy published a series of memoirs detailing some of her most interesting case studies. What you are about to read is a chapter from one of her books that was left on the cutting room floor. I was given the manuscript by an acquaintance, who, at the time worked as an intern at the publishing house that distributed her books. The story, as my acquaintance relayed to me, was that Sandy had been insistent on printing the chapter exactly as you'll read it here, but after a lengthy back and forth with her editor was eventually persuaded to exclude the tale from her final draft. It was believed by those within the company that, if published, the anecdote might hurt her credibility in the medical world which in turn could have a negative effect on future book sales. Below is the unedited chapter, titled 'The Curious Case of Stephen Haim', exactly as Dr. Rieve had written it in her memoir.

HAD BEEN WORKING at Sequoya State Mental Health Center, a psychiatric hospital located in northern California, for three years when Stephen Haim was admitted under my care. He was a shy man with a soft voice and a gentle disposition. An avid reader, Stephen would spend much of his free time – of which there was plenty at Sequoya – losing himself in any book he could get his hands on, especially science fiction novels.

Stephen was a ward of the state. When I first met him, he was struggling with mild depression and a crippling drug addiction, but one thing he most certainly was not struggling with was his sanity. Aside from his dependence on illegal narcotics, the young man was as lucid and rational as any nurse, guard, or doctor in the facility.

So why had he been committed to Sequoya (for a mandatory six years no less) a hospital that housed criminals so mentally unstable that they had been deemed unfit for general lock-up at state penitentiaries? One might assume it was to get his drug habit under control, but the answer is a bit more complicated than that.

In the fall of 1989, Stephen murdered his older sister, Janice Haim, while under the influence of a dissociative hallucinogenic drug known as PCP. By the time he came down from his high, a full day had passed and he was locked inside of a holding cell at the county jail. His new surroundings had come as a great shock to his now sober mind, but even more troubling for Stephen were the circumstances involving his incarceration.

He maintained to have no recollection of the entire event and was horrified when he heard that he had murdered Janice, his only remaining family member, in cold blood. Stephen's claim of memory loss was not a new precedent. There have been many well-documented instances of people suffering blackouts while abusing powerful hallucinogenic drugs. After a series of long, rigorous police interrogations, hypnotherapy sessions, and multiple injections of sodium amytal it was determined that Stephen was in fact telling the truth. He was not lying about memory lapses nor was his memory somehow being repressed by a guilty subconscious. Stephen was dealing with full-blown amnesia and had completely forgotten everything that had happened. It was concluded that he had lost complete control of his faculties while under the influence of the drug and was therefore not fully responsible for Janice's death. Similarly, people suffering from temporal lobe seizures have, at times, been known to perform extreme acts of violence without even realizing it. In these instances, they are not considered culpable, but are still handled by the state and sometimes committed to mental health facilities for the benefit of their own well-being.

To make matters trickier, Janice was killed in such a gruesome manner that the psychologist overseeing the case advised the court not to inform Stephen of the horrific details unless he insisted on disputing the accusations levied against him. He did not, which was probably for the best since the evidence was overwhelming anyway. His hearing was held in-camera. This was done for two reasons. Firstly, to protect Stephen, already grieving the loss of a loved one, from learning the macabre truth about his sister's final moments. Secondly, to prevent the press from catching wind of the event and sparking up a media circus around a man who was already suffering a great deal.

The entire matter was taken care of swiftly and Stephen was sent to Sequoya where I would work with him for the next six years. In that time, I would get to know him quite well. As the primary psychologist treating him at the hospital, I was privy to all the details of Janice Haim's murder, but I made sure never to bring them up with Stephen, who had elected to remain ignorant to the grisly specifics involving his sister's death. My main focus was to help him battle his addiction and to aid him in overcoming the guilt he felt for killing her. My strategy was a success. Within a few months Stephen had put the drugs behind him and by the Spring of 1990 he had seemed to make peace with his dubious past.

Regardless, I couldn't help but feel sorry for Stephen – one of the few patients at the center not dealing with a debilitating mental illness, yet forced to mingle and interact with schizophrenics, manic-depressives, and people suffering from dissociative identity disorder. In my opinion, he was ready to leave the facility after a year, but because his stay at the hospital was court mandated he was forced to wait out the entirety of his sentence. To his credit, he had accepted the hand he was dealt, often telling me during our one on one sessions that he was merely thankful the judge's ruling hadn't been more severe. Nevertheless, once his mandatory time at the clinic was up, I was happy to proclaim to the board overseeing his release that Stephen was of sound mind and ready to reintegrate into society.

He was released on November 14th, 1995, still a relatively young man with his whole life ahead of him. I remember feeling a sense of accomplishment as he walked out the door, stronger than I had encountered with any of the other patients I had treated at that hospital. Often my job is to teach the people under my care how to manage their illnesses without becoming a danger to themselves and others. Stephen on the other hand was cured, his drug habit long-gone and his self-loathing no longer an issue. I felt confident that he would turn his life around and not slip back into the drug habit that had flipped his entire world upside-down. Two years later, after his probation lifted, I heard he moved up north and rented a house in a sleepy little town out of state.

In the summer of '99, I received a letter that Stephen had sent to my office requesting a telephone consultation. He needed advice about some recent problems he'd been experiencing and had written a phone number at the bottom of the page where I could reach him. If it were anyone else, I probably would have written them back with a recommendation for a clinician in their area that could help them. It goes against my code of ethics to give professional advice to patients no longer under my care, but I felt a sort of irrational guilt after watching Stephen waste so many unnecessary years locked away at Sequoya. Against my better judgment, I picked up the phone and dialed his number.

I was a bit disturbed when I heard how nervous and panicky Stephen sounded when he picked up the line. Right away I began to wonder if he was using again. I asked him if that was the case and he assured me it was not – he had even deliberately chosen an employer that drug tested so he wouldn't be tempted to revert back to his old ways. It was a relief to hear, but his reason for writing me was disconcerting nonetheless. Stephen Haim, a man I had never felt truly belonged in a mental institution, was beginning to grow concerned with the status of his own mental health.

He explained that the trouble was stemming from a strong, putrid odor, that he could detect whenever he was inside the house he was renting. Stephen described the smell as being akin to raw sewage. At first he thought there was a problem with his plumbing, but when his landlord sent a maintenance crew to his home to investigate, nobody but Stephen seemed to be able to detect the stink. He invited friends and neighbors over to get a second opinion, but still the phantom stench appeared to only be perceivable to him. It had gotten far worse in recent days. The odor was now more powerful than ever and yet no one else, no matter whom he asked, seemed to smell it at all. It was because of this he had decided the whole thing was in his head – and so he had contacted me for an opinion.

Indeed, it was a peculiar situation, though one I believed I had an answer for. I told him that the odor could very well be in his head, but that I didn't think it meant he was losing his mind. To me, the most plausible likelihood was that Stephen was experiencing some sort of olfactory hallucination induced by flashbacks from his days using PCP. These hallucinations, referred to in the medical field as phantosmia, are known to sometimes spring up in people with a history of abusing hallucinogenic drugs, even if they've been sober for years. I then explained to him, that the smell was probably harmless and would go away with time. However, phantosmia can also occur in people suffering from seizures, so just to be safe, I gave him the number of a nearby neurologist and asked him to set up an appointment to get checked out. He thanked me for easing his concerns and told me he would call the doctor later that week.

Stephen Haim would then drift from my mind until a second letter arrived at my office a few days later. The return address was identical to Stephen's, but to my surprise it had been written by a woman named Colette who claimed to be his fiancé. I was startled to learn that her reason for writing was to inform me that Stephen had recently committed suicide. His funeral was to be held over the weekend and she hoped that I would be able to make it.

I was extremely saddened to hear about Stephen's tragic death and even felt as if I deserved some of the blame. We had spoken so recently. If only I had been able to recognize the signs. Perhaps it was this same guilt that spurred me to cancel my plans and make my way up north for the weekend to pay my respects. I arrived in town the morning of the funeral. The ceremony was scheduled for early afternoon, but Colette's letter had requested I stop by to speak to her beforehand. I wasn't sure what it was she wanted to discuss, but I rented a car at the airport and headed straight over to the house to meet her.

I was greeted at the front door by a young woman with a sharp jaw and striking blue eyes. She introduced herself as Colette and invited me inside. We sat in the living room and made some small-talk for a bit, mostly about the time I spent working with Stephen at Sequoya, before she confessed the reason why she had asked me to come over. She told me that Stephen's final few days had raised a lot of questions about his unsavory past, questions she knew I had the answers to and that she was hoping I could share. I explained to Colette that there was only so much I'd be able to tell her due to doctor-patient confidentiality, but I would try to help in any way I could. She seemed mildly irritated by my answer, but nodded her head cordially in agreement, then began into her story about the circumstances that lead to Stephen's suicide.

Stephen's hallucinations had gotten worse after our conversation on the phone. It wasn't long before the horrible phantom odor he had complained to me about was accompanied by an equally foul taste that he couldn't get out of his mouth. Colette explained that he would go through half a bottle of mouthwash every day, but no matter how often he rinsed, gargled, and spit, the taste continued to remain. It had become so bad in fact that he had stopped eating altogether, which had lead to terrible stomach pains, headaches, and fatigue. As I listened to her speak, I wondered if this phantom taste could have also been a hallucination induced by his prior drug use, but when Colette started on the topic of Stephen's nightmares – dreams of himself repeatedly committing the same horrific act over and over again – my mind began to formulate another, much more fascinating theory.

This is where I detail the night Stephen Haim killed his sister.

On September 12, 1989, Stephen was alone smoking PCP in the apartment he and Janice shared. The drug sent him into a frenzy. As luck would have it, Janice arrived home just in time to catch him at the height of his drug fueled rage. Stephen strangled her on the living room floor. As he choked the life from her, he gnawed on her face, tearing flesh away, and mangling her features until her corpse was completely unrecognizable. The brutality did not end there. Stephen would take a pocket knife to Janice, making an incision in her body that ran from her lower abdomen all the way up to the base of her sternum. He would then proceed to devour much of her organs, including her stomach, liver, and large intestines. By the time police arrived at the apartment, they found a wild-eyed Stephen, covered in blood and excrement, still chewing on his sister's entrails.

This was the memory that was believed to have been erased from Stephen Haim's mind, yet years later, according to Colette's story, it had somehow resurfaced in his nightmares. Every night he was dreaming the same detailed, disgusting scene exactly as it had really happened. I theorized that the phantom smell and taste that had been tormenting him may have also been latent memories of the incident, manifesting themselves in his brain by dominating his sensory stimuli. The constant aroma of raw sewage lingering in his mouth and nose was actually Stephen's mind remembering the flavor of his sister's bowels. It seemed as though Stephen realized this as well and couldn't bear the burden of guilt his newly returned memories had placed on his shoulders. He used a razorblade to slice his wrists. His body wouldn't be discovered until hours later when the landlord stopped by the house for some scheduled repairs.

Colette finished her story abruptly, thanked me for stopping by, then ushered me quickly to the door before I really had a chance to weigh in on what she had said. I was surprised to find her suddenly anxious to get rid of me especially after I expressed my interest in further exploring Stephen's case. It was my opinion that the incident was a medical phenomenon and needed to be studied as fully as possible. She promised me we would talk more at the funeral, but that she had to take care of a few more arrangements before the ceremony got underway.

I waited for her to show me out, but she paused suddenly, frozen in place, hand on the doorknob, mind lost in deep thought. There was something that appeared to be troubling Colette, a thought eating away at her from the inside. Those striking blue eyes then glared up to me as that thought found its way out from between her lips.

"When you were treating Stephen at the hospital, did he ever tell you that he was sorry for what he did?" Collette swallowed and looked away. A pause before she met my eyes again. "You know. To his sister?"

A desperate curiosity emerged across her face and I felt a strange sense that she wasn't going to let me walk outside until I gave her an answer to her question. I wondered why she had asked such a thing in the first place. Clearly, Stephen had demonstrated more than enough remorse when he took his own life just a few days prior. Still, it seemed as though the grieving woman needed to hear reassurance from me. Perhaps, I thought, she required the assessment of a professional to put her mind at ease in regards to her deceased partner's ability to show empathy. I told her that in my opinion Stephen loved his sister very dearly and wished more than anything that he could have taken back what he had done. After hearing this, Colette then thanked me again for my time, opened the door, and sent me on my way.

I spent the next few hours in a daze. Never before in my professional career had I heard of memories manifesting themselves in such peculiar ways. The entire situation was so bizarre and I wanted to know more about it.

I arrived at the funeral later that afternoon. A small group had turned out to mourn the loss of Stephen. Most of the people there had only known him for a short period of time, but it was clear that he had made a favorable impression on all of them, just as he had on me when I first started working with him. Curiously absent from the ceremony was Colette. Given her relationship with Stephen, I would have assumed she'd have been the one greeting everybody at the door when they showed up. I found it odd that she wasn't around, but I imagined that perhaps seeing her fiancé inside a casket might have been too trying for her. I expected to catch up with her later, but even at the wake she was nowhere to be seen.

It was during the wake that I met Rami, the only person there who had known Stephen before he was committed to Sequoya. They had been close friends since they were kids and had even stayed in touch during Stephen's long stint at the hospital. I was surprised when Rami told me that he had been the one who had organized the funeral. Again, I expected this was a duty Colette had taken up, especially since she had made it seem that way when she hurried me out of the house earlier that day. Rami was shocked to learn that I was Stephen's primary doctor at Sequoya and wondered out loud how I had heard about the funeral. I told him about the letter I received from Stephen's fiancé, how it had requested I visit her at the house that morning where she then she recounted the tragic tale of his suicide.

My comment left him perplexed. He was certain Stephen had never been engaged. Even stranger, when I mentioned Colette by name he told me he had never heard of her before. A memorial wreath, decorated with old photographs taken of Stephen throughout the years stood at the head of the room where a few of his friends had given eulogies earlier. One of the pictures caught my eye. The photo couldn't have been taken long before Stephen was committed to Sequoya because he appeared to be around the same age as when I first met him. Standing next to him was a woman with a sharp jaw and an unmistakable pair of striking blue eyes. It was Colette. She looked exactly the same in the photo as she did when she greeted me at the door that morning.

Triumphantly, I pointed the photo out to Rami, explaining to him that this was the woman whom I had just spoken to, but his reaction didn't elicit the response that I was expecting. Instead of acquiescing once he realized who I was talking about, Rami became very quiet. We stood in an awkward hush for a long time as the rest of the wake carried on around us before he finally spoke again.

"I can't tell if you're joking or not," he said to me, his voice quivering under his breath. "but I was the one who snapped the picture you're pointing to. The name of the girl standing next to Stephen isn't Colette. It's Janice."

THE CRIME SCENE

J UST ONE MONTH PRIOR, the grizzled old detective celebrated his thirtieth year on the force. In the three decades he had been working homicide, the veteran lawman investigated cases and arrested people for crimes that he never even fathomed possible, at least, not until he had to write and deliver a fifteen-page report encasing the horrendous details of gruesome murders to his boss' desk. It was the kind of job where every morning, as he headed out the house, cup of coffee in his hand and a folded up newspaper under his arm, he prayed that work would be as dull and mundane as possible. Those were the good days – the ones where nothing of importance happened and he could get home before his wife fell asleep so the two of them could drink tea and watch old episodes of *Cheers* on the couch together. This would not be one of those days.

To any civilian spectator the scene would resemble that of absolute chaos. Ambulances and police cars were parked every which way all along the street facing off in arbitrary directions. A small army of officers formed a human wall around the area doing their best to hold back and mitigate the ever-growing crowd. Further down the block a cluster of news vans had assembled, each with a well coiffed reporter beside it, covering the spectacle as more and more details continued to leak.

The detective ducked under a ribbon of police tape and made his way towards the group of EMTs attending to a man lying on a stretcher. He flashed a badge to the paramedics and they stepped aside, giving him a clear path to their patient.

"Mr. Charles Hopple?"

The man had been casually chatting with the female paramedic holding a pack of ice to the side of his head. He turned an inquisitive eye towards the detective, "Yes? That's me."

"Mr. Hopple, I'm with the police department. Would you care to explain what happened here tonight?"

"Oh, why certainly, officer! My wife Marcy and I had just sat down to dinner and –"

The detective raised an eyebrow, "Dinner?"

"Yes, we were having dinner," Charles repeated with a hint of agitation in his eye, seemingly annoyed over having just been interrupted. "A delicious meal too, I might add. We weren't more than a couple of bites in, when he crashed through our front door like a mad man."

"When who crashed through the door, Mr. Hopple?"

"The lunatic, the screwball, the psychopath! Who do you think I'm talking about!? Now, if you could please stop butting in, officer, I'd like to continue. This whole incident has been very traumatic for me. Please just let me finish."

The detective turned his gaze from the man and looked up into the night sky. Though the constellations were slightly dimmed by the city's lights, he was still able to make a few of them out. The stars had always been a source of comfort for him. They reminded him of all the evenings he spent with his father as a boy, talking on the roof of his childhood home while watching the universe's cosmic dance unfold before them.

He took a slow, deep, exhale then focused his eyes back to the man on the stretcher, "I'm sorry, Mr. Hopple. Please continue."

"Right. Well, you should have seen him! His eyes were crazed, like he just escaped from the loony bin. The nut-job screamed at the top of his lungs and rushed right for us while we were still sitting at our dinner table!" Mr. Hopple waved his arms around wildly, recreating the madness. "It was all very terrifying! I tried to stop him, but the man is built like a linebacker and as you can see, I'm – well, I've always been told I'm quite wiry."

"Crazed, huh?"

Charles swatted at the icepack with his hand, shooing the paramedic away as though she were some bothersome child. "Indeed. The man was a certifiable maniac tonight. He threw me against the wall – that's how I hurt my head, see? I think I may be concussed. It was horrifying to watch him in action, tears streaming down his cheeks while he pummeled my poor wife repeatedly over and over again in the face."

"She's on her way to St. John's uptown. The EMTs I talked to said she probably won't need reconstructive surgery."

"Oh thank Heaven! You've no idea how relieved I am to hear that. For once, detective I'm actually glad you cut me off. Now, where was I? Oh right, once he finished with her, he turned to me. He pinned me to the ground and snatched the carving knife off the dinner table." Hopple lifted his arm overhead like a wide-eyed Hitchockian villain about to dispatch of a throw away character. "My goodness he was strong! He held me by the throat, screaming at the top of his lungs, droning on and on about how he was going to make my wife and I suffer. That's when the police arrived – just in time I might add. It took a couple of your boys in blue to subdue him, but they brought him down. Score one for the good guys, aye?" Hopple nudged the detective with his elbow and gave him a playful wink. "Honestly though, I have no idea what would drive a man to act so insane."

"No idea, huh?"

The detective reached up to remove the weathered hat sitting atop gray thinning hair, which he then ran his fingers through, stopping only at the back of his neck to massage away the tension. Thirty years. For thirty years he had been working homicide in the city. For thirty years he had always prided himself on his ability to stay composed and act in a professional manner no matter what the circumstances. For thirty years the old man had headed up cases that ran the gamut from strange and unorthodox to downright sick and depraved. In all that time no matter how appalling, how offensive he found a particular crime to be, he had always remained cool, calm, and collected.

The detective felt his heart pounding emphatically inside his chest. His mouth had gone dry. He tried frantically to rein in his breathing, but couldn't prevent his lungs from drawing in and expelling air at a frenzied pace.

Thirty years. For thirty years he had been able to

keep his emotions at bay while doing his job, but everyone has a breaking point.

"YOU REALLY HAVE NO IDEA!?"

He grabbed on to the side of the man's stretcher and flipped it over, sending him tumbling down to the ground. Charles let out a *welp* and cradled his hands over his head in a feeble attempt to protect himself. The old detective stormed towards the cowering man, snatched hold of his collar, dragged him to his feet and shook him violently against the side of the ambulance.

"Well for starters, how 'bout the fact that you and your sick wife were eating his infant son for dinner!?"

THE FIGHT

DING DING
ROUND 6

The kid was fast. Damarco knew he'd be quick, he had watched tape on him, but he wasn't expecting him to be able to slip his left so effortlessly. It was like he knew it was coming before he even threw it. For a second, he began to wonder if the 19-year-old Russian circling him in the ring really was the better fighter. The promoters seemed to think so. The only reason he had even been given the fight was so the kid could pad his record with a recognizable name. "The Bronx Bomber" Damarco Looney – a name that used to mean something in the sport of boxing...used to. The kid had never been knocked out – hell – he'd never even tasted the canvas over the course of his short professional career and Damarco's hook was his best punch. If he couldn't land that then what chance did he have?

The kid connected with a solid cross to the jaw and for a brief second Damarco's vision faded, not all the way to black, but the Bronx Bomber had been hit enough times to know he had been rocked. To anyone in the nearly empty arena who may have been watching, it would have looked like the cross didn't even register. Damarco's head barely moved when the punch landed, but the kid's fist felt like a shotgun slug to the chin. It sent a wave of heat through his face that pulsed all the way to his ears.

He rushed the young fighter as fast as he could, wrapped his arms tightly around him, and hung on for dear life. A few seconds later, a much smaller man wearing a blue shirt and black bowtie managed to force his way in between the two heavyweights. The referee placed a hand on each fighter's chest and forced them apart with surprising power.

There were no more punches thrown in that round, thanks only in part to the Russian's inexperience. Damarco realized a more seasoned fighter would have smelled blood after the cross and tried to put him down. He was completely gassed, but luckily the kid had been respecting his power a little too much.

The bell rang and the two men dropped their fists. Damarco staggered to his corner and crumpled down on the stool his cut man had placed out for him.

"You doing alright, Champ?" The voice was gruff and husky. It sounded like how sandpaper feels. It was the voice of a man who had been drinking for 30 years, smoking for 40, and cursing even longer than that.

"Yeah, I'm good."

Damarco glanced up to see Richie's gnarled old face hovering just inches from his. He could tell his trainer was worried, but there was still hope in his eyes – the sight caused him to straighten up in his seat. The fight was far from over. He had taken his licks, but Richie hadn't given up and neither would he. The elderly man's cracked lips had bowed into an anxious frown. They flapped like two burnt pieces of bacon as he spoke.

"He caught you pretty good there, Champ, but I don't need to tell ya that!" Richie's voice garbled like a cement mixer. "Come on, you're too good to be walking right into that punch!"

Damarco knew he was lucky to have the old man with him that night. In reality, he was no champion, but Richie Bohannan was the top trainer in the sport. He was a man who only took the very best under his wing, a man who worked with real champions, yet there he was, crouched down in the corner of a washed up old boxer at a non-televised, ten round preliminary fight. When Damarco had showed up in his gym six months prior and told him he wanted to get back into the game, the old trainer didn't hesitate to take him on as his pet project. Perhaps he felt that he owed some part of his success to Damarco.

The heavyweight gazed out at all the vacant seats in the arena and remembered back to a time when people came to see him fight, back when he and Richie were rising up the ranks together. Before the drugs and alcohol had derailed his career. Before he had lost everything to a gambling addiction and a messy divorce. Before his little girl had-

"Champ?! Champ, you listening to me?! I said watch his shoulder! He's dipping his shoulder every time he throws that cross. Step around it, then nail 'em with the hook!"

The referee was standing right behind Richie now. He quickly informed them the next round would start in ten seconds, then hurried across the ring to tell the Russian's corner the same thing.

Richie buried a bony finger into the front of Damarco's bulky deltoid to accentuate his point.

"*Watch the shoulder, Champ.* He's leaving himself wide open for you."

The veteran nodded to his old friend then sprung up to his feet. Richie and the rest of Damarco's corner emptied the ring.

Ding Ding

ROUND 7

Aside from a few people here and there, the first fifty rows of the arena were almost totally barren. In a few hours, once the cameras turned on and the main event was ready to begin, the building would fill with celebrities and socialites, each of whom had shelled out exorbitant amounts of money just to be seen at the event. Damarco couldn't help but notice the woman in the shimmering black dress who had already taken her seat in the front row. She had hair like midnight and bright red lips, smooth olive skin and exotic features. The woman was gorgeous – there was no denying that. Even if the arena had been packed, Damarco was sure the beauty would have stood out in the crowd, yet he found her to be more off-putting than alluring. He couldn't explain why, but her presence upset him.

He wondered why she was there, all by herself, staring at him from the row of empty chairs. Her seat was worth an easy fifteen grand, and nobody with that kind of money ever showed up before the cameras started rolling. Was she famous? He didn't recognize her, but still she seemed familiar. Familiar and, in some strange way, repulsively beautiful.

The kid was more aggressive in this round. Damarco pushed the woman out of his mind and focused on weathering the young fighter's offense. The Russian threw a quick 1-2 and Damarco took it in stride. Richie was screaming something from the corner, but the old vet couldn't hear it. Another 1-2 followed by an uppercut and now his face was stinging. He threw a jab to keep the kid back. It didn't land and when the Russian countered with another uppercut he knew he was in trouble.

Damarco backed away, but not before swinging wildly with a haymaker, missing the kid by an inch.

Damn, he thought to himself. *Almost caught him.*

Still, it was enough to keep his opponent at bay. The kid had a look on his face like he just dodged a bullet and Damarco saw that at least one person in the ring believed he might still have a little left over from his days as the IBF heavyweight champ.

He caught a glimpse of the woman again out of the corner of his eye. She was standing at ringside now, gripping the bottom rope with her hand as she glared at him. Her stare was cold and distant. It burned a hole in his chest. He felt a bizarre urge to jump out of the ring and sprint down the Vegas strip until he was as far from the arena as possible.

The kid closed in on him in the corner and unleashed a brutal flurry. Damarco covered his face, but he was being bombarded, one ferocious blow after another. He ducked as low as he could. Each shot felt like it was rattling his brain inside his skull, and he knew he wouldn't be able to take many more, but the barrage ended suddenly and when Damarco looked up the kid was calmly walking back to his corner.

"Champ! You coming?!" Richie was already inside the ring, waving him over.

Damarco was sure the ref had stopped the fight. He hadn't even heard the bell, though apparently it had rung, signaling the end of the round. Luck must have been on his side because a few more seconds of absorbing the kid's punches would have been enough to end the bout. He stumbled over to his corner on shaky legs and collapsed on his stool.

"What's going on, Champ?! You don't look like you're even paying attention out there."

The referee jogged over to their corner and grabbed Richie by the sleeve of his shirt. He said something to him, but Damarco's ears were ringing too much from all the headshots to make it out. Richie was scowling at the ref. His usual sneer was even more crooked than normal. As his hearing began to come back to him, Damarco was able to pick up the last little bit of their back and forth.

"He's peachy, Steve!" Richie growled. "Don't worry 'bout him! You *should* be worrying about that punk over there rabbit punching my fighter every time they go to clinch! Now would you mind?! I'm trying to work here!"

The ref backed away and Richie turned to face Damarco.

"I can't beat him, Rich," the old boxer moaned. "My comeback, this whole thing, it was a mistake."

Richie shot a liver-spotted hand out and gripped Damarco tight around the wrist.

"You think I call you Champ for shits and giggles?

Back when we was comin' up together you were one of the best fighters I ever saw. Don't you give up yet! 'Member what you said when you walked into my gym six months ago?" Damarco nodded, took a sip from the water bottle that was being held in front of his face, then hawked what he didn't want to swallow into his spit bucket. His saliva came out as red as the gloves he wore over his fists. "Ya said you wanted to do it for Trinity. Ya said you knew she was watching you from heaven and you wanted to make her proud."

Trinity was Damarco's daughter. After the divorce his wife had won sole custody of their little girl. His public battle with drugs and gambling was enough to convince the judge that Damarco was an unfit parent. Trinity and her mother moved back across the country to New York and aside from the occasional phone call he had lost all contact with her. It had been two years since he last saw her when he received the call from Hackensack Medical Center's trauma ward. Damarco was in his sixth month at a rehab clinic in Malibu at the time. There had been an accident on the Jersey Turnpike. The car his eleven-year-old daughter was in had collided with a semi-truck. She died on the operating table in the hospital's ER.

Richie stared apprehensively into his old friend's eyes, waiting for him to say something.

"You're right," Damarco grunted. "I ain't just fighting for me no more."

There was nothing left to be said. The once great champion rose to his feet and began to bounce in his stance.

Ding Ding
ROUND 8

The kid had size and speed on him, he may have even been a more skilled boxer, but he was too young to have battled the demons Damarco had. The old veteran knew these demons had toughened him; they had made his skin thick and calloused. The Russian had never considered downing an entire bottle of oxycodone, he had never lost his fortune to lawyers and debt collectors and been forced to start over with nothing, and, perhaps most importantly, he had never been forced to bury his daughter. The fight was Damarco's last chance at redemption. No promoter would ever give him another shot at a comeback if he didn't win. He knew he had to make it count.

The kid came out of the gates swinging. Damarco bobbed and weaved, avoiding most of the attack and threw a few jabs to create some space between them. He set him up by faking with his left then landed a solid body blow that nearly doubled the Russian over, but the kid recovered quickly and squared up before he could capitalize. The Russian was looking anxious now and Damarco could see the frustration in his eyes.

Watch the shoulder, he thought to himself. *Look for the dip.*

The kid faked with his head and that's when Damarco saw his opening. The shoulder dropped just like Richie said it would. The cross was coming, but this time Damarco was ready for it. He stepped to the side and connected with a vicious left to the temple of the Russian's face that sent him reeling against the ropes. Damarco felt like he was back on top of his game again. He moved in on the kid and started teeing off on him, talking trash just like he did in his glory days.

The Fight

"Thought I was a washed up old man, didn't you? Thought you were gonna walk all over me?"

He peppered him with shot after shot until the kid wrapped him up. They wrestled around on the ropes for a few seconds. It was during the clinch that the woman in the black dress caught Damrco's eye once more.

She had moved to the ring steps, her blank expression and icy gaze still fixed upon him. Her stare was uncanny. Damarco couldn't shake the feeling that she was watching *him* and not the fight, as if everyone else in the arena didn't exist. Why did she disgust him so? He couldn't say, but he could barely stand being so near her.

He tried to get the official's attention. "Hey, where the hell is security?" He asked. "Why is she allowed to stand over there?" But the referee didn't acknowledge him. He was too busy prying the large men apart.

The woman was tall and gaunt. Damarco thought she may have been a model. Her cheekbones were prominent fixtures on her face – they jutted out below her eyes like two cliffs, descending sharply into the smooth brown sea of her skin. She did not open her mouth, her lips stayed sealed, steadfast. The sight of her made him want to cower in the corner like a wounded dog and still he could not understand why. He turned to say something to the referee again, but felt a sudden intense pressure on his left eye and then the world went black.

When the world came into view again, it did so not all at the same time. The light rig above the ring materialized first, followed quickly by the catwalk. Sounds came next. He could hear Richie's rough, scratchy voice shouting for him to get up. Finally, he heard the referee's count.

"four…"

Damarco tilted his head and saw the official standing over him. The kid had caught him with a good one. He hadn't been knocked out that cleanly in years.

"five…"

He pushed himself up on one elbow and glimpsed across the ring. The kid was watching him from his corner. His training staff was celebrating around him, but the Russian's face bore an intense, serious stare. Damarco's head was throbbing. It felt like that last punch had cracked his skull open like an egg.

"six…"

He struggled up to one knee. The woman was still standing on the ring steps. The lights of the arena reflected off her bare shoulders, and in that moment she looked both horrible and heavenly.

"seven…"

She reached out a long tan leg – the one visible through the high cut in her sequin gown – and stepped up to the ring apron. Her eyes were piercing – two dark onyx stones buried deep into the quarry of her face. They weren't just watching Damarco, they were devouring him. He felt that same inexplicable fear begin to amplify.

"eight…"

Oh God, he thought. *She's coming to get me. Why me?! Why is she coming to get me?!*

"nine…"

It was fighter's instinct that caused him to shoot to his feet before the official reached ten. He stopped his count and started his quick inspection of Damarco.

"Hey, you ok?" the referee asked.

"Yeah, get that woman off the ring. She's distracting me."

The ref gave him an odd look.

"Who, the ring girl? Round's about to end."

"No! The other one!" Damarco paused suddenly, realizing the official didn't know whom he was referring to. "Just forget it. I'm fine ok?"

The Russian had come out of his corner and was waiting like a caged lion, ready to pounce on Damarco as soon as he was given the word.

"If you say so," said the official. He backed away until he was halfway between two boxers. "Fight's on!"

The kid came at him fast. He was ready to end the fight. Damarco, flustered by the woman standing on the ring apron, couldn't do anything but throw his hands up in defense. He deflected two quick blows with his fists before the bell rang mercifully, saving him from slaughter.

"Champ! Champ! Get over here!" Richie was frantically waving his towel in the air, signaling Damarco to the corner. The old boxer hobbled over and sat down.

"Jesus Christ!" Richie spat. "Would ya look at that eye?!" He turned to the cut man. "Hey, Joey! Get a cold compress on his eye right now! We gotta get the swelling down!"

Damarco felt the cold metal instrument being firmly pressed to the flesh around his eye and it was only then that he recognized just how tender he was in that spot. Richie rumbled on.

"Now look, Champ – I ain't gonna lie – you're way behind on points, 'specially after that knockdown. It's time we start thinking 'bout going for the knockout-"

"Why's that lady allowed to stand on the ring during the fight, Rich?"

Damarco's question had caused the old trainer to stop suddenly in his tracks.

"The lady, Richie! The lady in the black dress! She stood on the ring all last round and I couldn't concentrate! She's still standin' there, look! Goddamnit, Rich! Don't you see her?!"

Richie's face sunk.

"Champ, you ok? There ain't no woman on the ring, save for the ring girl and she just hopped up there."

"The hell there ain't Rich! She's right there! You know what? Screw you and screw her! And screw that Russian punk too!"

The referee ran over to their corner.

"Ten seconds, guys."

Richie spoke with care to his good friend, voice rolling out from mouth as smoothly as his cigarette ravaged throat would allow it.

"Champ...what day of the week is it?"

"Saturday," Damarco answered. He was looking out across the ring at the woman, her detached awful stare had never broken from him. "The day I finally do right by my little girl."

He lumbered up to his feet.

Ding Ding

ROUND 9

Darmarco now understood that he was the only one who could see the woman standing in the corner of the ring. It was an idea that terrified him, yet buried somewhere beneath his horror he was beginning to feel a bizarre euphoria stirring inside him. The woman's presence was now fueling Damarco. It ignited a fire in his belly that had motivated him to win more than ever, if for no other reason than to spite his mysterious onlooker.

She wants to see me lose, he thought to himself. *But I'm not gonna fail.*

The Bronx Bomber needed a homerun. With only two rounds left, a knockout was his only conceivable shot at victory. His head was aching terribly, but he was no stranger to pain. Damarco pushed past the pounding in his skull and attacked the Russian. He backed his opponent into a corner then unloaded on him in a frantic attempt to put him down. The kid rolled out of it and stuck him with a couple of jabs. Damarco shook them off and again went on the offensive. He caught the kid on the ropes and threw everything he had towards his body, but once more the Russian was able to escape, this time connecting with a brutal cross to his engorged eye, causing Damarco to stagger back.

The air that filled his lungs burned sharp and he realized that in his desperation he had punched himself out. His fists felt like lead weights and he could barely hold them up to his face. Damarco shot a glance at the woman in the black dress. She had been standing motionless in the corner from the moment she stepped up to the edge of the ring, but now she was beginning to rouse from her frozen state. Slowly she paced down the apron, almost floating, her hand gliding along the top rope as she moved, all the while her terrible stare fastened firmly on Damarco.

The kid landed two more shots while Damarco's attention was diverted. He swung violently at him, trying to answer back, but felt his glove skip off the top of his Russian opponent's head. His heart was racing a million miles per hour. The air rushing in and out of his lungs stung like millions of tiny needles. His muscles were on fire and his head was throbbing worse than ever. Damarco knew the cross was coming, the kid had dropped his shoulder again, but this time he didn't have the energy to dodge it. The Russian's fist connected squarely with Damarco's jaw, rendering him unconscious before he even hit the ground.

There was darkness after that. Only darkness. Then out of the black void Damrco saw his daughter's face. He wanted to reach out and touch her, but he had no body with which to do so. He tried to speak, but alas he had no voice to communicate with. If he could, he would have told her that he loved her. He would have begged Trinity to forgive him for all his past indiscretions. He would have explained that he had dedicated the fight to her and that she was the reason he had tried to turn his life around. She smiled at him, her round face warmed his heart and for the first time in as long as he could remember he loved himself again, but this would not last. Slowly Trinity's face began to fade away, leaving Damarco alone in the empty black void again.

And then as quickly as the darkness came, the light returned – a horrible yellow light – the kind fastened to the rig that hung above the ring.

"seven…"

The referee was counting again and Damarco realized he was on his back.

"eight…"

Trinity. Damarco could only think his daughter's

name. He scrambled to his feet just as the official was reaching the count of nine.

"Hey, you ok, Bomber?" the ref asked.

"Fine. Slipped when the kid caught me."

Both men knew this was a lie.

The name of the referee inspecting Damarco was Steve Milton. He was a Brooklyn native who had been working in the sport for over thirty-two years. Damarco didn't realize it, but when he was sixteen Steve had officiated his New York State, Junior Golden Gloves championship bout and had been the one to raise his hand in victory that night.

Watch that kid, he had told his wife during dinner that same evening. *Best fighter I've seen come through New York in a long time. He's gonna be somebody someday.*

Steve had followed Damarco's career closely and was heartbroken after witnessing his fall from grace. Nevertheless, he respected the veteran fighter and wanted to see him redeem himself.

He looked into Damarco's eyes for any sign of life. He wasn't cognizant of his favoritism, but Steve knew that the fight was the Bronx Bomber's last opportunity at a comeback and deep in the depths of his consciousness, he dreaded having to be the one to hammer the final nail into the coffin of Damarco Looney's career. If it were any other man on any other night, Steve would have ended the fight then and there, but this was somehow different. A champion of New York – his New York – deserved better than a TKO. He deserved a fighter's chance.

"You sure you good to go, Bomber?" he asked again.

The battered warrior glared ferociously into Steve's

eyes.

"Let me fight."

The official stepped aside. Damarco put his gloves up and bit down hard on his mouth guard readying himself for punishment, but before the kid could get another shot in the bell rang and the round was over. Damarco slogged back to his corner, each step an agonizing exercise in fortitude. His head had moved beyond the point of pain, his face was numb. Damarco sat down gingerly and took a sip of water. It hurt too much to swallow so he spat it out into the bucket.

"Damarco," Richie started, his coarse voice rising and falling like a rocky mountain range. "I think it's over. Ya fought bravely-"

"No!" the old heavyweight interrupted. "I ain't goin' out like a chump. Don't you dare throw in the towel, Rich!"

"Ain't no shame in takin' *the L* here."

Richie looked into the pleading face of his old friend. Damarco's skin glistened with sweat and Vaseline. His left eye was almost swollen shut.

"I need this, Rich. There's only one round left. Don't take it from me."

The woman was standing in the ring now, right next to the Russian. Nobody was even acknowledging her. Damarco knew not to mention it to Richie. If he did, his trainer would have surely asked the ref to stop the bout for fear of his health. Richie was already gripping the towel so tight his knuckles had turned white.

"Don't stop the match, Rich. Let me go down like a fighter. It's what Trinity would have wanted."

For a long time Richie said nothing, then, he placed a

hand on Damarco's muscular shoulder.

"Good luck, Champ."

He and the rest of the crew exited the ring.

Damarco stood up in his corner and waited for the final round to begin.

Ding Ding

ROUND 10

The woman was now undergoing a gruesome transformation. Her smooth brown skin had become dry and brittle. It cracked and chipped, falling from her face in flakes like dried paint, revealing the deep raw muscle beneath, muscle that, once exposed to air, started to drip and ooze. It ran down her arms, legs, and chest, pooling in thick brown puddles on the canvas at her feet. Her hair had gone from black to gray to white. It dangled like loose cobwebs from her rotting scalp.

Damarco watched her intently, all the while keeping one eye on the kid who had just stepped out of his corner. The woman circled the ring, slithering behind the Russian like a grotesque shadow. Damarco's heart was pounding in his chest and he didn't know if it was due to fatigue or fear. His head was pounding too and every muscle in his body burned intensely, but nothing was going to stop him – not even the horrible thing stalking him in the ring. He couldn't give up.

The kid charged forward aggressively and Damarco realized his opponent wasn't just shooting for a decision victory, he was looking for the knockout. Damarco dipped under his first two punches, but couldn't escape a powerful hook that drilled him directly in his swollen eye. It felt like Hell had struck him. The woman hung back as the two gladiators traded blows. Her eyes had begun to liquefy into gooey tears that trickled down what was left of her cheeks. The kid pelted Damarco with another couple of shots that left him feeling dizzy.

You ain't been through what I been through kid, Damarco thought. *You don't know how tough I am.*

The kid's name was Dimitri Petrov. Damarco was right, Dimitri had never buried a daughter or battled a drug addiction like he had, but life in Moscow had been far from easy for the young man. His father passed away when he was nine, leaving his mother, who had no education or job, to care for him, his younger sister, and his baby brother. They had always been poor, but after the death of Dimitri's father, they couldn't even afford to eat three meals a day and often went to bed with rumbling stomachs. Dimitri's mom began dating a low-level mob enforcer. He was an abusive drunk who beat her ruthlessly, but her kids were no longer hungry, so she put up with his mistreatment.

Young Dimitri began training at a local boxing gym in order to escape his toxic household. Ironically, he only ever felt at peace while he was fighting. After his mother developed a chronic lung disease that rendered her weak and frail, Dimitri started spending every waking minute in the ring, hoping it would help him forget about his pain. As his mother's disease worsened, the human piece of filth that had attached himself to Dimitri's family had turned his attention to his younger sister.

One night, a fifteen-year-old Dimitri returned home from the gym to find his mother's boyfriend in his little sister's bedroom. Dimitri beat him to within an inch of his life and kicked him out on the street. It was the last he ever saw of the man, but his absence provided a new problem. His mom was sick, and his brother and sister were still too young to work, so he turned to the only thing that ever brought his heart any sense of tranquility – fighting. The boy fought in gyms and underground clubs for cash, where he knocked out men twice his age. A Russian promoter with ties to The States took notice of the boy and by the time he was eighteen, he was training in the US at one of the world's most reputable boxing gyms.

He sent the little money he made back to his family so that his siblings could eat and his mother could afford the medication she needed. His fight with Damarco would be his biggest payout to date, but even more than that, it represented a gateway to the big time – televised bouts, huge purses, enough money to help his family escape poverty once and for all. A week before the fight, the promoter promised him spot on an HBO card against a ranked fighter – someone Dimitri was sure he could beat – but only on the condition that he could knock Damarco Looney out first. There was no telling when another opportunity like that would come his way.

Dimitri had not battled the demons Damarco had, but he *had* battled demons – fear of failure, pressure to succeed. His mother's health and the future of his brother and sister rested squarely on his ability to inflict damage with his fists, and he feared that if he failed to put Damarco down, then they'd be out on the street. And so he showered the old veteran with blow after blow, hoping, wishing, praying, that his next punch would be the one that ended the fight for good.

The flesh had completely fallen from the woman's face and now only a brownish-yellow skull remained. It looked as if it had been just been unearthed after lying for centuries at the bottom of a grave. Her feet no longer touched the ground. She hovered inches above the ring like a specter. Damarco couldn't help but stare at the ghastly sight hanging in the air behind his opponent, but the kid was laser focused. He connected with a ferocious uppercut to Damarco's chin that caused his head to whip back violently. Damarco swung at the young Russian but caught nothing. The kid dipped inside and hit him three more times. He was moving like lightning. Richie shouted something from the corner, but to Damarco his voice sounded as if it was a thousand miles away.

The woman drifted towards the two men. She was vapor, she was smoke, she was lighter than air. She extended an arm of rotting flesh and coasted closer.

A photographer at ringside, who had only been there testing his camera before the important fights began, turned his lens towards the ring. It was professional instinct that caused him to start snapping pictures. The sound of the camera's shutter triggered more photographers, who in turn started snapping photos of their own, and soon the ring was bathed in the light of a dozen flashbulbs, twinkling like brilliant stars.

Richie was squeezing the towel so tight in his hand that big blue veins were protruding from his forearm. He was biting down hard on his bottom lip. It had begun to bleed and a tiny crimson drop was dribbling down his chin.

The ring physician was trying to get his attention. He hadn't been paying attention for most of the fight, but now he was. Exhibitions were never usually allowed to go far enough to require his expertise. He was pulling on the old trainer's shirt and yelling in his ear, but it was as if his voice simply travelled out the other side without a single word even registering.

"Throw the towel!" he was shouting. "Throw the fucking towel!"

Damarco dropped his arms, but the kid continued to swing his fists relentlessly towards his face.

The referee felt as though his body had turned to stone. Something inside him was holding him back, preventing him from stepping between the two men and calling for the bell. He couldn't hear the voice. He wasn't even aware of its existence, but it spoke to him and ordered him not to interfere. *Who are you to end "The Bronx Bomber's" career?* this inaudible voice asked. Then it said something else. *Let him fall like a champion.*

The few spectators in their seats had looked up from their phones and had taken interest in what was going on in the ring. Some of them cheered. Some of them called for more blood. Still others winced from the sight.

One of the spectators turned to his friend who was standing next to him.

"Is that Damarco Looney?"

His friend's face crinkled with a perplexed expression.

"Couldn't be," he said. "He retired years ago…didn't he?"

Damarco was trapped in the corner now. His vision was blurry, but he could still see the woman clear as day. Her arm passed through the Russian's chest. The punches he was eating were sending excruciating vibrations through his cranium. He tried to think, but couldn't. His mind felt thick and muddled. Left was right, up was down, his whole world had become a constant barrage of heavy fists, and through it all, the woman's horrible, decaying hand inched closer, ever closer, to the old fighter's face.

The Russian dipped his shoulder.

The cross was coming again.

An image of Trinity flickered through his mind.

The kid's fist stung Damarco's chin at the exact moment the woman's finger finally touched him and for the third time that evening, everything went black.

When Damarco opened his eyes, he was looking up at the lighting rig above the ring again. He lied on the ground, listening for the official's count – a count that never came.

He sat up with surprising ease. Just seconds earlier, his body had been shutting down on him, but now it was as if all his strength and energy had returned. There was no longer any pain in his head and his muscles didn't ache. Damarco reached his hand to his face to touch his eye. The swelling was gone. Stranger even, his gloves had seemingly been removed.

It was then that he noticed just how quiet the arena was. There were no more sounds of camera shutters at ringside. Richie's scratchy voice had vanished as well. Not even an occasional cheer from one of the few fans in attendance rang through the air.

"How long have I been out?" he asked himself.

But immediately after the words emerged from his lips he understood the question made no sense. If he had been knocked out long enough for the arena to clear, he'd have been in a hospital bed by the time he woke up. Where

The Fight

was everyone?

Damarco rose to his feet and immediately felt another presence in the ring. He spun around to see the same woman in the black dress standing opposite him. Her beauty had returned, no longer was flesh rotting from her face. Again she looked like an exotic model. Her sequin gown shimmered radiantly in the ring light. Something other than her face had changed as well. It was her aura. Damarco felt a strange sense of comfort in her company. He didn't fear her anymore. She watched him silently, but now her stare was somewhat soothing.

"Daddy."

The voice came from ringside, and Damarco nearly jumped when he heard it. It was a voice he knew – one he never thought he'd hear again. He glanced in the direction of where the words had come.

"Daddy, down here."

Damarco walked over to the ropes and stared down, not believing what he was looking at. It was his daughter Trinity, staring up at him, beaming like sunshine.

"Daddy, you're here!"

Damarco stepped through the ropes, hopped down to the floor, then wrapped his arms around the little girl. He wasn't sure if he was hallucinating until he felt her face pressed up against his chest.

"Trinity? Baby, it's you! But how? Where are…we…?"

He looked back to the ring. The woman in the black dress was still watching him quietly. She wasn't smiling or scowling. Her face was blank, removed from human emotion. He opened his mouth to speak to her, but before a word could get out, he felt a tug on his arm. Trinity was guiding him towards the exit tunnel.

"Come on, Daddy, let's go," she said to him.

Together, they left the woman in the black dress behind. Damarco didn't even think to look back to her. Trinity walked and he followed, gripping his little girl's hand tight. He feared that if he let go of her, she'd disappear and he'd lose her again. She was just how he remembered her. Curly brown hair, caramel-colored skin, a small gap between her front teeth. They wandered until they reached a large metal door labeled *EXIT*. It looked like any other door in the arena, yet there was something very different about it. It felt important – otherworldly even. Trinity stopped in front of it and smiled up to her dad.

"Grandma's here, Daddy," she said. "So is Milo."

"Milo? You mean…Milo, my dog? The one I had when I was a kid?"

"Yup," she answered matter-of-factly. "I've been taking care of him for you. He likes his tummy rubbed."

Damarco eyed the door, wondering what exactly was on the other side. He was sure by now that it wouldn't lead them to the Vegas strip. If he were alone, then he might have been afraid to open it and find out, but he had his daughter at his side, and she wasn't scared so neither was he.

He placed a hand on top of her head and ruffled her hair.

"Yeah," Damarco said with a smile. "I remember. He does like having his tummy rubbed."

He grabbed hold of the door's metal handle and tugged it open…

STORY NOTES

AT THE PATIO DOOR

There is something about the backdrop of Christmas that works so well in scary stories. Christmas and horror shouldn't go together, but they do. It reminds me of garlic flavored ice cream. That may sound disgusting to you, but I urge you to give it a chance. You might be surprised; it could become your favorite flavor. I know I was surprised by just how much I enjoyed writing this little holiday horror piece.

THE OCEAN'S COOL AIR

This story has undergone a lot of rewrites and has evolved over time with my writing. It's funny, I kept coming back to it, tweaking it again and again until I felt like it was something I could finally be proud of. I've had a lot of people tell me not to dwell so much on my writing – that once I finish a story I should just move on to the next one. But writing is art, and there's no right or wrong way to approach a piece of art. Some books take a long time to finish, some get done in a matter of days. The same can be said for stories.

GAS STATION BATHROOM

Part of the reason why I believe this story works is because we've all been in poor Shelly's shoes. Even though I live and spend most of my time in Los Angeles, I still call the bay area home. When I go back to the bay I usually drive my car up California's I-5. It's a long, boring stretch of highway, with nothing to look at but brown fields, cows, and gas stations with filthy bathrooms ripped straight out of this story. Where did you think I got the idea? Inspiration strikes us at the strangest times. Sometimes it's on the toilet.

THE WOMAN IN THE RED SUNDRESS

I had this picture of a woman floating around in my head when I wrote this short little story. She was sexy, intelligent, enchanting – most importantly – she was completely out of my league. If I were to see this woman walking down the street, I might shy away rather than speak to her. I'm bound by my own insecurities. What if she laughed at me? What if she rolled her eyes? It would break my heart. The protagonist in this story once struggled with the same dilemma, but unlike myself, he's freed himself from those shackles. He does what he wants, unobstructed by societal norms and insecurities. It just so happens that it took him jumping out the window of a city skyscraper to realize it.

PICTURE THIS

One of my more popular stories is Picture This. I think it's because a lot of creative people tend to follow my writing. I've heard from so many writers, artists, and actors, who have told me they identified with the protagonist in this story. Now, criticism is frustrating, but its also a necessity for anyone who wants to create art. Criticism helps us grow and improve.

I will say this though, there are so many people out there who use the Internet as their own personal torture chamber, jabbing content creators again and again, doing whatever they can to devalue their work. These people are called trolls, and anyone who has shared their art on the Internet has felt their wrath at some point. For the record, the protagonist in this story is not a victim. He's full of insecurities about his work and he uses them to justify the awful choices he makes when confronted by one of these trolls. It's ok to feel his frustration, but also important that all you artists reading this don't identify too closely with him. You should focus your energy on loving your art not hating your critics. When you do that, those nasty comments won't sting as bad.

THE AFRICAN BOWANA SPIDER

This story was an attempt to satirize some 19th century western authors. I wanted to write characters who would read Kipling's White Man's Burden, and nod their heads in agreement. Tweed gives off a sort of philanthropic racist vibe in the story, as if he's making the lives of all those "brown savages" in the jungle so much better by hiring them out to carry his bags during his sight-seeing vacation.

SR Tooms, who coauthored Decomposing Head with

me, the book in which this story was originally featured, actually suggested a different ending to give the story more of a dry, "British" vibe. It was just one little line at the very end that he added. I cut it out at the last minute, although I often ask myself if it was the right call. It makes me laugh every time I think about it. His version ended like this:

"Eight long spindly legs emerged from the doctor's mouth. Robert sipped his tea nonchalantly."

FAST ENOUGH

I once heard an apt analogy comparing short stories to card tricks. Both short stories and card tricks rely on subtle misdirection. Both rely on manipulating a mark or a reader. The key to writing an effective twist is to make those who are reading your story think one thing, just before bashing them over the head with a punchline. Such is the case in Fast Enough, a story that waits until the final sentence to ask "Is this your card?"

THE CLEAR BLUE SPRING

Aside from the Devil, I don't write about evil characters. I know that it might be a little strange to hear that coming from a horror author, but I don't believe in the concept of good and evil. We as human beings all exist on a moral spectrum. There is no black, there is no white, only shades of gray. Did the main character in this story do a terrible thing? Absolutely, but we should consider other factors before condemning his soul to hell. I try to make it a point to write people who make bad decisions, but decisions that we ourselves might be able to rationalize and understand. Should he have burned his house down? Even though his mom was a piece of crap, the answer is still a hard no. Should he have drowned his girlfriend? Well, if the Spring is as magical and as influential as the story would lead us to believe, if what it showed him was really true, then perhaps the answer is...maybe? As long as I can make readers feel a little sorry for someone who has killed in cold-blood, then I'm doing my job.

THE EYE OF RA

Ah, The Eye of Ra. The story I wrote to promote a forgotten Egyptian-themed horror film called The Pyramid. It really has nothing to do with the movie, but I'm thankful that I got the opportunity because it gave me the chance to write my first "curse story". This tale is an early stab at the concept of destiny vs free will, which comes up a little later in this book in another story titled, By Your Bootstraps.

A FAVOR FOR A FAVOR

The idea behind this story was simple. If the devil was still out and about, trying to cut Faustian deals, he wouldn't be very successful these days. We've all seen movies like Bedazzled, we've watched musicals like Damn Yankees, and yes, we've read stories like The Devil and Tom Walker, which was mentioned in Favor. Think about it, if the Devil tried to trade you anything for the price of your soul, you would need to be the stupidest person on Earth to accept that deal.

The kid says it himself:

"What's a lifetime of happiness compared to an eternity in Hell?"

Anyone capable of using an ounce of logic would be able to see they're getting the short end of the stick from the get-go. Today's modern Devil needs to adapt, which in the story he has no trouble doing. Just because he isn't trying to own your soul, doesn't mean he can't manipulate people for his own nefarious purposes.

SCHIZO

I don't really know where the Bird Woman came from. To me, she is the embodiment of all things that go bump in the night. She just gives me the creeps. Out of every character in this book, I would least like to be Donny Polk. Waking up in the night to have that nasty thing hovering over me would be enough to make me sleep with a gun under my pillow for the rest of my life. This little story was originally published in a book I wrote called Just A Little Terrible, and even though I find the ending to be a bit contrived, I still believe it was a strong edition to my "best of" collection. The biggest reason, of course, is that I will never NOT be scared of the Bird Woman.

TROLL BRIDGE

One thing a lot of people might not realize about me is that I'm obsessed with fairy tales. I've written two, one is called The Beautiful Burden and I've never published it. The second is Troll Bridge. There's a long tradition of dark imagery used in fairy tales. Go read Hans Christian Anderson's The Little Mermaid – or hell – anything written by the Brothers Grimm. Many of Disney's movies are adapted from some of the most twisted stories. With any luck, Disney will buy the rights to Troll Bridge from me and turn it into some magical, CGI song and dance with cutesy characters that can be slapped on everything from t-shirts to backpacks then marketed to your children at exorbitant prices. Although, if past is prologue they'll probably just wait for it to hit public domain. I'll probably be dead by then.

IMMORTAL

Something about the protagonist's unhealthy obsession with immortality tends to strike a chord with me. I too happen to obsess over things. I'm the kind of writer who goes over a sentence with a fine-tooth comb and I think David would be like that as well if he had chosen the art of prose as his passion. I fear that I'll wake up in ten years and wonder if everything I've been working towards was for naught. Is there a writer's version of the Philosopher's Stone or Fountain of Youth? I don't know. I doubt I'll be the one to find it if there is, so I hope I continue to stay passionate about this job for as long as I live.

NEPTUNE'S FANCY

I actually borrowed tidbits of this story from my mother. It was part of an unfinished piece of writing she showed me a little while back. Her version wasn't intended to be horror, and there certainly weren't any Lovecraftian elements, but I knew there was something there that needed to be explored. I hope I did the story justice with the 10K words I added to it. From what I've heard, the reception has been fairly positive so far, and Simon & Schuster will be publishing it as part of a Mr. Creepypasta's horror anthology, aptly titled, The Creepypasta Collection later this year.

THE OLD HOUSE

If you are familiar with the Internet Horror writing scene, then you may be aware of Nosleep, a forum on Reddit (it really is good for things other than stupid cat pictures and bastardizing the word meme!). Nosleep stories follow a rule, in that, the stories have to come across as "real". To achieve this, most are written in a first person, "forum post" narrative. The Old House was my attempt at that. There's nothing fancy about the prose and there's certainly no fluff. All you get is the meat and bones, and of course, a weird little twist at the end.

THE WENDALL LANE DIARIES

The house on Wendall Lane is an idea that I've been kicking around for years. I've even considered writing a novel about the place. Superficially, it comes across as your generic haunted house, but there's really a lot more to it than that. In my head, I think of the house as more of a Bermuda Triangle than an Overlook Hotel. It's a point in space-time where reality isn't right. I like to keep the scope of its supernatural powers to be ambiguous, but it opens up a lot more story telling possibilities than just ghost stories.

YOU SHOULDN'T

You Shouldn't is probably one of my favorite stories in this collection. I think it's a reflection of my true writing. I wasn't attempting to satirize a period like in The African Bowana Spider or write a forum post like in The Old House. The prose is 100% me being me, and I kind of like it. It's a little goofy, a little gross, and I just can't stop myself from sneaking in a cheeky line or two. Alan Palmer is me unfiltered.

THE PHONE IN THE KITCHEN

To me, the most unsettling thing about this story is the motive behind whoever the main character has been conversing with on the phone every night. This entity, be it ghost or something else, isn't interested in harming the protagonist. On the contrary, it seems to be using him for companionship. There is something creepy about a being with supernatural powers that is still so helpless that it's been reduced to impersonating a man's dead relatives just to connect with someone. It's both horrifyingly powerful and utterly pathetic.

BIG F'N ROACH

I hate bugs. Roaches are by far my least favorite things on the planet. The idea for Big F'n Roach came to me after a run-in I had with a nasty palmetto bug one night. The scene in the story where Jimbo winds up with a magazine and smacks a roach on the wall as hard as he can, only for it to not budge one inch actually happened to me.

It was one of the more emasculating things to ever happen to me, but it was also the moment this story was born. Yet another strange place inspiration has struck me. The narrator in this story, Bill Huckley, was actually written with Bruce Campbell in mind because I knew he was going to narrate it as part of a promotion for his show, ASH VS THE EVIL DEAD. If you read the story in Bruce's voice, it might give you some Ash vibes.

BY YOUR BOOTSTRAPS

One of the most discomforting concepts I've ever considered is the possibility of free will being nothing more than an illusion. I am by no means the first person to ever write about it. In the foreword of this book I mention Vonnegut's Slaughter-House Five, where Tralfamadorians, a race of intergalactic aliens, try to explain the concept to the novel's protagonist, Billy Pilgrim. Non-linear time comes up again and again in Vonnegut novels (as do the Tralfamadorians), and I believe it was Vonnegut who inspired Ted Chiang's famous sci-fi tale, The Story of Your Life, which also deals with the theme. I always found it kind of disturbing that the main characters in these stories end up accepting this notion of fate, with little push-back. After all, the thought that we aren't in control of our own destiny is a frightening one to me. I don't know if I would react as calmly as others if suddenly forced to face the idea as fact. Wendy Hope is forced to accept this notion, but I think she's just as disturbed by it as I am. Imagine knowing all your life that you would be committing such a horrible act, and not being able to do anything to stop it.

On another note, the bootstrap paradox in this story isn't actually Wendy, it's the brooch. The brooch is stuck in a closed loop with not point of entry. Never does it actually have a point of origin. I've always enjoyed a good bootstrap paradox story. Heinlein's All You Zombies and PKD's The Skull are two of my favorites.

THE CURIOUS CASE OF STEPHEN HAIM

When I wrote The Curious Case of Stephen Haim I was in the middle of a William Fryer Harvey binge, which is why it has – at least to me – the feel of those gothic ghost tales of yesteryear. The title is also a nod to 19th century penny dreadfuls. It harkens back to stories such as The Strange Case of Doctor Jekyll and Mr. Hyde and Doyle's The Case of Lady Sannox.

The idea for the story came from a chapter titled Murder in Oliver Sacks, The Man Who Mistook His Wife for A Hat. The psychologist who narrates the tale, Sandy Rieve, is also based on Sacks, a clinical neurologist who famously wrote a series of memoirs about his time working in the medical field. In Sacks' book, he described a man, who, much like Stephen Haim, had killed someone very close to him while under the influence of drugs. He too would develop amnesia about the event, and it was only after he suffered serious brain trauma that he would remember what happened. Sacks leaves a lot of his patient's story ambiguous, but it didn't take very long for me to fill in the blanks with a dash William Fryer Harvey and a touch of gross out horror to boot!

THE CRIME SCENE

This story was an exercise in subtlety for me. Throughout The Crime Scene we get tiny little clues into the nature of what happened as Charles Hopple tells his story to the detective. These clues, are given to us by the detective himself. Follow his mannerisms and one can deduce just how screwy this Hopple fellow might really be. Of course we don't find out until the end that the detective definitely knew something was up before he even started questioning the man.

THE FIGHT

I'm not sure if you could call the ending of this story sad or happy. Sure, Damarco is reunited with his daughter, but think of all the unanswered questions it leaves us with. The Fight is unquestionably Damarco Looney's story, and for him, you could say it ends on a happy note. But what about Richie, his trainer, who was too overcome with emotion to throw in the towel while his good friend was getting pummeled? What about Steve, the referee who let a fighter die on his watch, or the unnamed physician at ringside? I suppose these are questions that we'll never truly get an answer to, but that's ok because no story will give you the full scope of what happened to every character. We only get snapshots of moments, small pieces of these characters' lives. It's up to us to decide how we feel about the ending of this story. And that's why writing is art. Because it's totally subjective. You interpret a piece of literature just as you would a Picasso hanging on the wall of The Met.

ACKNOWLEDGEMENTS

Thanks to...

My mother and father for all their support. No way I would be writing without you believing in me.

Champ for being the sweetest thing on the planet. Yes, you have four legs and can't read, but I still love you.

Tooms for pushing me into publishing the junk I write. You opened a new chapter in my life.

Kirsten for putting this book together. I'm sure I'm difficult to work with.

Defne for all the encouragement and help. You were 100% behind me before anyone else was.

Spike for all of his help. Lots of people call themselves writers, your support made me a real author.

And everyone who has ever said a nice thing about my work. My writing is a reflection of who I am. Your kindness gives me a reason to wake up and continue to do it every day.

More by Vincent V. Cava

Just A Little Terrible
Dead Connection
The Creepypasta Comic Book

For more information, visit his website at
http://vincentvenacava.com/

www.ingramcontent.com/pod-product-compliance
Lightning Source LLC
Chambersburg PA
CBHW071046250626
47159CB00002B/384